# Silvermoon & Silver Mink

## HAVE A COLLECTION
## OF 48 GREAT NOVELS

## OF

## EROTIC DOMINATION

**If you like one you will probably like the rest**

## A NEW TITLE EVERY MONTH
## NOW INCLUDING EXTRA BONUS PAGES

**If you like one of our books you will probably
like them all!**

**For free 20 page booklet of extracts from previous
books (and, if you wish to be on our confidential
mailing list, from forthcoming monthly titles as
they are publshed) please write to:-**

## Silver Moon Readers Services
## PO Box CR 25 LEEDS LS7 3TN

or

PO Box 1614 NEW YORK NY 10156

Or leave name and address on our 24-hour answering manchine -
0113 287 6255 (phone or fax - UK only)
http://www.thebookshops.com/silver

New authors welcome

Printed and bound in Great Britian

# HACIENDA

## BY
## ALLAN ALDISS

### BONUS PAGES

# HACIENDA by Allan Aldiss

## 1 - CARLOS MAKES HIS PLANS.

Carlos Ortiz lay swinging in the big hammock that was slung across the wide porch at the back of the large and luxurious hacienda ranch house in Costa Negra, a small little known country in Latin America.

He lay sideways across it in the usual Latin American way, his muscular body stretched out comfortably.

He wore only a sarong in the warm tropical afternoon sun - a sarong which he had untied, displaying his hard, tanned figure - as well as baring it for the attentions of the two young girls that the hammock also held.

The girls were sisters, indentured servants, virtually a replacement for slavery, which had been abolished in the middle of the last century. They were coffee coloured, half Indian, with a dash of Negro and white blood. They snuggled up to their Master, one on either side - pretty young creatures with pert little breasts. Round their necks iron collars had been riveted from which hung discs giving the name of the estate, El Paraiso, and the numbers under which they were listed in the hacienda's official register.

By Costa Negra law, going back to the days of slavery, livestock was divided into cattle, pigs, horses, and slaves, the latter now replaced by indentured servants. The female indentured servant section of the register was further sub-divided into several distinct types of women.

Each type had been bred in El Paraiso quite separately for several generations, either for use on the hacienda itself or for sale to neighbouring smaller hacienda owners. Many of these were dependant on El Paraiso for replacing or building up their teams of young female indentured servants, or for crossing with them to prevent excessive inter-breeding amongst their own small stock.

The first type were plantation workers whose hacienda registration numbers were prefixed by a T, standing for Trabajadora, or female labourer. These women, mainly black, were carefully chosen to stand up to long hours of working docilely in the hot sun, picking coffee beans or cotton.

Second were household servants. Their numbers were prefixed by the letter C for Criada, or maidservant. They were chosen for their beauty, intelligence and obedience. They often had white blood in their breeding, and indeed the whiter they were, ranging from mulattos through quadroons up to octroons, the more valuable they were.

The final type, found only on the larger and more remote haciendas, such as El Paraiso, were pony-girls. Their registration numbers were prefixed by a Y, standing for Yegua, or mare. They were, of course, bred to have the long legs, speed, stamina and conformity needed to win the trotting races and dressage competitions that were so popular amongst the big landowners and the local peasantry - as well as in the more discreetly held show rings.

Once a a successful pony-girl had been earmarked for breeding, then to denote her special status as a valuable brood mare, the letter V was added after her number, for Yegua de Vientre, literally belly mare.

The oligarchy of rich landowners, who strictly controlled the outwardly peaceful country of Costa Negra, had long since learnt that young women rather than young men made an ideal and cheap labour force for the plantations on which they depended for their wealth. At the same time they had learnt that Indian men made excellent overseers, standing no nonsense from the women in their charge.

Strict laws ensured that the women remained their virtual property and indeed on the more remote plantations conditions were virtually unchanged since the days of slavery.

Originally many women, negresses, mulattos, mestizos and even poor white women, finding themselves threatened with starvation and misery, had willingly accepted the terms for female indentured service: service for a period of twenty years from the age of 21. Girls below twenty one, who were indentured servants, were legally considered to be 'under training'.

The system had continued to the present day, since it was largely self perpetuating, for all female children born to indentured servants were themselves automatically indentured in return for for their keep and upbringing.

Plantation owners were thus encouraged to take steps to ensure that the supply of of suitable female indentured servants did not dry up!

Carlos reached for one of the older girl's full breasts. The milk was delicious. Absent-mindedly he stroked the smaller pointed breasts of her sister. They were perhaps disappointingly small, but he knew that there was a simple answer to that problem - the same solution as he had used on her sister.

"I think Marguerita," he said decisively, "it's time you were sent to the the breeding pens."

The girl gave a gasp. She did not know whether to be proud to be selected or horrified at the thought of being taken by one of the plantation studs. If only she could be allowed to bear her Master a son! But then she knew that the landowning class were careful not to use their indentured servant woman to spawn numerous squabbling heirs - and coloured ones at that.

"Oh, please, Master!" she cried.

But he had something more urgent on his mind, for whilst the two dusky girls now gently licked and stroked Carlos's body, he reached down and opened a letter lying on the verandah table under the hammock.

HACIENDA

The letter was from his lawyers in the capital city. It told
him that Diana Carstairs, his young English cousin by marriage had been in touch with them. Diana Carstairs? Ah, yes,
he remembered meeting her briefly several years ago in London. He had a vague memory of a tall, rather lanky and quite
pretty schoolgirl, who had talked to him about her her athletic prowess. But she was now coming to Costa Negra in
two weeks time! But the letter went to warn him that she was
coming to to contest the will of Carlos's aunt who had re-
cently died, leaving the El Paraiso estate to him.

The girls in the hammock trembled as Carlos read this,
sensing his anger.

How dare she! For ten years now he had been running the
remote estate for his aunt who had lived in the capital. He
had had a free hand to run it as he liked - and he had done so
very successfully. Not only had the yields of coffee beans
been exceptionally high, but he had also shown considerable aptitude for breeding and training a a series of both
winning racehorses and pony girls.

And now this chit of an English girl was threatening his
very inheritance. And what did she know about plantation
life? Or of what what went on in the cruel macho police
state of Costa Negra?

It was true that thirty years years ago, a young English-
man, James Carstairs, had arrived in Costa Negra to seek his
fortune. He had married a wealthy heiress, Carlos's aunt,
and had bought El Paraiso. On his death Carlos's aunt had
inherited the estate. Now suddenly this English girl, Carstairs'
niece, had had the temerity to contest Carlos's right to El
Paraiso!

The letter warned that under Costa Negra law Diana would
have a good legal case for at least half of her uncle's estate
and advised Carlos to take immediate steps to defend his
inheritance - though they did not suggest how.

Carlos's knuckles whitened as he gripped the offending

letter and the girls were greatly relieved to hear wheels on the gravel approach to the other side of the house. Diverted by this fortunate event, Carlos jumped out of the hammock and went to the window that looked out onto the drive.

It was his great friend and secret lover, Senora Inez Mendoza, whose husband owned the neighbouring hacienda. Inez, he knew, enjoyed girls as well as men, and he saw that she was driving her little dog cart which was being drawn by a perfectly matched pair of slightly coffee coloured girls harnessed one behind the other.

Most of the tracks and paths that wound around the estates in the area were too narrow for a horse drawn carriage, or a car or truck, and it was therefore usual to use indentured servants to pull their masters and mistresses around their estates in little dog carts. These resembled Chinese rickshaws with shafts between which a woman could be chained, with if necessary another in front of her to to provide more pulling power.

The two sweating girls were naked, except for a small leather belly flap, that hung down in front over their intimacies from a wide leather girth strap that was buckled tightly round their waists. The front of the belly flap was prettily decorated with the brand mark of the Mendoza hacienda.

The woman nearest to the dog cart, known as the Wheeler, was chained to the shafts by two short pairs of chains that linked the shafts to rings on either side of her girth strap. Another chain was fastened to a ring on the back of the Wheeler's girth to another ring on the front of the dog cart.

It was this last chain that took the strain when the woman was pulling the cart forward. The chains on either side of the Wheeler enabled her to steer the dog cart by pulling on one or other of the shafts in response to her reins. They also acted as the backing and braking chains, making the woman act as a brake for the dog cart when going downhill and enabling her to push it backwards when reversing.

Both pairs of chains were tightly fastened so that the woman was held rigidly between the shafts by her girth straps. The slightest movement of her belly forwards, backwards, or sideways, was transmitted by the chains to the pony cart or its shafts, making the cart go either forward or backwards, or turn.

Thus, going down hill, the weight would be transmitted by the side chains onto the woman's girth strap, pulling her forward. However, as the back chain prevented her from going forward, she was forced to act as a brake, leaning back in order not to lose her footing.

The woman's wrists were also fastened to the side of the girth straps so that her elbows were well back behind her hips and she was unable to grip the shafts. This meant that to move the dog cart she was forced to thrust out her breasts and pull back her shoulders.

This in turn was an ideal posture for being made to trot along prettily with her knees raised in front of her, and her breasts swinging rhythmically in time with her trotting gait - something which would not have been so easy to achieve if she had simply been allowed to lean forward and use her hands to pull the cart along by its shafts with her hands.

The Wheeler's companion, the Leader as she was known, was also naked except for a short belly flap and the broad girth strap round her waist, and her wrists were also strapped to this girth strap. As she was placed ahead of the shafts, she had no side chains, but, as with the Wheeler, a short chain was fastened to a ring at the back of the girth, in the small of her back. This back chain was not led back to the dog cart, as was the case with the Wheeler's back chain, but instead was fastened to another ring situated in the front of the Wheelers girth strap.

Thus, as the Wheeler pushed forward, she was further pulled forward by the chain leading back from the Leader's belly girth. The driver in the dog cart could readily check the tautness of the chain linking the two women, and the chain linking the Wheeler to the dog cart, and use his long carriage whip to correct any idleness by either of them.

If the going was easy, then it was normal practice for only one woman to be used to pull a dog cart with an additional one often running along behind, chained by the neck to the back of the cart. If the going became particularly heavy or hilly - as was the path between the two estates - then the spare girl could be chained ahead of the Wheeler.

In this case, both women were fitted with tight leather bridles. A leather band went round each of their foreheads and was fastened with a buckle at the back of the head. To prevent this strap from slipping down their faces two steadying straps went across the tops of their heads, one from ear to ear and one from the front of the forehead to the buckle at the back of the head.

Just forward of the ears another short strap hung down and on either side supported a large metal ring. A big rubber bit was fastened to this ring and lay across the top of the mouth of each woman on top of her tongue.

To prevent a woman from getting her tongue over the bit it was fitted with a flat rubber projection that lay on top of her tongue, thus forcing her to accept the bit that controlled her.

To ensure that the bit was kept tightly in her mouth another strap went from both cheek rings, back behind her neck, where they were joined by a buckle. Another pair of straps hung down below the rings and were buckled tightly under her chin preventing her from opening her mouth to talk, or to try and spit out the bit.

To provide better leverage on the women's mouths, a further driving ring was brazed onto each cheek ring, and it was to this ring that the reins were fastened which led back to where the driver sat, carriage whip in hand. If the driver pulled back on the reins, then the driving ring would turn the cheek ring, and hence turn the bit in the woman's mouth, raising the stiff extension piece against the roof of her mouth.

To make the woman trot on faster, the driver relied, of course, on his whip.

To ensure that the women concentrated on their task it was normal to fit their bridles with blinkers on either side of their eyes so that they could only see immediately in front.

As Carlos well knew, it was all a simple and yet devilishly clever way of harnessing a woman to a dog cart - and in such way that she could be made to prance prettily along!

A young Negro boy postillion stood at the back of the dog cart on a little step with his arms folded. He wore Senora Mendoza's red and blue livery - red pantaloons, a little short blue coatee or bolero that left his little boy's chest naked and a red cap with a tall blue feather.

As Senora Mendoza drove the dog cart at a smart trot up the sweep of the hacienda drive to the front door, the boy groom jumped down. He ran up to the Leader and held her by her bridle. Senora Mendoza put her long carriage whip into the container at the side of the dog cart and stepped down.

"Keep them here, Juanito," she ordered. "Let them have just a sip of water. I don't want them getting colic."

The household maid servants showed her onto the back porch where Carlos was beaming with pleasure at the sight of his lover.

"Oh, you naughty boy Carlos! Two young girls in your hammock! You'll make me jealous!"

Then she saw the expression of anxiety on Carlos' face. "What is it darling? What's the matter?"

Silently, Carlos handed Inez the lawyer's letter. She read it quickly.

"The little bitch! Trying to rob you of your inheritance! You must shut her up quickly. What will you do?"

"Oh, I'll think of something ... Now let's forget this unpleasant matter. Tell me all about your visit to the other valley. What's the gossip there? How are the new stables getting on?"

"Well, I must say that Fernando has certainly got himself a beautifully matched pair of two white fillies for his spanking new stables!"

"What!" exclaimed Carlos. "White girls!"

"Yes!" replied Inez with a laugh. "Two pretty American girls - young school teachers who came to Costa Negra as tourists. They were arrested carrying drugs and you know how tough the police are about that! With no publicity they were sentenced to twenty years in prison and, after a short time in the horrendous conditions of our prisons, they quickly volunteered for what they imagined would be a life of ease on a hacienda!"

"Little imagining," mused Carlos, "that they would be auctioned as indentured servants!"

"Yes! Fernando saw their description in the list. Most of the big landowners fought shy of buying American girls, but he decided that, out here, his plantation was far away enough to be out of the public eye. So he bought them both cheap! Like so many American and English girls the're very tall and long legged, and being keen on tennis are quite athletic. So he's put them into training in his trotting stables. He says that locked up in his stables as pony girls, they'll have no opportunity to contact the outside world or escape . He even says that if they do well racing, then he'll breed from them and start a new breeding line!"

"Breeding from white women!" queried Carlos. "Well well!"

"Why not? They're only indentured servants, after all. And out here we can do what we like with them. He says they can jolly well earn their keep and that he wants to cross the determination and agility of the whites with the strength and

13

stamina of the blacks. I saw them shut up in his stables and then being being trotted round and round his menage on a lounging rein. They had been broken in and were coming on nicely. And I must say I didn't think that they'll ever escape! Indeed they looked such a pretty and submissive pair that I wondered whether I might copy his idea and ..."

"Good heavens," interrupted a suddenly excited Carlos. "You've given me a brilliant idea. Listen ..."

## 2 - MISS CARSTAIRS' PREDICAMENT

Diana Carstairs' turbo-jet circled the compact little airport, giving her a first glimpse of Costa Negra - lush green countryside and the seemingly distant mountains she had just flown over, blue with haze. It was the first time she had been outside of England, and she found it a thrilling experience.

The inter-continental flight from Heathrow to Central South America had been an excitement in itself. One of the stewards had been distinctly handsome. And here she was, about to claim a ranch. El Paraiso - even the name was exotic. What an adventure!

Now, as she stepped down from the little plane into the blinding sunshine, a police officer asked her name. He asked in English. What a relief, for she knew that she could not cope with Spanish. That was what they spoke here, Spanish.

God, it was hot!

It must be Carlos who had alerted them to look out or her. Good old Carlos! She remembered meeting him once. She had been a schoolgirl then, and she had been madly impressed by this tall dark handsome man from Latin America. He had seemed so suave, so self confident, and, if she dared to admit it, so wonderfully dominant and commanding. What a

14

contrast to the rather nice but weak brothers of her school friends.

Yes, she admitted to herself, she had had quite a school-girl crush on him. And now he was helping her. How generous of him, when she had come to reclaim the estate that he might have come to consider his.

The man led her to the terminal building, but the VIP lounge, as she supposed it to be, was a distinct disappointment. A bare room. A fat cigar-smoking man hulking behind a desk. Customs, she supposed, as she handed over the keys to her case. Two policemen with wicked looking guns in the waist holsters now stood just inside the door. It was quite cold in here, rather off putting in fact...

The fat man beckoned, puffing complacently on his cigar. He took the keys to her case and threw them to another man in uniform, then held out his hand for her handbag, opened it and turned it upside down. Less politeness now. Everything fell out, return ticket, driving licence, passport, everything. He opened her passport and started to examine it.

Then the man who was checking suitcase shouted and held up a small package wrapped in plastic.

"Drogas!" he shouted. "Contrabandista!"

Diana looked round from stony face to stony face, and then horror struck her, froze her breathless.

"I've never seen it before!" she said. She looked from stony face to stony face. "He must have put it there!"

"It is heroin," said the fat man. He spoke English quite well, but there was a malicious gleam in his dark piggy eyes. "You are a smuggler, Senorita! That is not nice."

"I'm not!" screamed Diana, "I'm not!"

"It is not advisable to smuggle drugs into this country, Senorita," said the fat man. "The penalties are severe!"

Diana staggered across the dark dungeon that had been

her home for the two weeks since she had been sentenced to twenty years in prison! Twenty years in prison - that was all that she had understood of her mockery of a trial, but it was more than enough.

Twenty years! She could not stand another day of this dungeon. It was in an old sea fort and the sea swept through a grill at high tide, washing away her wastes and leaving a muddy stinking surface that only dried gradually, in time for the next high tide. There was no comfort whatsoever, and, moreover, a heavy chain linked her ankles together, making even walking extremely difficult, even had the cell been bigger.

There was movement at the door...

The the judge from her trial!

A man carried in a trestle table and the judge produced a document resplendent with red seals and ribbon, and waved it in her face.

She was handed a pen.

"What is this?" she asked.

"Sign," he said.

She hesitated.

"Leave prison," he said.

A sudden relief rushed through her. Carlos must have arranged this! Eagerly she signed the magnificent document. Now all would be well...


## 3 - PLANS ARE MADE

Don Carlos Ortiz smiled happily as he put down the telephone.

His cousin the Minister of Police had just confirmed that Diana had voluntarily signed her indenture papers, which would be put up for sale at the monthly auction in a few days time.

It had really all gone off very smoothly, as it should do in a ruthless police state!

Should he really buy Diana's indenture herself, Carlos mused? Or would it be more amusing to let it be bought by one of the brothels? The thought of the proud and arrogant Diana being forced to offer herself to numerous men was very satisfying.

No, he decided, that would be too dangerous. Diana might escape, or manage to send out a message. Then all efforts to silence her could come to nought.

No, Carlos resolved, there was simply no alternative. Diana must be brought back to El Paraiso to serve as an indentured servant on the estate, where he could keep a close eye on her. Even if she did escape from the remote estate, she would probably soon be recaptured or handed over to the police by the local peasantry. There would be little chance of her escaping from El Paraiso or of smuggling out letters.

Moreover, mused Carlos, it would be amusing to have Diana under his control here, and to treat her as a genuine indentured servant on the estate she had come to Costa Negra to claim as her own. But under what heading should he have Diana entered in the estate register? She hardly had the physique to be a labourer. It might well be amusing to have her as a household servant - perhaps as his personal maid.

But would that be safe? Might she not try to escape or try to contact the British consul or her family back in England? That would be disastrous. She might get her hands on the estate after all. No, she would have to be kept under strict control and constant surveillance. So how should she be used on the estate?

Carlos remembered what Inez had told her about her friend Fernando buying two American girls' indentures and putting them both into his stables. Perhaps that was the answer! After all Diana was tall and buxom with long legs. She might make an excellent pony woman, and certainly there would be no escape from the stables - or chance of smuggling out a letter! No, as a pony girl, she would be well and truly silenced!

Carlos' eyes gleamed as he read the sales leaflet that had been sent to him:

Private and Confidential
State of Costa Negra
Ministry of Police

The following female prisoners, sentenced to hard labour, having voluntarily signed indentures for service in accordance with the law governing indentured servants, notice is hereby given that the indentures of these women will be sold by private auction at noon at the El Rosal prison in one week's time. The prisoners may be inspected between 9 and 11 a.m. immediately prior to the sale by those invited to the sale or their authorised representatives.

The Ministry of Police will undertake the delivery of each woman to the estate or brothel designated by the purchaser. After delivery the purchaser will be responsible to the Ministry of Police for the woman's safe custody until her sentence has been completed or the woman returned to the custody of the Police at the El Rosal prison.

Lot No 1
Mulatto. Aged 25. Pleasing appearance. 6 months pregnant, would make good wet nurse. Sentenced to 10 years hard labour.

Lot No 2
Nearly white mestizo. Aged 18. Pretty. Dark hair. Tall and slender. Obedient. Recommended for use in brothel or as household servant. Sentenced to 5 years hard labour.

Lot No 5
White. European looking. Aged 23. Tall. Buxom but slender. Very Pretty. Blonde hair and blue eyes. Highly intelligent. Speaks no Spanish. Argumentative and recalcitrant. Will need strict discipline and close supervision. Sentenced to 20 years hard labour.

Lot No 6 ...

Carlos smiled as she recognised Diana as Lot No 5.

The sales list had been confidentially distributed to those leading landowners and brothel keepers who were known to be in the market for fresh supplies of women for their estates or their brothels.

Meanwhile Diana herself, completely unsuspecting her fate, had been delighted to find herself in a bright clean cell with two of the other women who had signed indentures and who were going to be auctioned with her. As she spoke no Spanish and as they spoke no English she still did not learn what was going to happen to her. She just thought she was being rested and smartened up before being released.

The women's heavy leg irons were removed. Their clothes were brought back to them. Their hair was washed and set. They were given make-up and a big mirror. Instead of being supervised by a male guard, they were looked after by a friendly woman warden. They were encouraged to make themselves as beautiful as possible, and indeed the other two women knew that their fate largely depended on how much they attracted their buyers. They were given healthy and nourishing food, bathed daily, and had the run of a little garden.

Soon Diana had almost forgotten the horrors of the dungeon open to the tide, of the terrible leg irons, of the lack of any sanitation or bedding. She quickly recovered again and after several days was looking as radiant and gorgeous as ever. She simply could not understand why she and her companions had not been released. Why were they being kept in relative luxury but still locked up?

She was rather surprised when, one morning, their woman warder gave them little wrap round tunics to put on, under which they were to be naked. She thought she looked rather fetching as she looked in the mirror. The low cut top of the tunic showed off her breasts. The tunic itself was tied tightly at the side and showed off her small waist and the swell of her hips. It only reached down halfway down her thighs and showed off her long, good looking legs.

The woman wardress had paid special attention to ensuring that they washed and bathed themselves properly that morning. Diana sensed that something special was going to happen. She could see that her companions were looking anxious and excited. She thought that their moment of release must have come - but why the revealing little tunics and why were they not allowed to put on any underclothes?

She was soon to have the answer.

## 4 - THE INSPECTION COMMENCES

Suddenly the door of the cell opened.

Three burly male warders entered. Diana shrank against the wall, embarrassed at being seen by a man with nothing beneath her skimpy tunic.

They carried handcuffs and, without saying a word, went up to each of the frightened women, pulled her arms back behind her back and fastened them there with handcuffs. Diana cried out in protest, but of course no one understood her.

The women were led along a passage to a large room. There, several other women were already lined up, all similarly dressed in skimpy little tunics, and all carefully made up like herself with bright lipstick, rouge and eye shadow. Diana was the only European woman. She and her companions were lined up with the others. Facing them was a row of comfortable looking arm chairs.

Then the same hateful fat police officer who had arrested her at the airport, and who was in fact the prison governor, entered the room. The guards saluted. Diana saw that the women were becoming increasingly nervous - they knew that the moment of the sale was approaching, even if Diana did not.

The police officer had a list in his hand - the sales list. He called out the numbers, checked that the women were in the right order and pinned her lot number onto each woman's tunic. Mystified, Diana watched as the number five was pinned onto hers.

Then to make sure that the buyers would not confuse the women when they were later displayed naked, he went down the line, pulling back the wrap-around skirt and with a broad felt tip wrote her number on each woman's curved belly just below the navel.

Diana was appalled when she saw what he was doing to the other women. She suddenly realised that something awful was going to happen.

When he came in front of her and pulled back her short tunic to bare her belly, she screamed and tried to run away, but a guard held her tightly from behind by the scruff of her neck. With her hands handcuffed behind her back she was quite helpless.

Her screams of protest were ignored. No one seemed to understand English. The felt tip was on her belly, carefully outlining the figure five. Her naked sex and pubic hair were also displayed to the fat police officer.

Then some twenty or thirty men and women came into the room. They were all well dressed and chattering and laughing amongst themselves. Amongst them was Carlos's agent, carefully briefed to purchase Diana irrespective of the price.

The men were mainly agents and estate managers of the large landowners, though some of these themselves, finding themselves in the capital, had come to see what was on offer. Rich owners of remote estates were often interested in purchasing the indenture of a woman who had fallen foul of the law - usually as a labourer, a household servant or for their own sexual enjoyment. However they were also very conscious of the need to get a good outcross to prevent too much inter-breeding. Big estates whose breeding strains had a good reputation could sell their surplus offspring very profitably to smaller estates.

Those who went in for the absorbing hobby of breeding, training, showing or racing girls in the more isolated parts of the country, might also interested in such women - particularly if they had the long legs and good figures needed for speed and stamina in the races, and for winning in the increasingly popular show classes and dressage competitions.

Buying such an indenture could also be a very exciting investment, for quite apart from the prize money that they could earn for their owners, a pony girl's value could soar astronomically once she had won a few races or competitions - and so would that of her progeny.

As for the women who had come to attend the sale, they were mainly the Madams of the leading brothels of the city, keen to pick up a woman who would bring in the customers.

Carlos had also come to the capital to see the humiliation of the young English woman he hated, the mere chit of a girl who had tried to take away his inheritance. However he had not wanted to draw attention to himself or to Diana, and had therefore arranged with the prison governor to watch the proceedings through a convenient one way mirror that was often used by wealthy landowners to survey discreetly the girls on sale.

On this occasion Carlos was accompanied by Inez Mendoza. She had come partly to see and enjoy the degradation of Diana, about whom of course Carlos had told her, and partly because she herself was looking for another 'ladies maid' to join her little harem of pretty young girls - girls who were kept exclusively for the sexual use of herself and her woman friends and not allowed near a man!

Inez had been particularly interested in the description of Lot No 2 on the confidential sales list that had been sent to her; the pretty 18 year old nearly white mestizo - a type of girl whom she had found could be trained into a most satisfactory intimate maidservant for an older lesbian woman.

Inez and Carlos had given their agents instructions to inspect Lot No's 2 and 5 carefully, and to report on their findings before the actual auction. They were also to ensure that the women, when naked, were made to display themselves properly whilst they watched from behind the one way mirror.

Carlos had also told his agent to inspect Diana very closely from the breeding point of view, as he wanted to see her being humiliated. Moreover the agent was himself a very experienced breeder of indentured servants and his opinion on Diana's potential in this field would be worth having. The introduction of a little white European blood into the El Paraiso breeding lines might turn out very well!

Her hands fastened behind her back, Diana watched with embarrassment as the smartly dressed men and women settled themselves in their comfortable chairs. For them it was a social occasion, rather like a sale of yearlings at Newmarket in England. Indeed, although Diana still did not realise what was happening, there was distinct similarities for several of the young women would be bought to be put straight into training for trotting races, and to see whether she had the stamina, courage and physique to make a winner.

The governor clapped his hands.

"Senores y Senoras," he began, "welcome to our latest sale of indentures. I think you find that we have some very interesting lots to offer you. As usual we will first exhibit each lot individually and demonstrate its strength and possibilities and then we will give you all an opportunity to have a general look at them. Then finally they will be positioned for inspections of a more intimate nature!"

This last remark was greeted with a burst of cruel laughter.

"Then," the Governor went on, "after that, the indentures will be auctioned! ... Now first, Lot Number One!"

A guard roughly pushed the mulatto girl forward. With her hands handcuffed behind her back, her slightly swollen belly was pushed forward under her short tunic. Her big pretty eyes were darting here and there in obvious fear. She was a tall girl, coffee coloured, with long black hair and pretty delicate features.

"Lot Number One is a mulatto and aged 25," began the Governor. "As you can see her features owe more to her European blood than to her Negro ancestors. She was the mistress of an American doctor and is herself a partly trained nurse. She is six months pregnant by her white boy friend and is carrying her child well. It will be her first. Both on her mother's side and her husband's there is a history of predominantly female offspring and so there is an excellent chance that she will drop a quadroon girl."

The spectators were looking at the young dark girl with interest. Several were murmuring to each other and pointing at her, others were writing notes on their catalogues.

"She was arrested when carrying drugs," went on the

Governor, glossing over the fact that, as with Diana, the drugs were put into her handbag by the police after she had been arrested. "She was sentenced to ten years hard labour. Her lover was deported as an undesirable alien and has not been heard of since."

The Governor nodded to one of the guards, who came round and unbuttoned her tunic top. He slid it down over one of her breasts.

"As you can see, this young woman has good big breasts. She will be able to feed several young children and could play a most useful role as a wet nurse in a private household or rearing several children in your breeding pens. Her training as a nurse would make her ideal for this, and her good child-rearing hips would also make her suitable for regular annual breeding. She's good strong stock and if mated with a suitable stud her offspring should be very suitable for hard work."

Again he nodded to the guards. The dark young girl was led over to a row of baskets. Each was prominently marked with the weight in kilos of heavy stones that had been placed in it. The lightest was marked '10 kilos', the next '20 kilos' and so on up to '50 kilos'.

The two guards carried vicious looking dog whips in their hands. They gave the girl an order, and unlocked her handcuffs. She bent down, picked up the basket marked '10 kilos', and lifted it up onto her head. For a heavily pregnant woman it was quite a weight, but obviously she was capable of carrying more, for she was a well built girl.

The guards ordered her to put it down. Then they pointed at the basket marked '30 kilos'. She looked at it with horror and shook her head. Many of the watchers stopped gossiping amongst themselves and watched keenly.

One guard again pointed at the basket with his dog whip and the other suddenly brought his whip down across her buttocks under the short little tunic. She screamed, but she bent down and very slowly, slowly started to lift the basket up. Her muscles were straining. The guard raised the whip again. With a terrific effort she placed the basket on her head and held it there, balanced with both hands.

The guards gave her a new order. With a desperate effort she began to walk around the big room, showing what weight she could carry. Her knees began to buckle. The whip was raised again. She straightened herself up, her swollen belly lifting the bottom of the tunic well above her thighs.

Another word of command and she started to run, stumbling round the room. Normally the governor liked to keep a woman running with her maximum weight until she had gone round the room half a dozen times. But on this occasion with such a heavily pregnant woman, he did not want to run the risk of an accident that might lower her price, and after only one circuit of the big room, she was allowed to stop and put her basket back from where she had picked it up.

"So ladies and gentlemen," said the Governor, "you have seen that Lot Number One can carry no less than 30 kilos and run with such a load. I think you will agree that this is a remarkable feat for a girl six months pregnant. Indeed if she had not been pregnant, my guards even now would be seeing what she would make of the 40 and 50 kilo baskets. You can see that she is very good breeding stock, and represents a wonderful opportunity to get a new strong line into your breeding strains."

The poor mulatto girl, sweat running down her front from the exertion was taken back to the line of trembling, waiting women. Her hands were again fastened behind her back. Then the next girl, No 2, was thrust forward.

"The next item in your catalogue is a delicate little thing, almost white, Aged 18. She has a docile character and I think would do well in a brothel or as a household servant."

The governor went on describing the young girl's attributes and then, just in case a big landowner was thinking of buying her for his breeding pens, she too had to show what she could lift. In fact that she was such a slender young thing that she twice dropped the 20 kilo basket, bringing the dog whips down hard into her buttocks, and it was clear that she could really only run round the big room properly with the 10 kilo basket on her head.

And so the parade continued, until the governor cried:

"And now we come to our special item today. This very pretty European blonde young lady who will be a bond maid for a full twenty years. What will it be for her: to be the prize exhibit of a brothel, a fancied ladies maid, or the pride of the stables, perhaps a brood mare bringing an injection of new white blood into a well established breeding line?"

## 5 - DIANA IS PUT THROUGH HER PACES

Diana, with her hands still handcuffed behind her back, was brought forward in complete silence.

She blushed deeply as she realised that her brief tunic scarcely hid her charms. She blushed even more when the guard undid the top buttons, reached into the tunic and then held up in his hand one of her breasts, displaying it to the silently watching audience.

But worse was to follow, for the guard came behind her and, reaching forward, undid several more buttons on the front of her tunic. Then he jerked it back over her shoulders, baring both her breasts. With a cry she tried to turn away from the seated watchers, but the guard roughly pulled her back to face them.

Diana felt she could have died of shame as, still standing behind her, he again reached forward and this time lifted up both breasts in his hands, pointing them towards the audience, and showing off both their size and resilience.

Holding her still with one hand, he slowly began to rub first one nipple and then the other. Diana gasped with a mixture of shame and excitement as she felt her nipples and her breasts swell under his remorseless touch.

The Governor gave a nod, and she was made to lift first the 10 kilo basket and then the 20 kilo one. But the guards were not satisfied, and soon she was struggling and straining to lift the 40 kilo one, and then to run round the room with its appalling weight on her head.

Diana just could not believe that she could be made to do such a thing, but a few taps from the dog whips and she was struggling and sweating like her predecessors to show off her strength.

And so the show continued until all the lots had been properly displayed, and it was time for the spectators to come and have a closer look at the wares.

It was, understandably, two Madames from the brothels who first crowded round Diana, stroking her blond hair, and feeling her soft skin. One was unpleasantly fat, and it was she who went behind Diana, running a pudgy hand down her back and lifting up the little tunic over her bottom.

"Yes, I think that many an older man would pay handsomely to whip that charmingly plump backside. Let's look at her teeth -"

Then there was a scream as the woman jumped back, shaking her hand in pain. Diana had bitten hard, drawing blood! The other Madame smacked Diana's face hard, bringing tears to her face, but many of the other purchasers merely laughed.

Carlos smiled with delight as he watched. Her temperament would make her forthcoming taming, and breaking in as a filly, all the more amusing, and meanwhile it would also frighten off some of the other bidders.

He was also delighted to see that she was indeed a beautiful girl with a good figure. She had only been a school girl when he had met her before in England. As he looked at her half naked body through the one way mirror, he gloated over the fact that she was now a most attractive young woman.

For the next quarter of an hour, Diana, like the other women on display, was poked, prodded, felt, squeezed and stroked by almost all the men and women purchasers. She felt degraded and humiliated as her body was discussed in front of her, but the worst part was yet to come.

The governor clapped his hands and the purchasers drifted back to their chairs, exchanging views and comments on the women they had examined. Then the guards went down the line of the women, unlocking their handcuffs and fastening their wrists to straps hanging from the ceiling, so that their arms, bent at the elbows were held level with their heads. At the same time their tunics were completely removed so that the women were displayed stark naked.

Diana's embarrassment was even more heightened when she saw that the guards were coming down the line fastening each woman's ankles wide apart.

As her feet were separated to be chained, she could feel that, under her pubic hair, her sex lips were now open to the watching purchasers, and a blush spread across her cheeks and breasts, much to the delight of the watching Carlos.

Then the guards went back up the line fastening a collar round each girl's neck. From a ring, at the back of each woman's collar, a chain was led down to a pulley between her legs. A handle was fastened on the end of the chain, and a little stool was placed in front of each woman. Alongside each stool was placed a pair of thin rubber surgical gloves and a pot of vaseline.

The governor clapped his hands once more and with a polite gesture invited the purchasers to make more intimate inspections of any of the women in whom they were interested. Diana was horrified to see the fat Madame coming towards her, grim faced. She was going to get her revenge on Diana for biting her, seeking her revenge in a particularly humiliating way! She sat down heavily on the stool and slowly reached down to pull up the handle.

Suddenly Diana felt a downwards tug on her collar. The woman pulled harder and Diana found herself being forced to bend her widely outstretched knees and to lower herself until her sex lips were level with the fat woman's face.

With her neck pulled back by the strain on her collar Diana was unable to look down to see what the woman was doing. But she felt hands on her sex lips and gave a gasp; no woman had ever touched her there. She felt her lips being felt. She knew that they were already widely parted. She tried to close her legs together but the combination of her ankles being strapped wide apart and the pressure on her neck making her keep her knees bent, defeated her. There was nothing she could do to prevent the odious woman from feeling up inside her most intimate parts.

She could not wriggle away! It was awful!

Carlos watched the degradation of Diana with pleasure as the fat woman felt the tightness between her beauty lips, something she always did before buying a woman for her brothel. Indeed she now proceeded to feel and examine Diana just as she might any woman she was interested in acquiring.

Diana was very tight. The Madame knew at once that here was a woman who, though not a virgin, had had little sexual experience; a young woman who had felt that it was wrong to make love before getting married; a young woman who had being trying to keep herself pure for her future husband, just the kind of that many of her clients would pay dearly to take by force.

Earlier on she had noticed how sensitive Diana's breasts were. Now, calling over her friend, she asked her to take over the handle and to keep pulling it well up, so as to keep Diana's knees bent and her beauty lips well displayed.

Then, keeping one hand on Diana's stretched and open beauty lips, with her middle finger up inside Diana, she started to caress the young woman's breasts with her other hand. After a minute she started to caress Diana's nipples and was rewarded by a juddering shock that went right through Diana's body. In no time at all she began to feel a fresh mucous discharge inside Diana.

Diana was horrified at the way her body was betraying her to this repulsive fat woman, but she simply could not stop herself becoming aroused as the woman played with her.

Satisfied with her test, the Madame proceeded with the next part of her examination. Whilst her friend kept Diana's chain tight so that she had to display herself in the same wanton way, the Madame slipped the thin rubber surgical gloves onto her right hand. Then she dipped the middle finger into the jar of vaseline between Diana's feet. Next she reached forward with her hand between Diana's legs, feeling for her rear orifice.

Diana gave a little cry of protest as she felt the greasy finger pressing against her rose. She tried to close her buttocks, but she was held helpless. She felt the woman's finger pressing hard against her, and then beginning to feel its way inside her.

A second later and she felt a strange new feeling as first one finger, and then two, pushed their way deep inside her. She tried to writhe and wriggle in protest to squeeze out the invading fingers, but all she could achieve was a little sideways shake of her hips, and this only served to enable the probing fingers to go even deeper inside her.

Smiling, the Madame recognised from the feel of the girl and from her protests, that she was a virgin here. This would undoubtedly increase her value in a brothel! She moved her fingers up and down inside Diana and was delighted once again to feel with her other hand, still between the girl's beauty lips, a further flow of mucous. So the little slut was also sexually sensitive behind! She would indeed make a good little whore!

The fat Madame withdrew her finger and pulled off her glove. Now would come the final humiliation of this chit of a girl who had dared to bite her. Keeping the middle finger of one hand up Diana's beauty lips, with the other hand she started to stroke and caress her beauty bud itself.

"No! No!" Diana cried out, but to no avail.

The experienced madame knew what she was doing and gradually brought Diana towards a climax. Diana began to pant. Red blotches appeared on her breasts and neck. The mucous discharge became more and more copious. Diana was appalled. She was going to be made to have an orgasm standing up in front of all these people. It was too awful, but she simply could not help herself.

Seeing what was going on, several other purchasers came and stood round Diana. One of these was Carlos's agent, who watched carefully so that he could report later to Carlos. Because of the crowd, Carlos could not properly see the final act of degradation, as panting and with outstretched legs Diana approached her climax. However he would have plenty of opportunity to repeat it when she got Diana back to El Paraiso!

The Madame could feel Diana's body muscles gripping her finger in desperation as she approached her climax.

"Very good," she muttered, and then, so as to give the watchers a better view, she removed her hand from between the helpless beauty lips, just keeping one finger of the other hand on the girl's bud. Diana could not help herself crying out in protest as the finger was withdrawn from up inside her, but the madame had judged the moment exactly - Diana was already starting her climax. Her belly and thighs juddered and shook, she cried out aloud, and the discharge ran down the insides of her thighs.

She had indeed displayed herself to be a really randy young woman, a woman whose violent climaxes would give great pleasure to any man who purchased her body for a night!

Slowly Diana came to herself again. The fat woman had gone! The handle lay on the floor. Her neck chain was slack. She straightened her knees and stood up, her legs still held wide apart. She swayed weekly, exhausted from her orgasm, but she was held up by her wrist straps. No one paid any attention to her. The purchasers were gathered around two other women who were being put through their paces, just as she had been. She could see the rhythmically shaking belly of one of the other women as she was brought to her climax. She heard the woman's cries and the laughs of the spectators.

During the next half hour several other purchasers came up to her, sat down on the stool in front of her, pulled up the handle and pulled down her widely parted thighs so as to have a good feel up inside her both between her beauty lips and from behind.

One such watcher was a rather prim looking woman who looked rather like the headmistress of a girls school. This was exactly what she was! She ran a discreet 'school' for young girls outside the town. But although the inmates were dressed, treated and disciplined just like young girls, in fact they were young women of Diana's age. The school was run on strict convent lines and no men were ever allowed to enter the school, nor were the girls even allowed the opportunity to see a man, never mind talk to one!

This school was in fact a very high class brothel for rich lesbian women. Many wealthy women sent young reluctant lesbian partners to this school.

The headmistress was always on the lookout for new girls. She was seriously interested in Diana, provided she did not turn out to be too expensive. She realised of course that Diana was no lesbian, but that did not matter. Many of her wealthy clients enjoyed dominating a young woman who found it repulsive to have to please a older woman. Indeed it was by no means unknown for them to have a young woman kidnapped on the eve of her wedding and incarcerated in the 'school', where she would be dressed and treated as a little girl, and visited daily by her 'aunt', who would order her to undergo regular floggings until of her own free will she begged to be allowed to attend to the intimate requirements of the 'aunt'.

Several men, managers of large estates, also examined Diana intimately, but none so closely as Carlos's agent. Initially he paid great attention to her thighs and belly muscles. He had noticed Diana's stamina when she had been made to run, and he now felt that Carlos might well have inadvertently stumbled on the acquisition of an outstanding pony-girl.

However, as he checked Diana's conformity he could not make up his mind yet awhile whether she would be best as a trotting racer pulling a light racing cart, or as a dressage pony pulling a dog cart through a long and complicated series of tests designed to show off her driver's control over her, or as a show pony competing for looks and perfect bodily condition at the many local horse shows!

However, irrespective of the actual field in which she proved best, her breasts, so firm and prominent, would undoubtedly be a great asset.

There was a further matter that concerned him. In a climate where cows did not thrive and where their milk was suspect, many landowners liked their own human brood mares to provide them with milk, and considered that the whiter the skin of the woman the more delicious the milk. For this reason Carlos's agent also felt and examined Diana's breasts with great care, ignoring her little whimpers of pain and embarrassment.

Then Diana found herself undergoing a very detailed examination from this hard looking silent man as he sat between her outstretched legs, feeling very carefully and slowly right up inside her. Although he could never be quite sure whether a filly might turn out to be barren, from many years of experience of examining young women he had found that he could usually tell.

Diana bit her lips as he felt right up inside her, carefully probing, feeling and testing her reactions. It was all too awful and, innocent as she was, even she began to suspect with horror the purpose for which he was so closely examining her!

Carlos's agent did not arouse her. He had watched carefully when she had been made to climax by the Madame, and was satisfied that if required she could be quickly aroused. He was by no means convinced that it was always necessary or desirable that a pony girl, being covered by a stallion with a high stud fee, a fee which had to be paid each time a stallion ejaculated into her, should be brought to a climax or even aroused!

His own experience with both natural and artificial insemination had shown that a woman would often conceive more readily when she was 'cold' rather than when she was aroused. He had found that the right timing and a good deep penetration, whether it was by a syringe or by a stallion's own manhood, were more important than the extent of the girl's own arousal in achieving a good, and preferably multiple, conception.

Equally important was the positioning of the human mare so that the precious seed slid up inside her and did not run out!

Satisfied with his examination, he rose and left the room to go and report to Carlos, and shortly afterwards all the women were taken out of the room to pretty themselves up again for the actual sale.

Carlos was delighted that his experienced agent's recommendation to buy Diana for use as a pony and potential brood mare coincided with his own ideas. It would be an exquisite revenge to have Diana in his stables, and if she turned out to be a winner so much the better. Carlos had, in any case, been keen to introduce some fresh European blood into his stud and the idea of using Diana for this was one he found very exciting.

His agent thought that the combination of Diana's recalcitrant nature as described in the sales list, and her displays of temper during the examination period, would frighten off many of the would-be purchasers, and enable Carlos to buy Diana for a reasonable sum.

## 6 - AUCTIONED!

Meanwhile Diana and the other women had been taken back to their cells and told to beautify themselves again.

Her two companions made themselves look as attractive as possible - each desperately hoping to be bought as household servants, or even for a brothel. Anything was preferable to being a labourer on the coffee or cotton estates.

The door suddenly opened.

The same three big burly prison guards were there, and all three women were quickly handcuffed again, taken out of the cell and thrust into a little room next to the large one in which they had been so shamefully displayed and examined. They could hear the animated voices of the men and women purchasers. This was the moment of truth, the moment in which would be decided how their future years would be spent.

Diana heard the governor's voice. The door opened.

Two guards seized the pregnant mulatto girl with the number One pinned onto her tunic and, holding her by the arms, led her out. There was silence in the little room. They could hear the governor's voice again, and shouts from the men and women, cries which even Diana recognised as numbers. Bids! The girl was being auctioned! It just couldn't be true - but it was!

Diana heard the bids fall away and then the bang of the auctioneers hammer. The door opened again and the mulatto girl, looking very flushed, her tunic untied to bare her swollen belly and her light brown breasts, was thrust back into the room.

The guards seized girl number Two, and the door was shut again. Diana could hear the bids for the pretty near white mestizo girl. She was in fact bought by Inez's agent. But, of course, she did not yet realise that her fate was to be one of Inez's harem of young girls, forced into lesbianism, forced to serve their mistress and her friends, but forbidden the delights of the touch of a man. Minutes later she too was thrust back into the room, her eyes full of tears, her tunic untied and thrust back over her shoulders so that it hung behind her back from her handcuffed wrists.

Number Two was thrust back into the room. Dear God, thought Diana, now they'll be coming for me!

Moments later the two burly men did indeed seize her and take her out. She saw that a little platform had been placed in front of the seated men and women. The guard with the carriage whip stood behind it. The guards holding her led her up to the platform, up the steps to the top, and there they left her. There was a silence. Diana raised her eyes, which had been lowered in shame and embarrassment. The comfortably seated men and women were looking at her - these same awful people who had so degradingly felt and examined her earlier on!

"I'm English, please help me!" she called out, even though she knew that it was pointless. "You've no right to -

The carriage whip caught her across the belly. She doubled

up and screamed with the pain. She did not dare speak again.

The carriage whip was cracked just behind her. She jumped. It cracked again. She knew she must raise her head and show herself to the buyers. She was too frightened not to do so.

The governor started to auction her. Several bids were made. The governor made a gesture to the two guards who had taken her into the room. They climbed up the steps to where she was standing and untied her tunic. Slowly they slid it down over her now naked breasts. The bidding continued. Then they pulled it back displaying her belly, then pulled it back over her shoulders. They stepped down again, leaving her standing there, helpless, degraded and naked, completely exposed.

Unable to cover herself, with her hands chained behind her back, Diana dropped her head in shame. The whip cracked dangerously near to her. Quickly she raised her head again, raising her large firm breasts.

The bidding continued. She could see that the main bidders were the awful fat woman, the headmistress-looking woman and the hard faced man who had so intimately examined her.

Then the headmistress-looking woman dropped out of the bidding.

It was now between the fat woman and the man. Diana watched fearfully.

Suddenly the fat woman dropped out.

The hammer fell.

Carlos was now determined to accept his agent's advice to register Diana as a pony-woman on the El Paraiso register and to use her as such. However the sight of Diana's nude body, and of her humiliating bodily displays and examinations, had thoroughly aroused him.

He found the sight of Diana's firm breasts, her slender

waist and generous hips both attractive and exciting. He wanted to enjoy them and to enjoy them before Diana passed from the status of a filly to that of a brood mare! However he did not want to remove the animal status that he was going to impose on Diana by having her put into his private harem of pampered young girls kept purely for his own pleasure.

So - Diana would spend most of her time in the stables, but from time to time Carlos would have her moved to the kennels and to his own house - but trained to behave as a bitch, crawling on all fours and sewn into a dog skin!

Yes, Carlos thought, he would really enjoy watching Diana being made to live like a bitch, as the bitch she really was - the bitch who had tried to take El Paraiso from him!

## 7 - SHORN

Two days later Carlos arrived back at the hacienda after a long drive from the capital.

It was still morning, for he had spent the night with Inez Miranda at her hacienda - a long night of love and excitement.

Like Carlos, Inez kept several young girls in her household, nominally as indentured servants but actually as a harem of lesbian slave girls. Carlos and Inez had lain on Inez's wide bed, kissing each other and fondling each others breasts, whilst two young girls lower down in the bed had tickled and kissed them, bringing them to climax after climax, whilst having to remain pure and chaste themselves.

The next morning Carlos had continued on to El Paraiso and set about making preparations for the arrival of Diana.

He lay back on a comfortable sofa, giving his orders to Gamba, his half indian mestizo house-keeper, who stood before him, a short stocky figure dressed in black, her hands caressing the handle of a dog whip which hung from her belt. This was her sign of office, her sign of authority over the indentured servants.

"Gamba, I've got a new girl - a white one!"

Gamba's slightly slant eyes lit up.

"The police will be delivering her shortly, and I want you to get her ready to be handed over to Pedro."

"Ah, so she's for Pedro, is she? Well, she's certainly in for a shock!"

"And I don't want her recognisable," added Carlos. There was a distinct resemblance between Diana and her late uncle and Carlos did not want anyone on the estate guessing Diana's identity and perhaps alerting the authorities or Diana's family. "You know what to do?"

"Oh, yes!" laughed the mestizo woman. "She'll certainly look different by the time I finish with her!

"Well, take charge of her as soon as she arrives. She speaks no Spanish and I want to keep her that way."

"Shall I bring her to this house and do it here?" queried Gamba.

"Yes." It would be amusing to let the girl see the luxury and comfort which she dared to come and claim, and which she might have owned. It would make her future treatment all the more piquant! "Use my own bathroom to prepare her and then bring her to me, but don't tell her what is going to happen to her. Animals don't know what is going to happen to them, and nor should she! But it may sometimes be amusing for you and I to talk in English in front of her when we're discussing her!"

An hour later a black police van drove up to the front door. Gamba and two of her assistants went down the steps to meet the driver and his fellow armed guard.

"Sign here," said the driver, and Diana Carstairs was delivered under the false but common name of Carmen

Rodriguez!

Diana's real identity had disappeared with the burning of her passport and her other papers at the airport when she had been arrested. The prison records simply showed the arrest and sentencing for drug running of a Senorita Rodriguez, her subsequent volunteering for indentured service, and the sale of her indentures to a Senor Carlos Ortiz of the hacienda El Paraiso.

The guard unlocked the narrow door to Diana's cupboard-like cell. Quickly he handcuffed her hands behind her back and gave the key to Gamba. Then he gripped poor Diana by the arm and led her firmly out of the van, still wearing nothing but her inadequate tunic. Gamba's women assistants seized Diana's arms and led her up the steps into the big hacienda ranch house.

Diana looked around her nervously. At a little distance from the house was a group of other buildings. She would later learn that they were the plantation buildings: the drying sheds for the coffee, the storage barns for the cotton, the stables and the training area for horses and pony women, the pig sties, the big open barracks in which women labourers were locked up at night, the kennels for the guard dogs, and a sprinkling of docile and gelded little boys being reared to do some of the heavier work on the hacienda.

Moments later Diana was staring about her in wonder as she was taken into the large cool and luxurious house. She was taken upstairs and led into Carlos's grandiose bathroom.

Gamba untied her tunic and then, without a word, momentarily unlocked her handcuffs, took off her tunic completely and refastened the handcuffs. Diana eyed the dog whip hanging from her belt nervously.

Gamba spoke in Spanish to her assistants, and Diana was pushed naked into the large kidney shaped bath. She was held by the women and thoroughly soaped. She was scrubbed all over, rinsed off, rubbed down, sprayed with scent, and rubbed over with talcum powder.

Diana felt relaxed for the first time in several weeks. Indeed under the experienced hands of the women a rather voluptuous sensuality crept over her as they washed, dried, and rubbed her mound of Venus.

Then she was led over to a massage couch in the corner of the bathroom. She was alarmed when her wrists and ankles were fastened to straps at the four corners of the table, and struggled. But Gamba merely raised her whip menacingly and without a word of explanation fastened another strap round her neck. It was now impossible for her to make the smallest movement.

Two of the women started to soap her armpits. Then came the razor. But Gamba was not satisfied. She ran her hands over the shaven skin and whenever she felt a hair that had escaped the razor, out would come her tweezers. It was pluck after painful pluck until all was beautifully smooth.

After her armpits, they went between her legs, an area which Gamba and her assistants clearly enjoyed dealing with. First came the scissors, then the razor and then the tweezers again until this whole part of Diana's body had been transformed into looking like that of a child, and indeed it was then powdered just as if it was.

Diana was then untied from the couch on which she had lost some of her most precious feminine attributes, and made to sit on a wooden stool by a curious looking table, small but heavy.

The table was hinged, and in each half there was a small semi-circle cut-out halfway along the edge. Diana was made to put her neck into one of the cutouts. The other half of the table was then brought up and closed behind her. She felt the back of her neck fitting into the other cutout. Her body was now hidden below the table and all that that could be seen of her was her head, which appeared to be resting on the table!

Then out came the scissors!

When Diana realised what they were going to be used for, she gave a desperate cry and tried to raise her hands to protect her head. But all she could do was to scratch ineffectively against the under-side of the table.

Diana was shaken by sobs as she heard the scissors cutting her lovely long hair and saw the long tresses fall to the floor. Soon the cheeks of the shorn girl were covered in tears.

Gamba picked up the longer pieces, over 18 inches long, and told her assistants to sweep up the rest and throw it away.

"You see?" Gamba said to her. "Probably you'll see these again when they form part of your mane or your tail!"

It sounded horrifying, but Diana had no time to think, for after the scissors came the clippers. Then, to make sure that Diana had the proper shiny bald and unrecognisable look that Carlos wanted to give her, out came the shaving soap again and the whole of her skull was completely shaved.

A special depilatory cream was rubbed into her cranium to slow up the re-growth of her hair. Then her head was polished until it shone and glistened. A little blonde stubble would grow of course but would be hardly visible, and to keep her head smooth it would now be shaved, depilated and polished every week, and indeed also on the mornings of her big days on the race track, the show ring - and perhaps in the mating box, thought Carlos with a laugh as he watched the whole operation through a one way mirror into the bathroom.

Then Gamba carefully shaved off Dina's eyebrows - something that gave the girl an even more inhuman look. Yes, Carlos thought, Gamba had certainly made a good job of making the former Miss Diana Carstairs quite unrecognisable.

Finally, Gamba fastened a wide flexible stainless steel collar round Diana's neck. The women labourers and household servants had iron collars, but the pony-girls had more attractive stainless steel ones. The collar closed in a series of rings which fitted into each other. Gamba dropped a lead pellet down between the rings which now held the collar tightly closed round Diana's neck.

Then Gamba picked up a strange looking tool rather like a large pair of pliers. Dina felt the pliers being applied to the rings that held her collar closed - squeezing the lead pellet so that it locked the rings together. Only by first removing the lead pellet - a very difficult operation - would it be possible for anyone to remove the collar.

Later the the blacksmith would weld on the disc giving her registered number.

The collar itself incorporated the El Paraiso estate's distinctive mark of a diamond with the letter P mounted above it. In this way if a woman tried to run away she would be quickly recognised as a runaway from El Paraiso, and anyone finding her would be very tempted to hand her over to the police and claim the reward that always paid for runaway women.

Shaken by her ordeal and by the sight of her changed appearance, the now shorn Diana was ready to be taken to meet her owner. A lead was attached to her collar and she was taken naked and blushing down the stairs of the magnificent house.

She was led down to Carlos's office. As they stood waiting for an answer to Gamba's knock on the door, she was astonished to see the notice 'Oficina El Paraiso'. El Paraiso!

Surely this couldn't be the same El Paraiso?

Gamba knocked again, and opened the door. There was a sharp tug on Diana's lead, then, firmly gripped by Gamba's assistants, she was marched into the room. Facing the door was a large desk, and behind it a swivel chair. Seated on the swivel chair, but with his back to the door and to Diana, was a man busily writing into a large book on a table behind the desk.

Surely - YES!

"Carlos!" she called out, and started to run forward. But she was jerked back by her collar and instantly Gamba's dog whip came down hard across her naked buttocks.

"Silencio!" shouted Gamba. "Silencio!"

She brought her dog whip down again, and yet again. "Silencio!"

Diana jumped up and down with the pain, but she did dare to open her mouth again.

The seated man had paid no attention to this little scene, and remained with his back to Diana, still busy writing.

"Now get down!" shouted Gamba in English, followed again, when Diana seemed about to protest, by "Silencio!"

Diana knelt under the desk. All she could see were the back of the boots of the man she had taken to be Carlos.

Then he spoke - in English!

"Thank you, Gamba. Now just help me check the entry for this creature. We don't want any mistakes in the plantations's official register of livestock. The Government inspectors might come and look. Now, let's see. Type of livestock? Female Indentured Servant. Name? Ah, yes, Carmen Rodriguez. Breed? Well, I suppose, white. Type? Mare or filly? And if mare, date when first covered and by which stallion? I think we'd better leave this blank for the time being. Progeny and date of last mating. Again blank for the time being."

Diana's mind was in a whirl of disbelief. This awful man she had at first taken for Carlos could not seriously be referring to her!

"Date of signature of indentures?" she heard him continue. "Well that's no problem. Age? 23! Registered Livestock Number? Y755! You'd better write that number down, Gamba. Make certain you give the correct number to Pedro - and to the blacksmith! Now, Stable Name? Well what do you think, Gamba? How about Fancy? Or perhaps Passion?

45

She's got quite a passionate temperament, you know. You should have seen the disgusting exhibition she made of herself at the pre-auction inspection!"

"I think Passion will be very suitable," said Gamba.

"Right!" the man said. Was he speaking in English just to humiliate her? A Master asserting his authority over his new indentured servant? Her Master! She could feel her body responding to the word.

"Now make certain she learns to answer to Passion or to Y755," she heard the man say in a firm tone of voice.

"Of course, Senor, of course."

"And I know that we usually keep our fillies sewn up, but I think in her case laced up might be better. It's more flexible and makes it easier to get at her."

Gamba gave a laugh. Easier for her Master to get her! She nodded eagerly it would all the more enjoyable to arrange for the girl to be laced up!

Poor Diana was bemused by all this. Sewn up! Laced up! Suddenly, there was the noise of the chair being swivelled round. But as Diana was still kneeling under the desk, all she could see of the man were his breeches and his highly polished boots, which he was tapping with a short riding whip.

For a whole minute she was left there, kneeling in silence. It was, Diana realised, a very significant moment. She was being made to kneel humbly, under the desk, at the feet of the mysterious man whose face she still could not see, and who was now her Master.

Her Master! The very word sent a strange thrilling feeling through her trembling body. It was a feeling of excited submission, coupled with a feeling of fear that accentuated by the sight of the polished boots - and of the whip.

Finally, she heard the man give orders in Spanish. He rose from his chair. Diana could hear his footsteps as he left the room.

Moments later Gamba jerked her, by her collar, back from under the desk and onto her feet again.

Then Gamba drove her out of the room, holding her lead in one hand, whilst with the other she applied her dog whip to her rear.

## 8 - AN INTRODUCTORY THRASHING

Gamba and her two assistants led the now terrified and naked Diana through the big luxurious ranch house out into the warm sun.

She was still mystified about what was going to happen to her. She could not believe that the man she had seen in the house was really Carlos.

Hidden from Diana's eyes, Carlos followed behind at a discreet distance, anxious not to miss a second of Diana's forthcoming debasement. As he passed, household indentured servants curtsied humbly and nervously, their eyes on Gamba's dog whip. Outside, as they made their way to the stables complex, women labourers also bowed to him, again humbly and nervously, only too well aware of the complete power that he had over them.

They passed the kennels of the guard dogs, dogs which roamed the estate at night to frighten off any stranger, perhaps trying to make contact with a loved one serving as a female indentured servant on the estate. The dogs also served to frighten the women from trying to escape. At the sight of Diana, the dogs jumped up at the bars of their cages, barking ferociously.

Then they came to an attractive series of buildings, laid out in two wings of stabling.

There was, however, one sharp difference between the two wings. Whereas the one for horses held both geldings and mares, the other held only only women, for the system of indentured service in Costa Negra was applied almost exclusively to females. Men were too much trouble, stirring up unrest, trying to escape, and refusing to accept their fate. Moreover women indentured servants were ideal for picking the two crops on which Costa Negra depended: coffee beans and cotton.

Linking both wings was a row of buildings containing the services that were common to both: the tack room containing bridles, harnesses and saddles; the blacksmiths forge and workshop; the veterinary surgeons examination and operation room; the piles of manure; the bales of straw; the bins of bran and oats and, for the women, the adjoining vats for making the oats into porridge; the sacks of high protien nuts for both horses and women, and the trophy room where the cups and rosettes won by both horses and women were proudly displayed to visitors inspecting the livestock with a view to a purchase, or to discuss joint breeding plans.

Beyond these buildings were a series of paddocks with white painted fences. Some had higher close mesh fencing, topped with spikes or live electric fencing. These, Diana would soon learn, were for pony girls.

There was also a carefully laid out dressage arena for use both by horses and women, a show jumping arena with jumps for both mounted horses and mounted women, and a covered menage or riding school used in wet weather by both. There was also a circular exercising ring with very long revolving arms, to which both horses and women could be attached so that they could be made to trot round and round at a speed which increased the further out they were attached to the arms.

Diana's eyes were taken up by the large figure of an Indian peon, superbly muscled, who stood waiting for them at the entrance to the women's stable, a short dressage whip hanging from his belt.

Pedro was Carlos's stud groom, in charge of both his pony women and his horses, and as such had been sent to England to learn the latest techniques of training both horses and athletes.

Diana cringed with embarrassment at being led up nude to this frightening man. The fact that her head, mound and beauty lips were now shorn, served to make it worse. Desperately she sought to cover her body with her hands.

"Oh, please, please help me," she begged. "I don't understand what is happening to me."

Pedro turned in mock horror to Gamba. Inwardly, however, he was smiling. The girl had given him a perfect excuse to administer the initial thrashing that he liked to give a new pony girl, to teach her discipline and obedience, and to break her into her new life.

"You hear that?" he shouted, speaking in broken English, so that Diana would understand, "This creature - a mere pony girl - dared to speak! Pony girls never speak! They only neigh, like horses. And she dare speak to me, the Stud Groom. I thrash her immediately!"

He turned to the now trembling Diana. "Get down! Down on all fours, you impertinent young filly! Go on! Get down!

Diana hesitated uncertainly but was pushed down by Pedro.

"Now put head down in dirt! Go on! Put nose in dirt! You disgusting little insolent slut!"

With his foot, Pedro pushed Diana's face right down into the mixture of sand and horse manure.

"That better! Do not you ever dare speak again! Not one word! Pony women not speak - or tongues cut out. Understand?" He kicked Diana's face back into the dirt. "You understand?"

Tongue cut out! After all that she had gone through since arriving in Costa Negra, she could believe it! Terrified, not daring to speak or even look up, Diana, her face covered in filth, nodded.

"Good!" cried Gamba. "And to make sure you not forget Pedro now give you six strokes with whip! Get buttocks up! Higher! Right up! Higher - or you get twelve!"

Diana strained to raise her naked buttocks high in the air. She felt so ashamed and yet so frightened. It was unbelievable! Here she was, a well educated young Englishwoman, about to be thrashed by a South American Indian peon in front of a grinning half black mestizo housekeeper - it was just unbelievable!

"Better! But keep nose in dirt." Again with his foot Pedro contemptuously pushed Diana's face back into the filth and kept it there.

He paused. Then speaking slowly to give his words more emphasis, he continued.

"Now, I, Pedro, the head groom of El Paraiso and now in complete charge of you, give you good beating. Ten strokes! You will remember them with fear - and you will get another such beating if you you ever talk again, or if you ever insolent to me or my staff. Even dumb insolence will get you another beating! You understand? Do you?"

Trembling with sheer fright, Diana nodded.

"Good!" she heard the terrifying head groom say, followed by: "One!"

A scream came from Diana. She knelt up and clutched her burning buttocks in a mixture of shame and pain. They seemed to be on fire!

"Get down! Keep hands flat on ground!" shouted Pedro, giving Diana a kick. "If you move or call out again - that stroke not count!"

"Two!" There a long pause. Then suddenly the whip cut across her buttocks again. Somehow Diana managed to keep still and to keep silent. "Three! Four!" The strokes now came in quick successsion and were greeted by suppressed little gasps of pain from Diana

"Five!"

It was too much! Unable to stand the pain any longer, Diana rolled over on her back in the dirt, whimpering, but managing to keep silent. She looked up at Pedro besearchingly as he stood over her, but he merely looked down at her with disgust. His whip was raised in the air.

"Six!" cried Gamba, and Pedro brought his whip down across Diana's breasts making her scream with pain. Clutching her breasts, she rolled over again in the dirt, seeking to ease the pain in her breasts by rubbing them in the dust and dung.

"She's disgusting!" she heard the watching Gamba say contemptuously.

"Back on all fours! Hurry!" ordered Pedro, tapping his whip impatiently.

It was the first time he had ever beaten a white woman, a pure white woman. It was exciting and arousing. And to think that this white creature was going to be in his stables - in his power! But her skin was clearly more delicate and more easily marked by the whip than that of the black or coffee coloured mulatto, quadroon or mestizo women he was used to dealing with.

He was having to be careful to find a balance between hurting the white woman sufficiently to break her into stable life, and yet making sure that she was not really harmed. Fortunately he was an expert at whipping women - an expert with years of experience behind him.

"Raise buttocks again!" he ordered harshly.

Four strokes to go, thought Diana desperately. But better on her bottom than across her tender breasts.

"Higher! More up!"

Diana strained to raise her buttocks up high again. It was so awful having to offer herself to the whip in this way. Perhaps she would have felt even more humiliated if she had had known that Carlos was discreetly watching and enjoying the whole scene.

It was not across her bottom that the cunning Pedro brought his whip down next, but across her shoulders.

Once again poor Diana found herself rolling over in the dirt to ease the pain, whilst Pedro and Gamba laughed.

"Back on all fours! Hurry!" came the order.

Where would the next stroke be, Diana found herself wondering fearfully. Back across her buttocks again or across her shoulders?

But it was neither! Diana screamed again as the whip unexpectedly slashed twice across the backs of her calves. This was certainly not a beating that she would forget in a hurry!

"Now for last two strokes, something different," laughed Pedro. "Turn over onto back. Put hands flat on ground behind head! Bend knees! Now raise belly and body for whip. Strain up! Up! Up!"

Diana found herself straining to raise her shoulders and buttocks off the ground - raising her belly for the whip.

And indeed it was across her soft belly that the last two strokes fell, leaving her writhing in the filth for several minutes as the pain gradually eased.

"You'd better put her into her stall now," she heard Gamba say.

"Yes," agreed Pedro, "but first I turn hose on her. Stand still, Passion."

Diana scarcely recognised her new name. But Pedro picked up the hose which was used for hosing down sweating women when they were brought back to the stables after being exercised. He turned it on and washed the filth off Diana's face, off her bald head, off her breasts and belly and off her back and buttocks. It was deeply humiliating, being washed down like an animal. but at least it got rid of most the pain of the beating.

Then Pedro led her into the stable... and Diana gave a sudden scream.

## 9 - THE STABLES

Diana screamed again in a mixture of horror and sheer disbelief.

Facing the stables passage were two rows of what at first sight she had taken to be loose boxes for horses. But then she had seen they were different. They were cages and inside each cage was a young woman - some twenty of them, mainly fairly light skinned, and all silently looking at her through the bars of their cages.

The women were naked, except for a wide leather girth strap that went round their waists, from the front of which hung a sort of leather modesty flap like the sporran on a Highland kilt. Each flap was decorated with the crest of the El Paraiso plantation, and covered the women's intimacies.

Later Diana would learn that these modesty flaps were normally removed outside the stables, to make it easier for the pony-girls to raise their knees high in the air when being exercised at the trot.

But it was not the sight of these modesty flaps that had made Diana scream for the first time. Rather, it was that prominently branded on their bellies, below the navel and above their hanging modesty flaps, was the brand mark of the El Paraiso estate; a diamond with the letter P superimposed on it, followed by the letter Y, for Yegua or mare, and three numbers, different for each girl - their Registered Livestock numbers.

Two of the girls turned away and, as they did so, their modesty flaps swung away away from their bodies. Diana was shocked to see that each girl's mound and body lips had been completely depilated - just like own. But she was even more shocked when she saw that each girl's hairless beauty lips had been sewn up tightly, hiding the lips themselves and giving the impression of just a narrow little slit - like that of a little girl.

Diana gasped as she noticed that one or two of the girls appeared to be in an interesting condition with their brand marks magnified by their swollen bellies.

She would have been even shocked had she seen that, under their modesty flaps, the beauty lips of these girls were not sewn up but were closed by a tight criss-cross lacing like the lacing on a shoe. But the strong leather laces were not threaded through several pairs of eyelets, as in a shoe, but through several pairs of little silver rings that in turn were threaded through the girl's own beauty lips. At the bottom of each girls beauty lips, the ends of the laces were fastened together by a little padlock that hung down between her legs.

But for the modesty flaps, she would also have seen that, on some these girls' bellies, and on some of the others who were showing the signs of a recent interesting condition, the letter V had been added - showing that the girl was now one of the estate's brood mares.

Each woman wore a wide, shiny, stainless steel flexible collar round her neck - just like her own collar. But she also saw that fastened to a ring on the back of each woman's collar, behind the neck, was a heavy chain, the other end of which was secured to a ring set in the floor in the centre of each cage. The chains were apparently long enough to allow each woman to walk up and down her cage like a chained animal - which several of them were now doing.

But it was not this that made Diana give that second scream. It was the sight of the shiny brass nose rings! These, as she would soon learn, played a significant role in the training and control of the woman.

The inhuman look made her remember how being shorn had made her look inhuman too. But these women all had lovely long black hair hanging down their necks, making Diana feel very jealous and, at the same time, curious about why her own hair had been so ruthlessly removed.

As Pedro led her down the cobbled passageway, she passed a strange pulsating machine that had been wheeled along to the cage of a pretty buxom young light skinned woman. Had Diana been able to see under her modesty flap she would have seen that the girl was one of those to whose belly brand the letter V had been added, and whose beauty lips were kept closed by leather laces.

A narrow trap door in the bars at the front of her cage had been unlocked. Above it a strap went from the bars and round the woman's neck. Below it another went round her waist. The straps held the woman pressed up tight against the bars of her cage, forcing her to thrust her full breasts through the small trap door and into the pulsating suckers of a portable milking machine.

A young Indian boy was watching a small enclosed glass bowl into which the milk was falling in little jets, before being sucked off into a large container.

As Diana passed, she saw the jets fall away, the boy switch off the machine, make a note of the amount of milk given, unfasten the straps, push the young woman back into the centre of her cage and lower the trapdoor, before wheeling the machine down the passageway to another cage. She would learn that these young woman would be milked several times a day to provide milk for the big house.

Some of the girls in the cages were under training for the very competitive trotting races, harnessed to a racing sulky or chariot; others were bigger girls trained to carry the saddle and to jump; others formed part of a carefully matched team of two or four women used to pull the heavier barouches and phaetons and to compete in the driving competitions and marathons.

The cages were identical and were sited alongside each

other facing onto the central passage. The bars separating the cages were lined with a wooden partition some six feet high like the kicking boards in horses' loose boxes. But in this case they were there to prevent the women from touching each other through the bars.

The floor was just hardened earth except for a little strip of cement down the centre of the cage. The floor gently sloped towards the passageway to enable the women's liquid wastes to run down a channel in the cement which in turn emptied into the open drains which ran down either side of the passageway - just as in real stables.

Along one side of each cage was a shiny metal feeding and drinking trough some two feet long. It had its own trap door, quite separate from the main cage door, so that the grooms could pour food and drink into the trough without having to go into the cage.

Each cage was some twelve feet square - the same size as the horse loose boxes in the other wing of the stables. They were built of solid looking iron bars that constituted not only the four walls of each cage but also its ceiling, thus making escape from the cages impossible. The bars continued under the earthen floor so as to prevent the women from trying to burrow their way out.

Hanging from the bars on the front of each cage was a plaque giving the name, number, stables name and age of the pony girl, together with the name and estate of her sire and her dam, and the date she was first put into training in the stables.

A large plastic board was also fastened to the bars of the front of the cage, and a marker pen hung from it.

This board was divided up to show the woman's weight and date when she had last been weighed naked, the date of her next race or competition, the desired weight she was to be by that date, and instructions for her feed.

There were also spaces to record whether her latest wastes

were satisfactory; the date she last came into season; the date when she would, if desired, next be ready for covering, or the date on which she had been covered, which was followed by a capital P for Prenada, or pregnant, if the vet had confirmed this; the time when she was next to be exercised and whether by a groom or by the master or one of his friends; and finally any special instructions regarding her care or any punishments which had not yet been carried out.

The only furniture, if one can call it furniture, was a little wooden three legged stool. Two wooden planks fitted perpendicular to the floor constituted the edge of a rough sleeping area filled with straw. It was about six feet long and two feet wide and was intended to allow a woman to lie down and stretch right out.

To keep their back muscles well developed the women were only allowed to lie down at certain times, and even were only allowed to sit on their stools at certain times. The rest of the time thay had to remain standing or walking up and down in their cage, like real horses in a horse box.

None of the women in the cages could use their hands. They all had iron rings welded round their wrists. They wore a wide girth or belly strap, made of heavy leather round their waists at all times of the day and night. These wrist rings could be clipped onto rings on the side of these girths.

However, to keep the women's arms straight down the sides of their bodies, it was normal when they were in the stables for two leather extension pieces to be fitted to the sides of the girth straps. These extension pieces hung down the flanks and were held in place by a strap that went round the thigh above the knee. The wrist rings were then clipped to a ring low down on these extension pieces, thus drawing their arms down straight.

This arrangement had the additional advantage of making it quite impossible for a woman to touch her sewn or laced-up sex with her fingers when in the stables - a matter about which Carlos had strong views! They could also be used to prevent girls in milk from getting at their breasts to ease the pressure as their milk built up.

The extension pieces were normally only removed when a woman was taken out for exercising and her wrists were then fastened to one of the rings on the side of the belt itself.

It was indeed strictly forbidden for any of the pony women to use their hands for any purpose whatsoever, and even the cleaning of their hands and the care of their nails was carried out by the Indian grooms.

As Diana had already noticed, each of the women wore a stainless steel collar which was riveted round her neck and to the back of which was fastened a heavy chain welded to a ring cemented into the ground in the centre of the cage. The chain was long enough to allow the women to circulate freely in her cage, if one can call that the animal-like walking up and down to which they were reduced.

Thus everything was planned for, and provided so that the naked girl could move about in her cage and use the little cement strip with its cement channel. This was washed down twice a day with a hose and, at the same time, so was the body of each girl, as she stood straddling the little central cement strip.

Although a girl might sometimes have to stand in her own wastes, they were soon washed off her feet by the hose, and in any case this was no worse than being exercised bare-foot with the horses and other women in the covered menage or in the circular exercise ring or along the narrow paths of the estate - all of which, thanks to the presence of the real horses, tended to be strewn with some dung.

When he arrived in front of the cage number 34, Pedro opened the door using a key from the huge bunch that hung from his belt. Gamba and the others remained outside watching Pedro strap a wide leather girth around Diana's waist and over her belly. As her iron wrist rings had not been fit-ted, he fastened leather straps round her wrists.

He looked carefully at Diana's breasts, and decided to clip her wrist rings, for the time being, high up to the rings on the side of her girth belt rather than lower down to the belt extension pieces. These of course were normally used only when a pony girl was in harness so that her elbows were held back behind her, thus forcing her to thrust out her breasts and push back her shoulders.

Pedro felt Diana's breasts carefully. Clearly the effect of pushing back her shoulders lifted her breasts nicely and elimi-nated any droop. It would be sensible to keep her like that for a time to train her pectoral muscles better - even though it would be rather uncomfortable for the girl.

Then he picked up a heavy chain and padlocked it to the back of her collar. Diana saw with dismay that as in the other cages the other end was riveted to a ring bolt set in the ce-ment strip in the centre of the cage. Then she looked up at the bars over her head and down at the bars leading down under the earth floor. There would no escape from her cage!

Pedro let the chain go. It was so heavy that at first she had difficulty in remaining upright. Although she did not realise it, this was all part of the muscle training that Pedro made all his girls undergo, for with each step round her cell, the heavy chain forced the girl to use her muscles to keep her balance.

This was all part of Pedro's body building technique.

## 10 - DIANA LEARNS THE TRUTH

Carlos stepped out of the shadows where she had been hiding himself, and came and stood in front of Diana's cage. Such had been his pleasure at seeing his would-be rival to the ownership of El Paraiso, whipped, caged and chained as an animal, that he was already becoming thoroughly aroused. However he could not bear to miss one last chance to gloat.

"Carlos!" gasped Diana. "Is it really you!"

"It certainly is!" said Carlos, speaking in his heavily accented English. "And moreover a filly doesn't answer her Master back because she knows that if she does, then she will be thrashed for talking!"

"But," said Diana, "but it's me!"

"Yes!"

"Me! Not a smuggler! Me!"

"You!" said Carlos. "You who wanted to take my estate from me!"

"Oh!" said Diana. She began to understand. "OH!"

"Exactly! That could not be allowed! But now you are no threat! Now I can do with you whatever I wish!" There was a pause whilst Carlos let the significance of his threat sink fully into the frightened Diana's mind. Then he came into the cage and stroked Diana's now smooth head.

"Well, are you missing your lovely blonde hair? And your eyebrows? Your bald shiny head certainly makes you unrecognisable and more like an animal than a pretty girl!"

Diana could have killed him, but with her wrists tightly fastened to her girth belt, there was nothing she could do.

"And how do you like having a bald sex like a little girl?" teased Carlos. "Animals don't have pubic hair, and so you won't either. The first signs of any little hairs growing on your head or between your legs and Pedro will have them out with his tweezers! Just think of that! And when you've been properly trained I shall take some photographs of you. Perhaps I might even send some to your friends in England, to show them what you look like now! Would you like that, little Passion?"

Goaded beyond all reason, Diana could not help crying out: "No! No! Supposing I want to get married when I go back to England!"

Then she fell silent, remembering that she must at all costs keep silence, that pony girls do not talk!

"Did I really hear you dare to talk again? And to me! Do you want Pedro to give you another thrashing? You are a glutton for punishment, girl"

Diana fell to her knees in front to Carlos, and unable to put her hands round Carlos's feet, she just looked up at her Master with a look of silent submission.

"That's better my girl. Now you just remember what you are now: an animal! And just remember who I am - your owner and Master. Then we won't have any more of these girlish tantrums. And meanwhile let me assure you that you won't be seeing England again - or getting married! Now it's time to get on with the next step of your conversion to be being just one of my fillies!"

He laughed and, turning to Pedro, gave him an order in Spanish.

Pedro came forward again. This time he had a long cloth in his hand and with it he proceeded to blindfold Diana.

Quite unable to see what was going on she felt herself being pushed towards the front of her cage. She felt part of it being opened and remembered seeing a trap door in the front.

She felt her head being pushed forward and then straps being fastened round her head, round her neck, and round her waist. All her body was being held pressed tightly against the bars. She felt quite helpless.

She heard Carlos laugh and say something to Pedro - once again in incomprehensible Spanish.

Then she heard something being wheeled up the passage-way towards her cage. There was a clattering noise as if from little surgical bowls and a hissing noise as if from a gas burner. Something was being heated or sterilised.

She heard Pedro and Gamba bustling around, talking and laughing in Spanish about something. She wondered what they were doing, what was happening. Her head was now clamped so that it could not move - and her nostril was gripped and pulled forward by an unseen hand.

Then suddenly a long red hot needle was driven through her nostril and turned several times. She screamed with the pain and shock. She felt something being threaded through her nose and then felt the weight of something hanging from it. She remembered the nose rings on the other women. "Oh no!"

Pedro stood back and proudly looked at the brass ring that was now hanging from Diana's nose. The combination of the girl's shiny bald head and this shiny nose ring gave her a strangely inhuman look that his Master would greatly appreciate.

The police in Costa Negra were responsible for returning all runaway indentured servants to their Masters for punishment and to help the police, hacienda owners had to mark their indentured servants as such. It was normal therefore at the El Paraiso hacienda for female indentured servants to be nose ringed in this way. It clearly marked a girl as an indentured servant and so served as a very effective deterrent to trying to escape.

But in Diana's case there was also another reason for her being nose-ringed. She was destined to be a pony girl, and Carlos had found that attaching reins to a pony-girl's nose ring was often a very effective alternative, or addition, to reins attached to a bit.

He had also found that, for carriage girls, a rein running down from the nose ring, down the legs and back to the driver, gave excellent extra control - particularly in dressage competitions where exact control was so vital. A short tug on this rein would hurt the girl and wake her up. It could be used either to warn her that she was not properly obeying the orders her driver was indicating with the reins and whip, or to warn her of an impending new order.

Now Diana felt something hot near her face as Pedro carefully brazed together the two ends of the ring. Then Pedro's hands were on her nipples, rubbing them into hardness and pulling them out. Held standing bolt upright as she was, with her breasts sticking proudly out through the bars of the cage, and her hands held fastened to the leather girth strapped round her waist, there was nothing she could do to protect them.

Suddenly she cried out as a bulldog clip was carefully placed on one nipple, making it even more inflamed and erect.

Once again she heard the noise of Pedro and Gamba bustling round and then of something being handed to Pedro. She felt Pedro holding her breast steady. She breathed with relief as the painful bulldog clip was removed from her nipple by Gamba, but then screamed again as it was placed on one of her now hairless body lips.

The sudden new pain made her judder and thrust her breast forward, giving Pedro an ideal target for his second red hot needle. Holding Diana's breast still, he drove the needle through the nipple.

The brass ring he threaded through the nipple was smaller than the nose ring. Carefully he ran the the ring through the nipple and then brazed the ends together so that, like the nose ring, it could not be removed.

Moments later the cage again rang to Diana's screams as the bulldog clip was first placed on her other nipple, and then suddenly taken away and placed on her body lips again. Once again the sudden pain made Diana thrust her breast forward. Once again Pedro was holding the breast steady and once again Diana's involuntary movement put her in the ideal position for him to thrust his red hot needle through the second nipple.

Gamba wiped the three little holes with surgical spirit and rubbed a healing cream into them to ease the soreness and pain.

Like nose-ringing, nipple-ringing was an essential part of Carlos's plan for training Diana for her new role as a pony girl.

Firstly, they would often be used for attaching to a second pair of reins to supplement those attached to the bit rings. Just as a difficult horse can be better controlled in a double bridle, so a difficult woman like Diana could be controlled better with separate pairs of reins going to her bit rings and to her nipples.

Pressure on one side or other of the bit ring is not, in the case of a human, a very accurate way of steering a pony girl. They will however respond much more exactly to pressure pulling their breasts to one side or the other, since this also makes them move their shoulders. They can be steered more accurately between the obstacles during a carriage driving and dressage competition.

Carlos planned that Diana would always be ridden out, even at exercise, in a double bridle, so that her delicate and sensitive breasts could be used to responding almost automatically to the slightest sideways pull.

The second reason for nipple-ringing Diana was a more aesthetic one. In the show ring, judges, when judging the conformation of a filly, looked for breasts that pointed straight ahead, with a nice deep narrow valley between them, rather than the more widely spaced type of breast.

Both Carlos and his agent had noticed, when Diana's breasts were exposed at the prison sale, that although otherwise excellent, her breasts did tend slightly to point outwards. Carlos was therefore anxious to start training them to lie closer to each other by joining the nipples with a tight chain that would gradually be shortened. In this way her muscles would gradually adapt themselves to give the pleasing and attractive conformation that the judges would be looking for.

Diana now had three very striking and highly visible rings

through her body. Her blindfold was removed and she was unfastened from the bars of her cage, told to remain standing up and to look at herself in a mirror held by the grinning Gamba.

When she saw her nipples pierced with little rings, and in particular the one through her nose, a fresh bout of tears sprang to her eyes, but as they rolled down her cheeks she was again blindfolded and taken back to the front bars of her cage.

She was secured to the frame as before, but this time her legs were fastened well apart. She also heard a stool being placed in the passageway just in front of her. Anyone sitting on it would be level with her beauty lips...

Once again she heard Pedro and Gamba bustling about. Once again she heard something being handed to Pedro. Then she felt Pedro's hand on her beauty lips. She felt them being compressed tightly together and and then pulled forward.

Suddenly she received a stroke of the whip across her naked buttocks. Her belly jerked forward, inadvertently offering herself. Instantly Pedro thrust his red hot needle through the two lips he was holding tightly together.

Diana screamed once again. But already Pedro was threading two little rings through the holes. Then with a special pair of pliers he the closed the ends together. Diana's beauty lips now now been fitted with a pair of little rings, one in the middle of each lip.

Three times more the same process was repeated. Then Pedro stepped back to admire his handiwork. Each lip now had four little rings, neatly spaced along its length.

He carefully threaded a leather lace through the rings so that the lips were now held closed by a criss-cross pattern. Then he locked the two ends of the lace together a little padlock-like fastener that hung down between her legs. As the rings had only just been fitted to the girl's beauty lips, he was careful not to pull the laces too tight. That would come later and meanwhile the weight of the padlock would gradually increase the tension on the lace until the beauty lips were slowly pulled tighter and tighter together.

Diana gave a gasp of horror as she felt the metal rings closing her body lips and guessed what had been done to her. Only if the little padlock was unlocked, and the laces eased, could she be penetrated. She would have been shocked had she realised that she was potentially a far too valuable filly for her Master to run any risk of an unauthorised fertilisation!

Diana may not have realised that, but she still felt utterly ashamed at the realisation that someone else now had control of her body. Already her whole appearance had been altered. Now her very sexuality was being controlled.

Indeed, ownership of a pretty young blonde European girl, Carlos had decided, was quite a responsibility. Diana's eventual mating would be a very serious matter, for her progeny could prove to be extremely valuable, if Diana did as well on the race track or show ring as her agent had forecast. There must be no mistakes or accidents. Carlos had full confidence in his stud groom, but he was was well aware that Diana would be regarded as almost irresistible to many of the stable lads and under-kennelmen with whom she would come in contact.

It was for this reason that he had given instructions that Diana was to be infibulated by being laced up, as soon as she was taken to the stables. It was a little operation that he had thoroughly enjoyed watching.

It was also an operation that gave him an extraordinary feeling of power - he, and not the hated Diana herself, was now in complete control of her body. And a very exciting body it was too!

Now Pedro rubbed a little healing ointment around Diana's infibulating rings. It was a very effective Indian ointment that he had successfully used before on women being ringed.

Unable to control himself any more, Carlos turned to Pedro.

"Put her down on her knees," he ordered, "but keep her breasts through the bars."

Quickly Pedro adjusted her position.

"Go, go quickly!" Carlos now ordered Pedro and the others. "Go down to the end of the corridor and wait."

Smiling, they left their Master alone with Diana. Carlos's hand pressed his manhood through his breeches. With one hand he pulled down the zip-fastener. In his other he held his riding whip. He was on fire with excitement.

Looking at the naked and blindfolded Diana, fastened helplessly at his feet to the bars of her cage, Carlos was on the edge of a climax. Diana's breasts were held temptingly in front of him, thrust out through the bars of the cage - the jet white breasts of an Englishwoman, so much more exciting than the coffee coloured ones of the girls he kept in the hacienda house.

Carlos raised his whip, took careful aim and brought it down across Diana's breasts. Diana gasped and juddered, and that judder almost brought Carlos to his own climax of pleasure. Never had he so enjoyed dominating a young woman! But he was determined to retain control. Marguerita and her sister awaited him back in the ranch house!

Still holding the whip with one hand, Carlos pressed the other to his surging manhood, gasping with pleasure, a pleasure made all the stronger by the knowledge that Diana would have realised that it was her pain, her awful pain, that had been the trigger for Carlos's pleasure. The girl's mouth was wide open in horror. A feeling of enormous satisfaction coursed through her veins.

He thrust his erect manhood towards her open mouth.

"Go, slut, lick!"

Terrified by the threat of the whip across her breasts, Diana thrust out her tongue - and touched his waiting manhood.

Appalled she jumped back.

Carlos brought his whip down across her breasts again.

"Go on, lick!" he screamed. "And now take it in your mouth. Go on, deep down. And now suck!"

He tapped her breasts with his whip, driving any feeling of hesitation right out of her mind. She would do anything to escape another stroke of his whip across her breasts. Timorously at first, and then with more confidence, she began to suck the large manhood in her mouth. Never had she done such a shameful thing, but she found that in some strange way she was rather enjoying being made to pleasure her cruel Master.

Carlos looked down again at the beautiful girl kneeling helplessly at his feet, her head going backwards and forwards, her mouth gently gripping his manhood. His glance took in the ring in her nose, the two hanging from her nipples, and the infibulation rings between her legs. A feeling of power surged through him. This English girl was now completely under his control! And to think that this now humbled creature had seriously thought she could challenge his ownership of El Paraiso!

Satisfied with having exerted his authority over her, Carlos stepped back and adjusted his dress. Then, without another word, he walked away down the passageway and made his way back to the house, followed at a respectful distance by Gamba and her assistants, leaving a shattered Diana standing forlorn and helpless, still blindfolded and fastened to the bars of her cage.

Her bottom was still smarting from her thrashing and her nose and nipples were uncomfortable from their ringing. Had it not been for Carlos's awful taunts she would not have believed it was all really true. But it was! Oh, how she hated Carlos!

Or did she?

She was ashamed to admit it, even to herself, but the truth

was that there might be worse things in this world than being the plaything of such an obviously powerful and commanding man!

## 11 - BRANDED!

Diana heard the footsteps of her Master, as she had now in some strangely exciting way begun to regard Carlos, die away. She was left there, blindfolded and tied to the bars of her cage, and thinking over all that had happened.

Suddenly she was unfastened, though her wrists remained strapped to her girth belt. Her blindfold was removed and she blinked in the sudden light. Feeling weak from the pain and shock, she staggered over to the little stool. She could feel the weight of the chain fastened to the back of her collar. Awkwardly she lowered herself down on the stool.

"Get up!" It was the angry voice of Pedro. "Fillies only sit or lie down when bell rings as signal. Two rings for permission to sit on stool. Three rings for lying on straw. No bell has rung! So you just walk up and down cage - like other girls."

Scared by Pedro's threat, poor Diana started to walk up and down the front of her cage - just like a caged animal, as was intended. The heavy weight of the chain fastened to her collar made her concentrate the whole time on keeping upright, leaning forward or sideways - and thereby exercising her muscles - again just as was intended.

Soon it was the hot weather siesta time, and Diana heard a bell ring three times. She saw the girls in the cages across the passageway go and lie down.

Gratefully she tottered to the wretched straw covered small sleeping area in the corner of the cage. Tired out, with her backside and breasts neatly marked by the stripes of her beatings and her nipples and nostril still very sore, she lay down, pulled down by the weight of the heavy chain, and for two whole hours slept.

She was awakened by the squeaking of the opening of her cage door, through which stepped Pedro. He gestured to her to get up. Then he unfastened the chain from her collar and replaced it with a short lead. He gave her buttocks a sharp tap with his his ever present dressage whip, and motioned her to step out of her cage.

Then, holding her by her lead and guiding her by his whip, he drove her across to the blacksmith's workshop.

Carlos was already waiting there, his eyes gleaming. This was something he could not miss! He had given orders for the next stage in Diana's transformation to take place now, since the girl would take several days to recover - and the sooner she was fit enough to start her training the better.

The burly Negro blacksmith's assistant was blowing the fire into a white heat whilst the blacksmith himself was holding pieces of red hot iron with his pincers, and was banging them into shape to fit Diana's delicate wrists and ankles - for although only wrist rings were needed to fasten Diana's wrists to her girth belt, nevertheless Carlos felt that like all the other indentured women, Diana should also be fitted with iron rings on her ankles.

Pedro held the naked Diana quite still whilst the blacksmith carefully measured her wrists and ankles. Soon he judged that the rings he was making were the right size and flung them into a bucket of water to cool. Welded onto each ring was another a smaller ring to enable a strap or chain to be secured to it.

The rings were placed loosely round Diana's wrists and ankles, then came the welding. The blacksmith put an asbestos cloth round Diana's wrist under the steel ring. Then picking up his welding torch and placing his goggles over his eyes he carefully proceeded to weld the two ends of the metal ring together.

As Diana watched, horrified, the whole process was then repeated for her ankle rings. Carlos was smiling. Fitting a girl with wrist and ankle rings had almost as much effect on her psychologically as did a nose ring.

The blacksmith picked up the disc hanging from her collar on which her Registered Number was engraved. He neatly welded together the ends of the small steel ring with which the disc was attached to her collar. It would now be a major task to remove the disc.

Pedro put a thick leather hood over Diana's head and buckled it tight with a strap that fastened behind her neck. Two tiny holes enabled her to breath but she could see nothing and the thick hood would muffle her screams.

He unbuckled her wrists from her leather girth and she felt them being fastened, by her new iron wrist rings, high above her head. She was held on tip toe, her belly well pulled in. Then she felt a wooden pole being pushed against the small of her back and straps being fastened to the rings on her iron ankle rings. She was now quite helpless and unable to move.

Although she did not know it, she was about to be branded.

It was normal for discs showing the crest of the estate and the Registered Number to be attached to the collars of female indentured servants. As a further precaution against escape it was also normal to have this crest and number tattooed onto their bodies.

However, in the case of pony girls, too much money was involved to rely on tattooing. Not only did the Coast Negra Pony Girls Breeding Society refuse to register any girl unless she had been clearly and permanently branded with the crest of her estate and her registered number, but, to prevent fraud, the stewards of all race meetings, dressage tests, shows and driving competitions, would eliminate any girl who had not been properly and permanently branded.

Thus branding formed an important part of stable life.

Not only did it have to be done prominently and correctly, but also in such a way that it did not look unsightly and detract from the value of a girl.

The neat branding of a potentially valuable pony girl required considerable expertise and skill.

Diana gave a little shudder as Pedro wiped her now prettily exposed tummy with a cleaning cloth soaked in antiseptic. The blacksmith removed a small red hot iron from the fire. It was the branding iron for the El Paraiso crest: a diamond surmounted by the letter P. He looked at it carefully, judging its heat, and then, holding it up, nodded to Pedro.

Suddenly Diana felt Pedro pinch her buttocks painfully. She jerked her head back - and her belly forward. It was just the movement that the blacksmith was waiting for, and he drove the branding iron hard onto Diana's belly just below her navel.

There was a smell of burning flesh. Diana screamed with the pain and tried to jump backwards but was stopped by the pole pressing into the small of her back. As she screamed again and again under her hood, the blacksmith kept the brand pressed hard against her soft skin until he felt that the right degree of penetration had been achieved - too little and the brand would not be permanent, too much and the girl's appearance would be ruined for ever.

Carefully the blacksmith pulled back the brand. Diana stopped screaming, but they could hear her sobbing. The blacksmith stepped back, smiling contentedly.

Carlos stepped forward and looked carefully at the brand. It was perfect - provided that the scarring process was not allowed to be too quick, or the girl was allowed to scratch at it!

He nodded at the blacksmith, who first of all squirted some red pigment into the now open wound to make sure that the brand would be a bright red, and then rubbed a little ointment into it to hold up the healing process and so get a good scar.

The blacksmith now turned to the heating of the second branding iron. This was a flexible iron that could be altered to hold the various letters and numbers that made up a girl's Registered Number. He checked with the number on Diana's neck to make sure that the numbers in the branding iron was correct. It would be too late afterwards!

Diana was still panting from the pain of the first brand. She did not know that another one was coming. Pedro patted her head and as if he was going to undo her hood. Slowly she stopped panting and became more relaxed as Pedro stroked her head through the heavy leather hood.

She felt the blacksmith's hand on her belly again, but thought that he was just rubbing in more ointment.

Then suddenly came the even worse pain of the bigger second brand, a brand that was several inches long - and which was placed immediately below the first. The curved branding iron fitted her belly exactly, but to make quite sure that the numbers were being properly engraved into her flesh, the blacksmith was slightly swivelling the two handed brand so as to make sure that the end letter and the end figure were equally well marked.

Finally he pulled back the branding iron. It was perfect! Another touch of the pigment and the special ointment to delay the healing process, and it was all over.

Diana's new wrist rings were untied from above her head and instead fastened to her girth strap. She longed to use her hands to rub the wounds, and ease the pain, but was quite unable to get at her brand marks which were now covered with a gauze bandage temporarily taped to her belly.

The hood remained in place.

Staggering, she was led back to her cage. A very strong sleeping pill was thrust down her throat under her hood by Pedro, and her heavy chain was fastened again to her neck. She was pushed down on her back onto the cement strip, onto which a little straw had been placed.

Her wrist rings were unfastened from her girth strap and instead fastened, once again above her head, to rings in the floor.

Half asleep, she felt her legs being pulled apart as her ankle rings were tied, wide apart, to other rings set in the floor, on either side of the cement strip.

She was now held, flat on her back, with her beauty lips positioned immediately above the little shallow drain in the cement strip. Not only would she be quite unable to scratch at her brand, or rub it against the floor, but her her liquid wastes would run harmlessly away into the bigger drain in the passageway. It had all been carefully thought out!

Tied helpless, and drugged, Diana almost immediately fell into a deep sleep on her pile of straw. Only then was the hood removed.


Little did Diana dream of the preparations that were being made for her future treatment.

She would be kept on her back for three days whilst her brand healed slowly - very slowly.

Tomorrow she would have to be wormed as a precaution, like all new arrivals in the stables, and proper regular worming carried out thereafter.

Her brand scars would have to be examined to make sure that there was no premature sign of healing over and that the marks would be clear.

She would also have to be closely examined to see that

there was no sign of her coming into season, for the pain and shock of the branding often upset a young woman's monthly cycle - not that a woman in season was treated in the stables in any way differently to the other women, any more than was a four legged mare in season. However Pedro liked to record everything properly and to be able to report to Carlos as each woman came into season each month.

Tomorrow Diana would have to start getting used to being fed mainly on porridge, made from the same oats as were fed to the horses, and mixed with the same high protien horse and cattle nuts as the horses - nuts to which vitamins and trace elements had been added.

It would of course take her stomach a little time to adapt itself to this diet, but Pedro had found that this problem could be solved by the judicial and periodical use of a good dose of castor oil. Indeed he tended to regard this as a cure for all the little feminine problems that occasionally affected the women in his charge.

The great advantage of this diet was that it was one which the grooms found easy to feed to the caged women. It was also one that had produced excellent results, not only on the race course but also in the show ring where a woman's condition was most important.

Diana, tied down flat on her back, would be fed for the time being by Pedro, or by the young Indian boy, Juan, the stable lad who was going to be personally in charge of her. Later, however, she would have to get used to feeding from her trough, lapping up everything that was put in it - for sometimes one of the younger grooms might put something unpleasant into a new girl's trough, so as to have an excuse for flogging her for not eating her food.

Unable to use her hands for eating, she would also learn to keep the trough spotlessly clean with her tongue.

Another matter which Diana, sensuous as she was, would have to get used to, was the complete impossibility of getting any sexual relief, since in the stables her hands would be kept chained tightly to her side. This of course was deliberate, for the owners of valuable women did not want them wasting their energies in self abuse.

Indeed one of the responsibilities of the young stable lads was to make sure that the girls in their charge had no opportunity to touch themselves. It was Carlos's frequent boast the only relief one of his pony women might get, was when she was driven with a beaded under-rein running between her legs, a rein with which Carlos might play to gently bring a girl to orgasm, an orgasm which, as Carlos was fond of explaining, was only achieved at a smart trot!

Finally and perhaps most important of all, Diana would have to start getting used to wearing a bridle and bit, and to wearing blinkers.

It would all be quite a programme for the wretched young English girl who only a month previously had been a carefree and beautiful young woman who had just come down from University. But meanwhile all that mattered was the forming on her belly of a neat and clear scar from her branding.

## 12 - A TASTE OF STABLE LIFE

Diana stirred in her sleep, half awakened by the noise of the stable lads pouring the girls' early morning feed of watery porridge sprinkled with cattle nuts into their feeding troughs.

Diana felt much refreshed after her long sleep. Although she did not realise it, it was three days later - three days during which time she had been lying drugged whilst her brand slowly healed.

Slowly she remembered where she was and all the terrible things that had been done to her. However the pain from her branding had eased off, as had the pain from her piercings.

She tried to get up, but her wrists and ankles were tied to rings set in the floor. Then she remembered being tied down flat on her back on a little straw spread over the cement strip in the middle of the cage.

She raised her head. She heard a rattling sound: it was the heavy chain, still fastened to her collar.

A few minutes later, a young Indian boy came into the cage. It was Juan, her stable lad, who although she did not know it, had looked after her whilst she was drugged, giving her special refreshing and nourishing drinks.

He smiled at her, said something in Spanish and proceeded to unfasten her wrists, deftly clipping each wrist ring to a little ring on the side of her girth strap.

Then having poured Diana's ration of food into her feeding trough, he came back and unfastened her ankle straps. Then he left the cage, locking the gate in the bars, and passed onto the next cage which was occupied by a pretty young mestizo girl.

Diana staggered to her feet. The weight of the chain fastened to her collar still threatened to unbalance her and she found she had to lean against its heavy weight. Rather unsteadily she went over to the front bars of her cage. She looked down at the unpalatable mess in her feeding trough with revulsion. Although she was feeling hungry, she was scarcely tempted by the cold porridge and cattle nuts. Anyway, with her hands chained tightly to her sides, how was she going to eat?

As well as feeling hungry, Diana looked anxiously around the cage for some sign of where and how she was expected to relieve herself.

She looked over the wooden screen bolted onto the side of her cage and was deeply shocked to see her pretty next neighbour lower her face into the trough in her cage and start to lap up her feed, occasionally raising her porridge covered face to swallow the mixture better.

Shocked, Diana turned away and looked through the bars of her cage towards the cage across the passageway from her own. She saw that its occupant, an attractive young half indian woman, was squatting awkwardly over the little cemented strip in her cage, her arms chained to her sides as Diana's were, her legs apart, her knees bent.

With a sudden shock Diana saw that she started to relieve herself onto the cement strip underneath her. Diana could see that the water was running down the little channel in the cement, which was sloped down towards the passageway. There it trickled into a larger collecting channel which ran the length of either side of the passageway in front of the cages, being covered with a wooden plank in front of each cage door.

Diana shuddered. There must be some other way! She could not just do it in public like that, like an animal. She bit her lips and squeezed her thighs together, for her need to relieve herself after her long sleep was very strong.

Just then Pedro came and unlocked the door to her cage. He stepped into the cage and without saying a word stood there looking at her naked body, naked that is except for her broad girth strap, tightly buckled around her slim waist. Silently he looked her up and down, pleased to see the recovery that this evidently resilient young woman had made.

Diana blushed with embarrassment under his silent unsmiling gaze, but with her hands chained tightly to the girth strap, she was unable to cover her breasts or her bald shiny sex.

Pedro sat down on the little stool and, pulling Diana's heavy chain, made her stand right in front of him. In one hand he held his dreaded dressage whip, with which he tapped her buttocks to indicate that she should bring her belly right up to him. Then he put down the whip and to Diana's great embarrassment reached up with both hands to part the now hairless lips of her infibulated sex, looking for any signs of her coming into season.

Diana jumped back, shocked by the idea of her most intimate feminine parts being handled by this repulsive looking man. Pedro put his hand down to pick up his whip and Diana, terrified and whimpering, brought her belly back to him - anything was better than the whip! He again parted her lips and examined her closely. He was pleased to see that there were no signs of her branding bringing her into season prematurely.

Then he removed the gauze from her belly and examined her brands. Perfect! As he rubbed a little healing jelly on the brands Diana looked down to see what he was doing. The heavy chain made it difficult, but she saw the outline of her brand marks. My God! She remembered the Registration Number on the disc hanging from her collar. Now it was also emblazoned in bright scarlet on her body!

Then he fastened a little leather modesty flap onto the front of her girth strap. It was decorated with the emblem of El Paraiso. It made her feel owned by Carlos, but at least it covered her humiliating brand and her shaven body lips.

Pedro stood up and, as she stood there in front of him, helpless with her wrists fastened to the sides of her girth strap, he pulled a short length of light chain from his pocket. He clipped one end onto the rings through Diana's left nipple, and then gently pulling both breasts towards each other, he clipped the other end to the other nipple so that the two breasts were pulled slightly together.

He tightened a little bottle screw in the middle of the chain, pulling the two breasts closer still, uncomfortably tight, giving just the effect that judges of pony women looked for.

Then he moved the stool over to the cement strip, and with his whip indicated that she should stand on the strip with her legs apart. He tapped the back of her knees with his whip to show that she should bend them and soon had her in a half raised squatting position. Then he held the lips of her sex apart and started to whistle just as he would to encourage a horse to stale, his eyes watching her beauty lips expectantly.

Poor Diana was appalled as she realised what she was expected to do. Never had she had to perform in such a humiliating way with a man's hands, the hands of a simple Indian, holding her open. The whistling was having its expected effect on her, and this was hastened when he moved one of his hands momentarily up to her belly and rubbed her bladder.

This time he was not disappointed, and, blushing with shame, Diana performed, enabling him to check that there was nothing wrong with his new young white charge in this department.

It was now time to make her eat. Pedro was a firm believer in the old stable adage of 'A little and often'. He led her over to the trough. In its bottom was a metal ring, specially fixed there to make reluctant women eat. Attached to the ring was a three inch length of chain terminating with a clip. He bent Diana over the trough and pushed her head down towards the feed that awaited her, then clipped the chain onto her nose ring.

Diana was now held bent over the trough, her mouth touching the pile of runny cold porridge. She heard Pedro impatiently tapping his boot with his whip; she heard him swishing it through the air; she felt him tap her buttocks with it as if checking just where he was going to bring it down. That was enough! She started to slurp the wet porridge down into her throat, slightly raising her head periodically to help her swallow, as she had seen her neighbour do.

Pedro smiled and waited until she had swallowed it all, then he unfastened her nose ring and indicated with his whip one or two little morsels that were still lying in the trough, making her lick them up and then polish the whole trough with her tongue. He had sprinkled the food with the contents of a package of worming powders to complete the course that she had been started on whilst drugged.

These powders would take a couple of hours to take effect so Diana found herself fastened, again by a little chain from her nose ring, to the bars of her cage immediately above the cement strip. Because of the cross bars that held the upright ones rigid, her nose chain forced her to remain standing, swaying on her feet to counterbalance the pull of the heavy neck chain.

With growing disbelief, Diana watched the other women being groomed, hosed down or led out - treated as human fillies or mares. Only her own recent experience in the capital of Costa Negra made her realise that such inhuman treatment could really happen in the 20th century.

Slowly she felt a familiar feeling in her belly becoming increasingly strong. She just had to relieve herself! But not here, not chained by the nose in a standing position to the bars of the cage! Time passed. No one came to release her. No one paid her any attention. The passing stable lads merely glanced at the strip of cement on which she was standing. Finally she had to open her legs. Because she was held upright by her nose chain she could only slightly bend her knees. She just had to thrust her buttocks back. She closed her eyes in shame, awaiting the inevitable.

Suddenly, the stable lad, Juan, stood before her, outside the bars of her cage. He was carrying a polaroid camera. He opened the cage door, and stepped in. The flash went off repeatedly as he photographed her straining body from the side. He bent down to scoop a specimen of her wastes into a little sterilised glass bottle and took it off to the laboratory for checking, leaving Diana there, like any other caged animal.

An hour later Juan came and hosed down both her cement strip and herself, pointing the hose through the bars. Having hosed down her face, breasts and belly, he reached through the bars, unclipped her nose ring, making her turn round, and reclipped her to the bars by fastening the chain to a ring on the back of her collar. Then he hosed down her back and buttocks, before unfastening her completely from the bars, leaving her totally appalled.

## 13 - DIANA STARTS HER TRAINING

Pedro arrived to start Diana's training.

First of all she was fitted with heavy military type boots so as to get her muscles well toned up by the extra weight. Then her hands were clipped to higher rings on either side of her broad girth belt, so that her elbows and shoulders were held well back, forcing her to hold her breasts well up.

Her modesty flap was removed, displaying her hairless mound and beauty lips.

The other pony women all watched through the bars of their cages as a white woman was led down the passage, being treated just as they were. Diana was the first white woman ever to be kept in the stable cages of El Paraiso!

She was taken across to the covered riding school or menage. A sweating young real four legged thoroughbred filly was being led out just as Diana was led in, a sight which only re-emphasised her animal status.

Stark naked, except for her girth belt and her heavy boots, she was made to run round and round the riding school, trotting almost without a single stop. She was tied by her collar to a long lunging rein which Pedro held in one hand, whilst with his other he cracked a long carriage whip just behind her hindquarters, or in front of her belly, to regulate and alter the speed of her trot.

Diana was being made to learn the difference between the controlled or prancing trot in which she had to raise her knees high in the air and throw her head well back whilst only advancing slowly; the normal trot in which she had to concentrate on swinging her breasts in time to each step; and the extended or racing trot in which she had to reach out with her legs and take long strides.

Although she was an intelligent woman, she took a long time both to learn just what was intended and then how to do it. Her first day in riding school was a painful experience, but slowly, with the aid of the whip, she was forced to concentrate on the three separate trotting paces.

On her second day, Pedro put her into blinkers and an exercise bridle.

The blinkers were partly to help accustom her to the bit, and partly to deprive her of the ability to see anything that was not right in front of her, and so make her concentrate purely on her trotting.

The leather bridle fitted her closely and held a thick rubber bit tight into her mouth. A plastic flange, attached to the bit, kept her tongue well pressed down so that she could not, like some dangerous horses, get her tongue over the bit.

The lunging rein was fastened to the ring of her bit, giving Pedro greater control of her.

The blinkers were fastened to the cheek straps of the bridle and were of two types, firstly the kind usually seen on horses that simply prevented the animal from looking sideways, and secondly the more severe type that only permitted her to peer through a little hole some two inches in front of her eyes. After a couple of days of this second type, Diana was allowed to run with the first type of blinkers.

Pedro would keep her at the exhausting prancing trot for what seemed hours, making her sweat profusely from the effort of raising her knees sufficiently high. Unable to see

Pedro because of her blinkers, she learnt to obey the slightest touch of his whip on her buttocks or belly, and the slightest jerk of the lunging rein on her bit. Fear of the carriage whip was uppermost in her mind as she ran round and round, getting more and more out of breath, her breasts bouncing.

Then would come the relief of being allowed to switch into the normal trot - though here she had to concentrate, on exaggeratedly swinging shoulders and breasts in time with her legs.

Pedro was a firm believer in varying the pace as a way of getting a girl fit, so this would be followed by a sharp spell at the extended trot - at racing speed. Now the whip would drive her on as, panting with exhaustion, she was made to run faster and faster.

Sometimes she would catch a glimpse of Carlos looking down from a little balcony and occasionally calling down to Pedro in unintelligible Spanish. Sometimes he would come down into the menage to inspect his new acquisition. Diana would feel the carriage whip on her belly and begin prancing on the spot. Then, still keeping the lunging rein taut, Pedro would accompany Carlos over to where Diana was still straining to raise her knees.

Unable to see because of her blinkers, Diana would hear them, as they stood alongside her, evidently discussing her progress. She would feel Pedro's whip on her thighs and stomach as he pointed out how her muscles were adapting to the prancing trot, and then Carlos as he touched her breasts, discussing the way they were beginning to hang more together.

Then she would be made to stand quite still, with her head raised in the air, whilst Carlos ran his hands down over his new pony's sweating body - invariably ending up by parting her exposed beauty lips and exciting her beauty bud. Soon he would have Diana panting from desire - and then with a laugh would take his hand away. Ponies do not have orgasms!

Diana's body soon began to show the effect of this hard training in the riding school, coupled with her simple diet. Her breasts were being steadily pulled closer and closer together by the gradual tightening of the little screw in the chain linking her nipples - a reshaping that was helped by the constant bouncing and swinging of her breasts in the menage.

Her thigh and belly muscles had hardened, her back muscles were now stronger, her breasts were more sensitive and her nipples were getting bigger and more pronounced thanks to the constant pull on her nipple rings. Well pronounced nipples were essential for a successful show pony.

Pedro was delighted with Diana's progress, and after several days also had her exercised for several hours a day in the circular automatic exercising ring. Here, fastened by the neck to one of the long arms of the slowly revolving exerciser she was made, together with other pony girls and real horses, to run continuously round and round.

At first she was fastened on the inside of the long arms where she only had to run slowly to keep up, but gradually she was moved further out until she joined the real horses near the end of the arms. After an hour on the machine she would be staggering as she was led back to her cage, fastened to her heavy neck chain again, and allowed to rest for a short time on her straw bed.

At last Diana was judged to be ready to be harnessed to a light surrey trap. So, after hosing her down, washing her all over, rinsing and thoroughly rubbing her down with a hay wisp, Juan took her across to the large coach house.

This held a large assortment of carriages, racing carts, light carts, four wheelers and two wheelers, some intended to be harnessed to horses, some to women and some even to a mixture of both.

Diana was to start pulling the simple light four wheel narrow surrey. For this no extra harness was required. The lower rings on the side of her now beautifully polished belly strap were simply attached by two short chains to each of the shafts. One of each pair of chains led back and took the strain when she was pulling forwards, the other chain led forwards and was intended to make her act as a human brake when going down hill, or when, for instance, the surrey was being parked in a tight space.

The chains held her belly absolutely rigid, so that her slightest movement was transmitted to the shafts.

The fact that she had to pull by pushing her belly forward kept her erotically upright - ready at any moment to be ordered to show off her paces by breaking into the prancing trot that she dreaded.

To enable her to use her shoulder muscles as well as her belly, a chain could be passed round each of her bent elbows and also attached to the shafts, so that she could now also pull with her arms. However at this stage Pedro felt it was important to get her used to using her belly muscles properly and so her elbows were not attached to the shafts.

The surrey itself had four light rubber bicycle wheels and a well upholstered comfortable driving seat which was shaded from the hot sun by a fringed canopy. At the side of the driver's seat was a vertical tube for holding the carriage whip.

Diana herself was now fitted with light running boots, and a more elaborate bridle which was really more like a muzzle. This was similar to that worn by Inez Mendoza's pony women, with straps over the top of her head and around her forehead supporting two cheek rings, which in turn kept the heavy rubber bit firmly in her mouth, and to which were also attached the one pair of the twin driving reigns.

The other pair of reins were, of course, attached to her nipple rings. This rein gave excellent control, since the fact that both breasts were linked by the tight short chain, made her respond even better to the slightest sideways pull on the reins.

A short bearing strap held her head back in a stiff proud position, with her chin well raised. This strap linked the buckle at the back of her head to a ring at the back of her collar. Two blinkers made of thick leather were fastened on either side of her eyes.

A stiff plume was fastened high on her forehead. This had been made from Diana's own long and distinctively blonde hair and at the sight of it she could not prevent two big tears from filling her eyes and rolling down her cheeks.

But she was in for more surprises, for she saw another sort of plume, also made of her own hair. This curved upwards at the base and gave the impression of her having a tail.

For show purposes the base was attached to a plug which was inserted into her rear orifice. The plug had a small circular indentation round it which enabled her sphincter muscles to hold it firmly in place. For longer periods, such as when she was taken out to exercise, the base of the plume was attached instead to a thick strap hanging down from the back of the girth.

In both cases, Pedro showed her how a jerk of the buttocks could attract attention or drive away the numerous flies that assailed her hindquarters.

Before forcing the bit into her mouth, Pedro had carefully applied lipstick to her lips and now he used the same bright red lipstick on her nipples and quivering sex lips.

With her head pulled back she could not see what had been done to her, but Pedro certainly found the matching red lipstick gave a most pleasing effect.

Two pairs of reins led back to the surrey, one leading to her bit which was more intended for braking and for steadying her, and the other, leading to her nipples, was for accurate steering, particularly past obstacles in the dressage and driving competitions. In this way, the driver, even if lounging back on the cushions of the surrey, would have no difficulty in controlling the vehicle, using the reins for steering and braking, and the whip to increase speed.

No brakes were fitted to the surrey, and as with Inez Mendoza's dog cart, the weight of the surrey when going down hill, or suddenly stopping, was transmitted by the front chains to the pony's girth strap, and thus to her belly, so that she herself was forced to act as the brake - provided of course she did not lose her footing!

So it was that a surrey, pulled by a naked and harnessed Diana, and driven by Pedro at a smart trot, swept up to the steps of the hacienda. Carlos stood waiting at the top of the steps, dressed in breeches and boots.

He took a look at Diana's bridle and at the adjustment of the two pairs of chains that harnessed her girth strap to the shafts. Then, helped by the stud groom, he mounted the surrey and settled himself down comfortably in the shade of the fringed canopy. He picked up the reins and the carriage whip, and looked down at the girl now reduced to the level of a common carriage horse.

"Well, Passion," he called out in English, "now I'm going to show you the estate you tried to take away from me! Trot, you lazy slut, trot!"

## 14 - HER MASTER'S FAVOURITE FILLY

There is no doubt that Carlos had obtained great satisfaction and pleasure from using Diana as his personal filly, making her pull her smart little surrey around the estate as he made his daily inspection. To be pulled by a naked sweating white woman with a beautiful body was indeed exciting, especially as he had noticed, with amusement, that the more he used his whip on her flanks, or to arouse her beauty lips, the more she was beginning to look at him with unashamed admiration.

Carlos was tempted to use Diana for his pleasure - just as he used his private harem of pretty young maidservants. But it was awkward to use her in the stables and to take Diana into his household as a maidservant, even temporarily, would surely be asking for trouble. The girl would have plenty of opportunity to try and escape, or at least contact her friends and relations.

No, he must stick to his original plan. Diana must remain in the stables and he must obtain his pleasure from humiliating her there.

The harnessing of the filly to the surrey did not involve the need to cover any of the lower parts of her body. These were left nude, with the sex bound tight together by the criss-cross leather lacing. This enabled Carlos to make his filly stale whilst still rigidly harnessed between the shafts. She simply spread her thighs when stopped - just as a real filly would do.

Increasingly, however, to Diana's desperate embarrassment, as her body adjusted itself to her new diet, with its frequent small feeds, so she found herself needing to relieve herself further when between the shafts. This she had to do at the trot - again just like a real filly. This was even more humiliating than standing over the cement strip in her stable.

A small plastic bucket of water and a sponge were hung from the back of the surrey and were used by the young Indian postillion, who normally stood at the back of the surrey, to clean her hindquarters when necessary.

Naturally this sponging of one of her most intimate parts was deeply humiliating for Diana, but there was nothing she could do or say as she stood helpless and bitted between the shafts, her legs spread, whilst the Indian boy washed her.

Another humiliation Diana often had to undergo was when Carlos decided to rest in the shade of a tree. Dismounting from the surrey, he would lie on the grass sipping a cool drink. Then he would order the postillion to bring Diana, still rigidly harnessed between the shafts, to stand in front of him.

Carlos would then amuse himself by running the tip of his carriage whip up and down over the most sensitive parts of Diana's body. She was a very sensuous young woman, and the fact that it was virtually impossible for the human fillies to touch themselves kept her madly frustrated - and even more sensitive to any titillation. Thus Carlos found it easy to arouse Diana with his whip, despite her shame and the lacing that kept her lips tight together.

He was careful not to allow Diana actually to reach a climax, and was interested to find that after these arousal sessions he had to apply his whip harder to keep her at a fast trot.

On one occasion, keen to check that his policy of not allowing his pony women to get at themselves did result in them being able to run all the faster, he decided to make a little experiment - to bring Diana to orgasm!

First he carefully unlocked the padlock that kept the lacing taut.

For the helpless Diana, her head pulled back by the bearing bit, so that she could not see what Carlos was doing, her muzzle and reins held by the postillion whom she also could not see because of her blinkers, her tongue silenced by the big bit, her breasts chained together by her nipple rings, and her belly held in by the tight girth strap, it was indeed a degrading experience - and yet also an extremely exciting one.

She could feel herself getting wetter and wetter between the legs as the shameful whip tickled both her nipples and, between her little infibulation rings, her beauty lips. She was almost overcome with excitement when the tip of the whip was replaced by the tips of Carlos' fingers - and even more so when they started playing with her now exposed beauty bud itself.

She could not help glancing down at Carlos with adoration and gratitude. Her Master was pleasuring her!

As she came to a shattering climax she was so ashamed to feel her juices running down her thighs, which of course she had had to hold wide open, open to Carlos's fascinated gaze.

Naturally Diana was weakened by her exertions, even if they had been involuntary, and by the copious flow of her juices. It was her first orgasm since her arrival at El Paraiso. Carlos had to apply his whip even harder than ever to keep the girl trotting properly all the way back to the stables.

Carlos drew the obvious lesson from his experiment: that he was quite right not to allow any of the sluts in his stables any sexual relief. Just as with his four footed fillies, sex should be reserved only for breeding. But he had been fascinated at the erotic sight that Diana had presented when being brought to orgasm whilst rigidly harnessed. He had found Diana's body disturbingly attractive. He remembered his plan to move her for short periods from the cage in the stables to the dog basket in his bedroom!

However, there was another little experiment that he first wanted to perform first, and one day Diana found herself being fitted with an extra rein. It ran from her nose ring, through a ring in the front of her girth strap, down between her legs, through her infibulation ring, up through another ring in the girth at the small of her back, and back to the surrey. Where the rein ran through her legs, large beads had been threaded onto the rein, the purpose of which she did not at first understand.

On this occasion Carlos left the postillion behind and was

alone in the surrey. As her Master drove her off at a brisk trot, Diana suddenly felt the under rein being slowly tightened. With her head held back by the bearing strap at the back of her head, she was unable to relieve the pressure from the under rein by lowering her nose. Soon she felt the big beads pressing against her beauty bud, pressing between her sensitive sex lips and rear entrance, and running up and down through her infibulation ring.

Then she felt the pressure being tightened and relaxed by her Master in time with her strides. It was devilish! Feeling herself being aroused, she slowed down.

But when the carriage whip cracked across her naked back, she quickly increased speed again. Ashamed but helpless, she could feel the beads inexorably arousing her. She was getting wetter and wetter as she trotted!

Again the whip cracked down, this time across Diana's hindquarters, making her keep up her steady pace, whilst Carlos steadily continued to arouse her with the under rein.

It was not easy for the excited Carlos, seated comfortably behind the straining Diana, to judge Diana's state of arousal. He was delightfully surprised when Diana suddenly half jumped into the air, her buttocks trembling, her breasts shaking, as she was gripped by a violent climax.

Then he brought his whip down again and again - determined to keep Diana running, determined to deny her the pleasure of stopping to enjoy her orgasm, determined to impose his authority on the sweating, quivering young woman as he brought her towards another enforced climax.

Poor Diana was made to keep on trotting, not only during that first orgasm, but during the second one, and finally during a third one, whilst Carlos laughed and enjoyed his feeling of power over her.

Then, tottering at the shafts, Diana was kept at a smart trot all the way home.

Pedro had timed Diana pulling a light racing cart round the practice track and Carlos had been delighted when he had reported that she was a very promising filly with a good turn of speed. However, trotting races would not be starting for several months. It was now time for Diana to spend a little time in the dog basket in his bedroom.

## 15 - FROM STABLES TO KENNELS

Diana's temporary departure from the stables occurred whilst Inez Mendoza was staying with Carlos.

They had spent a night of frenzied love in Carlos's huge bed, together with several of Carlos's pretty and terrified young concubines, whom Carlos had had specially forcibly trained to please them both.

The next morning, as the two wealthy lovers relaxed in bed over breakfast, Inez pointed to a large empty dog basket in the corner of the room.

"What's that for darling? It looks rather large for a dog!"

Carlos laughed. "That's for Diana!"

"Goodness!" laughed Inez. "Couldn't we fetch her now?"

"Why not?" agreed Carlos. He rang the bell and the half Indian housekeeper appeared. "Gamba, I want you to go and collect Diana from the stables. Clean her, wash her, douche her inside, scrub her down and scent her, then bring her to me."

Carlos turned to Inez. "I've had a special dog skin made for her."

"Wouldn't it be easier to have her tattooed?"

"Oh no! That would spoil her appearance when she goes back to the stables. Anyway I'm really looking forward to the feel of her dog skin whilst I make her lick or caress me."

"Ah!" smiled Inez, "Of course!"

"Anyway, you'll soon see!" chuckled Carlos. "It'll be very exciting, once the little bitch has been properly trained. Of course, there'll be the risk of picking up a few fleas. That's why she's going to be one of the short haired kinds!"

Laughing, the two lovers kissed and embraced.

Two hours later Gamba led a wide-eyed Diana into the drawing room of the large cool house, naked and ashamed.

Ever since Carlos had started to amuse himself by bringing his white pony girl to an occasional climax, Diana had had felt more and more attached to her Master, becoming almost besotted with him. The first couple of climaxes might have been involuntary, but then she soon found herself hoping that her Master would again bring her to a peak of excitement.

Now her girth strap had gone but her hands were handcuffed behind her back and she was held by a lead fastened to her nose ring.

With Gamba was the tough looking half Indian kennelman who was in charge of the guard dogs and who would be responsible for advising Carlos on the care of his new pet.

Diana was at first horrified, and then rather fascinated, as the kennelman and Gamba started to put the dog skin onto her. It was deliberately a very tight fit and followed every little bump and crease of her body. But she was horrified when they started to sew it up tightly, and she realised that it could not be removed except by cutting the stitches.

The skin was of natural tanned dog skin. The arms and feet terminated in little paws which held her fingers and toes quite rigid, so that she could not hold anything.

To keep her on all fours, light chains ran from her wrists to her knees. Each chain was only a foot long, so that she would have to learn to run along moving her hands and knees first on one side and then the other.

The skin went right up to her neck but left her breasts

naked. Her soft little bottom was also left naked, giving a strangely erotic effect. She was also naked between the legs, between which hung down her little infibulation padlock. Elsewhere the skin fitted her like a glove, a veritable second skin.

Extra strong pads had been securely fitted to the knees and to the paws, so as to protect the dog skin from wear and tear from contact with the stony ground.

Looking in a long mirror Diana was delighted to see how beautiful and erotic the dog skin made her look. It was rather exciting! If only it was not sewn on her!

But she was horrified when her head was now completely enveloped in a matching head piece that was also sewn onto the dog skin round her neck. Peering through two little holes in front of her eyes, she saw that she was now completely anonymous - her face had completely disappeared. There staring back at her was a very realistic looking dog, rather like a pug, with a flattened black rubber nose.

Her stainless steel collar had also disappeared from sight beneath the dog skin, and she was fitted with a strong leather dog collar over it, to which a lead could be attached.

On either side of her head were two erect ears that led down to her own hidden ones. In the front of the headpiece, as well as the holes for her eyes, there was a little slit, below the black nose, for her mouth. She reached forward with her tongue and felt a plastic serrated edge. The slit over her mouth could be closed by a half hidden zip fastener!

She saw that under the black nose was another little hole that fitted over her nostrils. It was through this that she was breathing.

Gamba closed the zip fastener over her mouth.

"We don't want the little bitch trying to bite her Master," she laughed, "or trying to talk!"

Diana found that her chin was tightly held in a strong leather cup that prevented her opening her mouth, thus ensuring her dog like silence - except for little barks and snuffles. The muzzle would only be unzipped when it as time for her to have one of her daily meal of dog biscuits and porridge - or if she was given a bone to chew.

In the stables, her feeding routine might have been the normal equestrian rule of 'a little and often'. But now her kennelman would insist on the normal canine rule of just one meal a day. It would take her stomach a little time to adjust, and she she would soon find herself begging for titbits from her Master.

The zip fastener, which was soft and of plastic, would also, of course, be unzipped whenever the bitch would be required by her Master to use her tongue to excite her - a service which her Master was determined she would be made to provide repeatedly and often!

Now dressed up in her dog skin, and made to move about only on all fours, it was time to start her house training. Carlos and Inez followed as she was led out by the housekeeper to a little patch of sand near the house.

Here she was taught by Carlos himself, carrying a dog whip, to put herself into the proper position for a bitch relieving herself; slightly squatting, with her hind quarters thrust back and her hind legs a little separated to avoid her dog skin getting wet or dirty.

It took Carlos a little time to train Diana to get herself just right, not only in the right position but also over the right part of the sand, depending on the type of performance. He used her dog whip to make the human bitch move her legs and hindquarters until he was satisfied, and then making her practice, again and again, taking up the correct position.

Carlos also trained her - and this took several strokes of the dog whip before she would do it properly - to sniff around for some time before performing, for this patch of sand was also used by other dogs! Then she was taught to cover up her performance with sand, scratching it up with her paws, just like a real dog - but not before her offering had been inspected.

This routine was strictly insisted on by Carlos, who saw that this little ceremony, repeated several times a day, would greatly help make Diana think and behave like a real bitch. Of course this training would require close supervision by the housekeeper and her staff, whom the little bitch now had to obey. The coloured housekeeper and her assistants would all enjoy watching this humiliation of a white woman. Indeed there would be no shortage of volunteers to take Diana 'out for a walk'!

The effect of all this on poor Diana was a mixture of horror and pride: horror at being treated as a dumb animal, and pride in being trained personally by her handsome Master. At least she was with him for much of the day. And, she had to admit, being her Master's little dog was really rather exciting.

## 16 - NEW COMPANIONS

The kennelman arrived and took a good look at the new bitch in his care.

Then as it was normally going to be kept in the kennels, when not required in the house, he suggested that that it should be taken to the fenced off area adjoining the kennels. Here the big doberman guard dogs were allowed to run during the day, together with the blood hounds used for tracking any escaping servants.

"It's important," he explained, "that they get used to their new companion and associate her as one of them. These are fierce dogs and we don't want any fights!"

He also suggested that her lead should be fastened to a special little chain that now linked her nipple rings to her nose ring.

They tried this out and quickly found that it was the ideal way of keeping her at heel without any annoying stops and tugs on the lead, for even if she dropped even slightly behind the chain would pull all three sensitive rings - a most effective way of keeping the creature at her Masters's heels, with her head and eyes docilely down.

Leading Diana up to the fence that kept in the dogs, Carlos ordered her to sniff along the grass growing at the bottom of the fence, and then at what seemed a likely place, a fence pole, she was ordered to drop a little liquid visiting card so that the dogs would be able to identify her in future - another routine which she was going to be made to perform daily.

A large number of dogs were now sniffing at her through the fence as Carlos held her there. Only a slight reddening of her naked breasts disclosed that, under her tight leather headpiece and zipped up mouthpiece and muzzle, she was blushing with the shame and humiliation.

"Well! The little bitch has certainly aroused the interests of your dogs!" laughed Inez, speaking in English. Then she pointed to a cage set slightly apart. "Which dogs are those?"

"Oh these are the bitches on heat - the hot bitches. They are shut up here partly for their own protection and partly to prevent the stallion dogs from fighting over them. They'd kill each other if the hot bitches were allowed to be free."

"And they'll kill each other over Diana when she comes on heat," laughed Inez. "You'd better put Diana in with them when she does - and you won't want her in the house then."

"Oh don't worry," Carlos smiled. "We've made special arrangements for her. Come and see the cage we've prepared for her right next to the hot bitches. She'll normally be in it most of the time."

It was quite a large cage. Two planks, fixed to the bars of

the roof, gave a little shelter from the rain and sun, and under them there was a pile of straw. A solid looking chain lay on the ground at the end of which was a heavy collar when put around her neck would enforce a very restrictive form of bondage - just like in the stables.

Suddenly Inez laughed. "I've just had a rather lovely idea, darling." She started to whisper something into Carlos's ear.

"Oh! Yes, but would it work?"

Again Inez whispered something into Carlos's ear. Diana saw Carlos's eyes brighten in astonishment and excitement.

"Wonderful!" he cried. "I'll invite some friends to come and watch! We'll have a little party. And the joke is that no one will ever guess who is under that dog skin. But, by God, I will!"

Then Carlos started to lead Diana back to the main kennels.

"Now, little bitch, let's see you say goodbye to your little friends. Come on, splash the post properly! Hurry up! I'm not going to wait all day."

Carlos started to whistle to encourage Diana to perform, tapping her naked buttocks threateningly with his dog whip. Diana looked up imploringly at her Master, but all that could be seen of her face were two small holes in her leather head piece, behind which her tear filled eyes could only just be seen. It was so hopeless! She would have to go through with it! She would have to perform, have to drop her visiting card, like a real little bitch visiting a strange kennels!

Obediently, she stretched her buttocks up and outwards so that she would wet the post properly.


## 17 - NEW DUTIES

Back in the house again, Inez and Carlos began to devize

other ways of amusing themselves with the new bitch, pinching her breasts as they hung down between her paws, pulling on her nose and nipples rings, or, having removed her muzzle, throwing a ball or bone for her to retrieve.

"Fetch!" would order Carlos, and the bitch, on all fours, had to obey and bring back the ball or bone in her mouth and then sit up on her hindquarters, begging for it to be thrown again. "Drop!" Carlos would order and the bitch had to drop the ball or bone at her feet.

They taught her to catch a lump of sugar which they made her balance on her nose for several minutes before ordering: "Catch!" If, as often happened at first, she was clumsy and dropped the sugar, then of course she was corrected with the little dog whips that they carried, or by Gamba whose self esteem was being greatly increased by being able to control and beat a white woman.

Of course these tricks were learnt under the threat of the dog whip which was only too frequently brought down across one of the bitches exposed buttocks, across one of her delicate breasts or sometimes down between her legs, making her cry out under her muzzle and try to beg for mercy.

"Little dogs do not talk," was the invariable reply of her implacable Master, and Dina soon learnt that if she wanted to try and please her Master then there was only one way: to sit up and beg, with her buttocks on her heels and holding up her two paws in front of her.

It was an hour later, and the two lovers were lying back side by side on Carlos's large high bed. They were playing with each other's bodies, and moaning with delight. Then one of the two pretty young mulatto girls gently drew a long ostrich feather through Inez's beauty lips.

"This is wonderful, darling," cried Inez.

"Indeed," smiled Carlos, picking up his dog whip again, "but now you're going to have even more fun - from a little dog who can understand orders!"

He waved the two mulatto girls out of the room and leant over the side of the bed to where Diana was kneeling on all fours, her lead fastened to the bed post, and her mouth still closed by her zip fastener muzzle. She had been half shocked and half excited at the noises she had heard coming from the bed above her, but above all she felt so jealous of Inez.

"Up little dog!" Carlos ordered, untying the lead and giving Diana's naked buttocks a sharp tap with her dog whip. "Come up on the bed."

Awkwardly, because of the way her wrists and knees were chained together, Diana got onto the bed. Peering through her little eye-holes she saw the handsome, tall and naked Carlos, and the shorter and plumper, but equally naked, Inez. A mixture of excitement and jealousy surged through her. She had been so longing for her Master to take her to his bed - but not like this, not with Inez there, too.

"Get your nose down, little dog," cried Carlos as he held the lead in one one hand and pushed Diana's head down between Inez's legs with the other.

"Oh it's lovely, Carlos," Inez cried. "But I must try her tongue!"

She lent down, pulled Diana's head up by the long ears, and unzipped her muzzle. Then she gave Diana another sharp tap on her bare bottom, and the lead a little jerk, and lay back.

"Now get back down and use your tongue as well this time!" she ordered. Moments later she felt something soft and moist, busily applying itself just below the equally moist rubber nose.

"Oh yes!" she cried out. "Oh yes!"

Then as Carlos watched, fascinated, she called out a series of orders, marking each with a cautionary tap of her dog whip, or an impatient jerk of the lead.

"Now little dog, move your tongue slowly up and down,

keep that black nose gently wriggling, push your tongue inside, deep inside, wriggle it ... Oh yes ... Now raise your head a little and lick my beauty bud, higher, higher, now suck ... suck! Ah! Ah! Ah!"

As Inez erupted into a climax, Diana now found herself enjoying being made to perform in front of her Master. It was as if she enjoyed being made to feel that she was not worthy of being used by her Master, and must merely please his mistress. She could feel herself becoming moist and excited. She tried to reach down and touch herself, but with her hands transformed into stiff hard paws, she found it difficult really to give herself pleasure. And then her action was seen by the watching Inez.

"Watch out!" she cried. "The little bitch is trying to play with itself!"

With a shock of anger, Carlos brought his dog whip down hard across Diana's buttocks.

"My God!" he screamed. "Get your paws away you disgusting little slut! Don't ever let me see you trying to do that again!"

Poor Diana felt so ashamed.

"Now raise your buttocks for the whip!" Yes, thought Diana, raising her bottom, she really did deserve to be punished. Again the dog whip came down. "Never try and do that again!" He began to punctuate each word with another stroke. "Never! Never! Never! Do you understand? Never!"

He turned to Inez.

"I thought we might have trouble in that way and I've had a little change to the dog skin made. You'll see it later, but now it's my turn to enjoy the little bitch!"

Poor Diana soon found that Carlos was even more demanding than Inez as he lay on his back, the whip ready in his hand. She saw his hardening manhood and prepared to pleasure him. But that was not where he wanted to feel her soft little mouth and tongue.

"Lower down, little dog," he ordered raising his knees.

Soon her tongue muscles felt tired. But the increasingly demanding Master drove her on and on, using the dog whip with increasing strength.

"Now bark!"

"Whoof!" Diana managed to cry out. "Whoof! Whoof!"

Inez laughed aloud and Carlos himself found it increasingly exciting as he felt Diana's tongue straining between his legs to make the little barking noises.

"Go on! Do it again!"

"Whoof! Whoof!" came the obedient little barks.

"Now, little dog, get behind me and use your tongue again!" Carlos ordered hoarsely as he turned and began to penetrate Inez's exciting body.

Then Carlos and Inez started to build up to a thrilling climax, greatly augmented for Carlos by he feel of the hot little tongue behind him. But not only was Diana, hidden behind her dog mask, having to play her role in helping Inez bringing her Master to his climax. In addition, she realised to her shame, the more she was made to aroused her Master, the more she also indirectly gave pleasure to Inez, who was being more and more aroused by Carlos's increasingly virile manhood.

Soon Diana could hear them calling out in pleasure whilst she herself was left feeling just frustrated and increasingly jealous of Inez. Then, just as on previous occasions when she had been made to pleasure her Master, she felt an increasingly thrilling feeling of servile submission flowing through her body and exciting her. She was now just his property - to serve him and his girl friends as he wished.

Then an emotionally and physically exhausted Diana was made to curl up silently by the side of the bed, her lead again tied to the bed post, and her mind reeling, whilst the two lovers slept in each other's arms.

An hour later Diana was kneeling on the floor. She still wore her headpiece, but her dog skin had been removed and she was otherwise naked.

Gamba was busy sewing sewing something white onto the dog skin, whilst Carlos and Inez waited impatiently. At last her task was completed, and Diana was again sewn into the skin. She felt something strange between her legs, pressing against her beauty lips. Peering down she saw something white gleaming, where before the dog skin had just been open.

"Look!" she heard Carlos say. "Look at how that little grill covers her beauty lips!"

"Darling, how clever! Press studs! She'll never be able to unfasten those with her paws!" Inez bent down for a closer look and felt the grill. "Goodness! Although the grill itself is flexible, I can see that it's also hard enough to stop her touching what's underneath! How brilliant, darling!"

"Yes," agreed Carlos. "The little bitch is going to be a good girl! But she can still spend a penny through the holes in the grill, and the kennelman can unfasten the studs to wash her everyday."

"And, of course," laughed Inez, "you can always unfasten the grill!"

"Exactly!" gloated Carlos.


## 18 - DIANA IS INTRODUCED TO HER NEW LITTLE LOVERS

It was immediately after this that Diana was taken to her kennel by the kennelman.

An extra heavy collar and chain were fastened round her neck, and she was left alone in her cage, watched eagerly by twenty five pairs of eyes: those of a dozen fierce Dober-

mans in their adjoining cage on one side, by half a dozen
bloodhounds in their cage at the back of hers, and by half a
dozen hot bitches from their cage on the other side.

Like the other cages, Diana's was open to the sky and had
a cement floor which was slightly sloping down towards a
drain, so that droppings could be hosed away twice a day. It
also had a raised bench, strewn with straw, for sleeping. The
bench was sheltered from the sun and the rain by a couple of
sheets of corrugated iron.

In a corner of the cage was a drinking trough. Otherwise
her cage, like the others, was completely bare.

For two whole days Diana was kept in her cage, dragging
her chain along as she crawled around it, doing her business
on the bare cement and curling up on the straw covered bench
to sleep.

Every morning the kennelman would come and let out
the other dogs and take them off for a short walk, before
flinging scraps of meat onto the cement for them to fight
over. He would also fling some into Diana's cage and then,
calling her over to the bars, he would reach down and unfasten the zip fastener over her mouth, holding up five fingers
to show that she had five minutes in which eat and drink.

Later in the morning he would hose down the cages, spraying a little water on the dogs. In the case of Diana, he would
also unfasten the press studs that kept her plastic shield fastened over her beauty lips, which he would then wash with
his hose, and then examine closely, before replacing the
shield.

Left alone with her thoughts, and always feeling hungry,
Diana was appalled at what had happened to her and at the
same time found herself now besotted with her Master, whom
she regarded half with hate, but now half with love.

She also found herself looking forward to her Master's
visits to her cage. She would bound over to the side of the

cage, eagerly greeting her Master with a series of little barks.

She longed to be able to touch herself and was deeply humiliated by the way the combination of the plastic shield, of her laced up beauty lips, and of her now stiff paw like hands, prevented her from doing so. She was even more humiliated when, once again ineffectually trying to get at herself, she heard the laugh of the kennelman who, unnoticed by her, had been watching her vain attempts.

In the evening the Dobermans were let out to roam around the estate buildings as guard dogs for the night, and light was switched on, illuminating Diana's kennel. There was no privacy - not even at night.

Then one evening when her Master came over to see her and discussed her in Spanish with the kennelman. She recognised the the repeated use of the word 'Manana'. What on earth, she wondered, was going to happen tomorrow?

Carlos had invited several friends over to watch the spectacle, for the mating of a bitch was always a big event in the kennels.

Chairs and an awning were placed around the cage so that the guests could watch the spectacle comfortably and in the cool of the shade. There was also a table, covered with a spotless white table cloth, for cold drinks and light refreshments.

Diana, crawling around her cage, could not understand what was going on. After she had been given only a very light meal the kennelman checked that her muzzle was fastened really tightly, for Carlos did not want to risk Diana biting or crying out her name.

Then the kennelman came into the cage. Standing astride Diana, as she knelt on all fours, and facing her hindquarters, her gripped her flanks with his knees to hold her steady. Then unfastening the press studs he removed the plastic grill, so that she was fully exposed.

Diana was used to him doing this to wash her, and although it was highly embarrassing, did not at first suspect anything untoward. But this time he pulled a little key out of his pocket and unlocked the small padlock that had kept her infibulated for so long and eased the leather lacing so that her lips were now no longer compressed.

Holding a pot of oil in one hand, he bent down and carefully greased the now exposed lips. Then, with his finger, he inserted some grease inside her to facilitate an easy and deep penetration.

Then he rubbed a little scent on her bare buttocks to arouse her lover, and went out of the cage, carefully bolting the barred entrance door behind him.

Diana was left all alone again, worried and anxious behind her heavy dog mask, mystified by the preparations that had been done to her body.


An hour later Diana saw Carlos, with Inez and several other guests, nonchalantly strolling over to the cage and its surrounding arm chairs. Several of the guests were beautiful women, and there was one very good looking young man, though he was not she thought as handsome as Carlos.

They surrounded the cage, pointing out to each other the unusual points of Diana's attire. Then they sat down. Servants brought cool drinks. But there was nothing for Diana on all fours in the warm sun under her dog skin. Then Carlos clapped her hands for silence.

He spoke in Spanish.

"Ladies and Gentlemen, Thank you very for accepting my invitation to come and see my new bitch being covered. She's been kept in this kennel for several days now and my kennelman feels that she is ready. You will see that we have fitted her with a plastic shied to ensure her purity - and to augment her feeling of frustration. Indeed, my kennelman says that if he hadn't kept her locked up in this cage, then she'd have been offering herself to every male animal on the estate!"

This was greeted with general laughter. Diana was left wondering what he had said that had produced so much mirth.

"Now we're very lucky for Inez has brought with her a very suitable lover for my bitch. She says he's a randy little chap - and that she's been practising him for today's event on several of her women labourers. So he should know what to do, even if the bitch doesn't! Anyway here he is!"

The guests all turned to look and then burst out laughing. There was a little round of applause as the Indian kennelman produced a strange looking creature that at first glanced looked just like Diana.

Diana gasped behind her mask. It was indeed another human being, also sewn into into a dog skin! It seemed very small however. How cruel she thought, to turn a child into a dog.

Its buttocks were bare like hers, and she saw that they were black, very black. Poor little piccaninny, she thought, another dog-girl.

Then as the creature turned away from her, she saw dangling down between its legs a little sack-like object. Then as it turned sideways on, she gave a gasp as she also saw hanging down beneath its belly a large black manhood, surprisingly large for such a small creature!

This was no child, this must be a dwarf! She remembered reading somewhere that male dwarfs have normal sized manhoods...

My God! No! She tried to open her mouth to scream a protest, but her tight muzzle allowed only little whine to to be heard.

"You see," Carlos laughed, "the bitch is getting excited at seeing her lover!"

With that he sat down, and to her horror Diana saw the kennelman lead the dwarf-dog up to the cage, open the door and let it in with her.

It sprang at Diana as if to attack her but then stopped dead at the sight of her hanging breasts. Diana, on all fours of course, was paralysed with fright, a paralysis that was helped intentionally by the sheer weight of her heavy chain. For a real bitch the weight was sufficient to make her stand still for the dog, and it had almost the same effect on Diana for whom it had been made even heavier.

The creature came slowly and suspiciously up to Diana sniffing her scented hindquarters, and then, to Diana's horror and just as he had been taught to do, he licked her sex lips to taste her juices.

Diana now fully realised what was going to be done to her. She again tried to cry out in protest but the muzzle still held her mouth firmly closed. All that came out was a little whimper that excited both the dog and the spectators. She tried to crawl away from the horrible creature with its poking nose, but she could only do so very slowly because of the weight of the chain. She tried to kick at the dog as he stood worrying her hindquarters, but because of the chains that linked her knees and her wrists, she could not do so.

Suddenly an electric shock went through her. The kennelman had touched her naked hanging breasts with a long cattle prod, an electric prod used for driving huge beasts.

"Now, bitch," she heard Carlos say, "excite your playmate's manhood with your front paws!"

The cattle prod touched her helpless breasts again and she screamed under her muzzle.

"Go on!" Carlos repeated. "DO IT!"

Diana simply could not stand more of that awful pain. She just couldn't! She turned towards the dwarf. Never in her wildest dreams had she ever imagined she would have to do this! The electric prod came forward again, menacingly.

Then, slowly and hesitantly, she reached forward to touch the dwarf's huge manhood which was slowly rising up into erection. Nervously she touched it with her paws, then started to stroke it.

This is what is going to master me, she was thinking despairingly - and in public for the amusement of her Master and her friends. This was what she was going to have to receive up inside her!

She saw the good looking young man watching her intently and the sophisticated and beautiful young women smiling at each other. What a crowd of cruel swine they all were!

Then the goad came through the bars again. "Now gently nuzzle it!" said Carlos in a harsh voice.

Nuzzle the dwarf! No! At least with her mouth firmly muzzled she could not be ordered to lick him. But this was almost as bad. No! Never!

She shook her head, but immediately the goad again touched her breast and this time remained touching it for several seconds whilst, impeded by the heavy chain, she tried to get away. The pain was terrible.

Suddenly the pain ceased, but she could feel the prod still touching her breasts.

"It will be switched on again in five seconds time, if you don't start nuzzling," came Carlos' voice. "Four! Three! Two!"

But Diana, beaten, had bent her head down to rub her plastic nose against the dwarf's manhood, thankful for once that the zip fastener over her mouth was firmly closed.

The two human dogs were now left to get used to each other for several minutes. Then the kennelman opened the cage door and stepped into the cage. He turned Diana so that her twitching hindquarters were nervously pointed towards the dwarf. Then standing astride Diana and facing towards the dwarf-dog that was standing behind her, he bent down and made her display herself.

Then gently calling the dwarf towards him, the kennelman

encouraged him to mount her. Diana felt his paws grip round her slim waist. She felt the hairy dog skin on her naked buttocks and then suddenly she felt his manhood parting her beauty lips. She tried to shake him off, but the kennelman, still standing astride her, held her firmly in place.

"Do that again, you little slut, and you'll feel the goad," called out Carlos in mock anger, secretly delighted by the spectacle of reluctance that Diana was putting on.

Then suddenly Diana felt the dwarf penetrate her. She felt him going further and further inside her. She felt him growing in size. He was thrusting at her violently! In and out, in and out!

Horrified, she felt her body reacting to the powerful thrusts. Horrified she felt herself becoming more and more aroused. She simply could not stop herself.

Then she began to realise that she was actually enjoying being made to perform by her Master in front of her friends.

The kennelman stepped aside and left the cage. The dwarf and the woman were now united in the most intimate way that a male and female can be. For a second Diana remembered her boy friends in England. They must never know about this, ever!

There was a sudden flash as Carlos took a photograph of the embrace of Diana and the dwarf, both in their dog skins. There were several more flashes as he took more photographs from different angles.

Then suddenly Diana felt the dwarf's seed shooting up inside her. It was revolting! The dwarf went on emptying himself into her. As he did so she herself erupted into a violent climax.

She heard the audience clap. It was too awful!

Then she felt a curious sensation; instead of now feeling the manhood inside her grow smaller, it seem to swell up and get even bigger. It was stuck inside her! Vaguely she remembered stories that of real dogs and bitches being stuck together for hours. Did this also happen with dwarfs? Oh, no she thought!

She could feel the dwarf pulling at her, trying to get free. Then, like a real dog, he lifted a leg up over her back, so that they were both kneeling on all fours, facing away from each other, hindquarters locked to hindquarters.

For a full five minutes they were locked together. She could not cry out for help and there was absolutely nothing she could do about it.

Then the kennelman came into the cage carrying a couple of buckets of water, which he suddenly proceeded to empty over the lovers. A few seconds later, the dwarf slid out of her and was taken out of the cage. The spectators gave a little clap.

Diana had had her first mating!

The servants came and served more iced champagne, and cucumber sandwiches. Even Diana was allowed a bowl of water which she had to suck up through the grill on the front of her muzzle.

"Ladies and Gentlemen," announced Diana in Spanish, "we have not finished! Inez has also brought another dwarf - a rather younger one that has developed a preference for using a woman in, shall we say, a rather different way! So, ladies and gentlemen, our little bitch will again have to excite him by displaying herself, but this time she also then have a rather nasty surprise!"

Moments later, Diana was horrified to see the kennelman leading another dog-dwarf up to the cage.

She tried to scream in protest, but all the eager audience heard were little grunts.

The kennelman put the new dwarf into the cage. He seemed a little smaller, thought Diana, but as before only his glittering little eyes, his black bare buttocks and his black hanging manhood and testicles were visible through his dog skin.

Like the other dwarf, he bounded up to Diana, sniffing her eagerly. Diana was so shocked that she scarcely noticed that the kennelman, before leaving the cage, again smeared a little grease between her legs - and this time, not so deep down.

"Now little bitch," Carlos called out in English. "This time you're going to arouse your little friend properly by displaying yourself - and by proffering yourself. You're going to twitch your little beauty lips in front of him. You're going to rub them up against him. And if you don't, then the cattle goad will make you!"

Diana was again appalled, but the kennelman pushed the goad through the bars of the cage again. Quickly she turned her hindquarters towards the dog! She thrust out her backside! She opened her legs! The goad came towards her and the spectators were delighted to see that she was trying to make her sex lips twitch!

The dwarf became aroused. He came towards her. The goad also came towards her again, and she forced herself to slowly back down towards the dog, seeking to rub herself against him.

It was a very erotic demonstration of the power of Carlos over Diana. Carlos found himself becoming aroused as he watched Diana. Terrified of the goad, she was making herself excite the dwarf, using her animal instincts as to how best to do so.

Suddenly the dwarf mounted her, gripping her with his front legs. Suddenly she felt his manhood thrusting against her, but this time thrusting against her bottom. She tried to wriggle away but the dog held her firmly and, thanks to the carefully placed grease, with a sudden thrust penetrated her where no man had previously entered.

She could not believe what was happening. The dwarf had made a mistake! Could no one tell him! And it was so painful!

Diana was screaming her protests through the muzzle, but all that anyone heard were little cries as if of pleasure. It was the first time that she had been taken in this way. She had never thought that such awful thing could happen to her, and by a dwarf dressed up as a dog!

She felt utterly subservient as the dwarf thrust in and out. It was an experience she would never forget - nor the dwarf who was riding her in such a masterly manner.

Once again came the flashes from Carlos's camera as Diana's performance was filmed for posterity. Finally, she felt the jets of sperm squirting up inside her, and when they ceased the two of them were even more tightly locked together, by the tightness of Diana's rear orifice, than she had been with the first dwarf.

This time the kennelman waited a full ten minutes before throwing his buckets of cold water over them. And then, under the threat of the goad, poor Diana had to wait while her muzzle was untied and then she had to lick the dwarf's manhood clean.

Carlos had rightly judged that Diana was now too ashamed to try and call out to the spectators - she just wanted to get it all over as quickly as possible.

Finally the dog was led away. The kennelman came into the cage and again stood astride Diana who was still kneeling on all fours. Once again she was made to show her beauty lips to the laughing spectators and then, bending down over her buttocks, the kennelman carefully replaced her little infibulation padlock. Blushing under her dog mask, Diana felt her lips, her now sullied lips, being closed tightly together and heard the click of the padlock.

There was another round of applause - for the kennelman, not for Diana - and the spectators started to drift away, leaving Diana alone, shamed and defiled.

For a whole day she was not washed or hosed down. She

could still feel, or imagined that she could still feel, the slimy semen of the dwarfs up inside her two orifices.

However, although she did not share a common language with her kennelman, she did share his confidence that there would be no untoward results from her performances with the dwarfs. Both knew that it was a very safe period for her.

## 19 - ESCAPE AND RECAPTURE

"You're going to be taken back to my verandah now," said Carlos in English with a cruel laugh. "I'm going away tonight to stay with Inez, and tomorrow we'll send for you again. Then, after you've been properly shampooed, we'll see how performing with a couple of dog-dwarfs has affected how you perform with us!"

He turned on his heel, leaving Diana furious and ashamed. The thought of being made to satisfy the two lovers yet again filled her with despair - but she could not help also being rather excited at the prospect of pleasing her Master

She knew only too well what would happen. Chained to her dog basket in her Master's bedroom, she would have to watch through her little eyeholes as the two of them excited each other. Then she would be untied and made to lie between them as they rubbed themselves against the prickly hairs of her dog skin. Then her muzzle would be removed and she would have to lick first Inez and then her Master, bringing each to an orgasm before being muzzled again and put back into her basket, leaving the two satiated lovers to sleep in each others arms.

Later that day two servant women came down to the kennels and collected her, leading her back to the big house. She was put back into the kennel on the verandah, but in the absence of their strict master they did not bother to fasten her collar to the kennel's own chain. Instead, they simply locked the door to the little cage.

That evening Diana was 'taken for a little walk' to relieve herself on the sandy patch. The coloured girl who held her leash found it very exciting to make a white woman behave in such a humiliating way. Making sure that Diana's muzzle was firmly secured, she put her through the full routine of squatting on all fours to relieve herself and then scratching up the sand.

The chains linking her wrists and knees had been removed when she was taken back to the house from the kennels as Carlos felt that she was now sufficiently cowered to remain on all fours anyway.

The coloured girl had therefore enjoyed 'walking' Diana all the more, knowing that this white girl was crawling along behind her on all fours only through fear of the whip. Indeed she found it all so exciting that she failed to properly lock the little door to Diana's kennel-cage after the walk.

Kneeling on all fours in the kennel, for it was only two and a half feet high, it was some time before Diana discovered that the door was unlocked!

It was getting dark and she knew that no one would come near until morning. This was her chance to escape! But did she want to? She was she realised half in love with her Master - he was the most exciting and dominant man she had ever met. But he just ignored her feelings, treating her as a performing animal, making her perform tricks for the enjoyment of his mistress, or having her shamefully mated with the two dwarfs as a show for his friends. It was all too much. She hated him! Of course, she must escape!

Desperately excited, Diana, still sewn into her dog skin and unable to use her hands which were now her front paws, waited for the lights of the hacienda to go out one by one. When everything seemed quiet, she gently pushed the barred door of her cage open and crawled out.

For the first time since she had been transformed into her Master's pet bitch, she stood up! She was free! If she had not been so tightly muzzled she would have cried out in delight and joy. She would run away and expose Carlos for the monster that she was! She would get possession of El Paraiso and make Carlos her plaything!

Softly she started to make her way through the hacienda buildings. After all this time she had spent pulling Carlos' surrey around the estate she knew her way very well. Silently she hugged the shadows of the big silent buildings. There was no sign of life! No one had seen her!

Then suddenly just as she passed the last building she heard the dog. One of the guard dogs! She had forgotten the guard dogs! They were let out at night specially to prevent intruders - or escapers!

The dog came bounding at her, snarling. It was one of the terrifying Dobermans! One of those who had been in the kennel next to hers.

The dog was about to leap at her throat when suddenly he stopped and, recognising Diana's smell, turned and went off. Diana realised that she was all alone again. Everything was quiet.

She started to run across the plantation towards the hills.

Dawn found Diana high up on a bare hill overlooking the estate and still sewn into her dog skin. She was exhausted after scrambling upwards for what seemed like miles. She found a little stream, and lowering her muzzled mouth into it, she sucked up the cool water. Refreshed, she lay down by the side of the stream, wondering what to do next. Her thick leather muzzle prevented her eating anything even if she could have found anything to eat. She would rest and then try and make her way to a village.

Diana slept for several hours, then she was awakened by the sound of hounds baying, a sound that was coming closer!

Carlos had returned early that morning to be greeted with the news that Diana had escaped.

He had smiled as he gave orders for the hunt.

His two favourite bloodhounds had been brought to Diana's kennel to get her smell and had immediately set off in her tracks. They had checked where the Doberman had found her, and then had set off for the hills, followed by Carlos and the kennelman, both mounted on horses.

Half an hour later the bloodhounds had found the stream where Diana had fallen asleep. Carlos and the kennelman had exchanged glances. They must be getting very near now! What a relief! thought Carlos. It was time Diana went back into the stables. It was obviously too dangerous to treat her as a pet bitch.

But she would have to be punished first!

A few minutes later Carlos heard the bloodhounds barking. They had their prey at bay! He galloped up. Diana, her eyes looking terrified behind her dog mask, stood with her back to a tree, whilst the bloodhounds bayed at her feet.

The kennelman got off his horse and slowly walked towards her. She tried to shrink back even further against the tree. The kennelman gave a word of command to the bloodhounds and they felt silent. Without a word he gripped her collar.

"You ungrateful slut!" shouted Carlos. "I let you enter my personal service - and what do you? Try and run away!"

Petrified, Diana hung her masked and muzzled head in shame.

"Well, just look what we do to run away women!" she heard Carlos cry out.

The kennelman pulled out a small rifle from its long holster strapped to his saddle. He handed it to Carlos. Slowly he took careful aim at Diana's skin covered belly. Diana tried to scream for mercy but her muzzle simply reduced her scream to a whimper. She heard a shot ring out. She felt a sudden blow in her stomach, a sudden pain and then oblivion. She fell to the ground, the tranquilliser dart sticking into her belly through the dog skin.

## 20 - PUNISHMENT

Diana regained consciousness slowly.

She was in a small cell, lying on a simple cot. It was the first time that she had slept in a bed of any type since her arrival in Costa Negra.

Her dog skin had been cut off and so had her dog mask. She put her hands up to her mouth - there was no muzzle. Her hands were free. She looked down. She was wearing a simple cotton skirt. It was the first time she had worn any clothes since her arrival at El Paraiso!

She sat up in the bed. She felt something tight around her waist. She put her hand down. There was something hard between her legs!

Quickly she pulled up her skirt and looked down.

Something shiny, made of metal chain-mail, had been locked over her sex lips with little chains. It was heart-shaped. Was it a sort of chastity belt? She put her hand down to touch it. It was raised over her beauty bud. clitoris. It was not so much a chastity belt, she realised, as a purity belt, designed to prevent a woman from playing with herself, from rubbing her clitoris, from touching herself.

But why?

Little did she then realise the extent to which Carlos did not allow any relief to a woman who was about to start her training as a racing pony!

Shocked by the simple effectiveness of the purity belt, Diana swung her feet to the floor. They were chained! A light chain only about eighteen inches long linked her ankle rings, making her have to walk with little mincing steps.

She looked in the mirror above the small wash basin. She saw her shaved bald head, her nose ring, her nipple rings and her naked breasts, which after their training now hung much more closely together. Shocked by her animal like appearance she turned away.

The door opened. A stern looking armed guard entered. Diana covered her bare breasts with her hands in an automatic gesture of modesty. Without saying a word, the man put down a tray of simple food and fruit juice, and left the room. She felt like a prisoner enjoying a last meal.

For a whole day she was allowed to rest, to sleep and day dream. The nutritious food soon had her fully recovered from the exertions and excitements of her abortive escape.

Then they came for her - three large masked men, part-Indian overseers dressed like executioners in black tights which showed off their bulging manhoods. They wore black shirts under which their muscles rippled, and black masks that half hid their cruel faces.

They seized Diana and marched her out of her cell and into the open area outside, making her hobble along on her chained feet.

She blinked with amazement in the bright sun. There was a lot of shouting of orders as large groups of women were being drawn up in smart military formation. They were divided into different companies, each company wearing simple dresses of different colours, and each company under its own male overseers.

The overseers were former army drill sergeants recruited by Carlos to supervise and discipline his women labourers. They wore well pressed military type uniforms and peaked caps. They carried short dog whips as a sign of their authority.

The women all wore heavy military boots and were stamping smartly as the overseers wheeled and halted their companies, and then numbered them and brought them to attention.

To the right of each company, evidently in the place of honour, was a group of half naked women - naked except for coloured scarves, their army boots and and shorty blouses that left their swollen bellies exposed so that they could be seen and easily checked by their overseer. They had been chosen by their overseers for their stamina, physique, good looks and docile character to enable the company to meet its quota of the next generation of indentured servants for El Paraiso.

Whereas the rest of the women were standing at Attention with their hands to their sides, the half naked ones were standing with their hands on their heads to display their bellies better.

Tapping their dog whips against the palms of their hands, the overseers were proudly striding up and down in front of these expectant women. Clearly their state did not excuse them from the strict discipline that these former drill sergeants imposed on all the women under their control - just as it did not excuse them them from a full day's work, labouring in the fields.

Indeed, a few of the women had been fertilised by their own overseers - in itself a simple way of rewarding the overseers and of giving them a weapon with which to enforce discipline amongst the terrified women of their company.

But the majority had been mated, under the supervision of their overseers, with one of the estate's own breeding studs. These were a small number of men with a proven ability to throw female children with the right characteristics. Not only were they used for mating with selected indentured servants but alternatively, as Carlos had begun to experiment with, used to produce the vital ingredient for artificial insemination - not only of his own female indentured servants but also, for a fee, of the indentured servants on neighbouring smaller estates.

An increasing number of plantation owners, both large and small, were realising that just as artificial insemination could be cost effective alternative to keeping expensive bulls to cover their cows and heifers, so too it could be a cheaper and simpler alternative to keeping young studs to cover their female indentured servants. Moreover, it had the added advantage of eliminating any emotional attachments.

The number of women in an expectant state was large since the annual production of young female indentured servants was as important a crop for the El Paraiso hacienda as were its crops of coffee and cotton. Indeed most of the women in the companies had numerous red chevrons tattooed onto their arm, looking rather like a sergeant's stripes, each denoting the successful delivery to her master of another future servant - something which also earned a handsome bonus to their overseer.

The women all looked very alike, except for a few women that Carlos had acquired from other estates to bring in new blood. This similarity was the result of generations of carefully selective breeding to produce the distinctive El Paraiso breed of labouring women.

Whilst Diana was marched through the assembled women, there was a rustle of whispers as the women saw that she was a white woman - a shaven, ringed, chained woman, naked to the waist, but still, to their astonishment, a white woman.

Suddenly Diana saw what the women were paraded around - a gallows! She was being marched to the gallows! She was going to be hung! Struggling she was forced up the steps. The rope was fastened round her neck and her hands were tied behind her back.

"No! No!" she screamed. The executioners stood back.

Then suddenly came the commanding voice of Carlos, riding his horse on the outside of the parade. He gave orders in Spanish. It had been amusing to frighten Diana, but the spectacle was also intended to warn them all that the punishment for trying to escape from El Paraiso could be death.

Now he announced that the death sentence for Diana was to be remitted. Instead she was to be flogged - flogged in front of the other women as a lesson to them all.

The executioners unfastened the rope round Diana's neck. They untied her hands. Then they held her and slowly removed her skirt. They unlocked her purity belt, displaying her bald and tightly laced beauty lips to the watching women.

Then they her marched across to a raised platform that held a special stocks. It was mounted on two strong wooden supports at a height of about four foot. Diana's neck was put into the hole in the centre of the stocks, and her wrists into the smaller ones on either side. The top of the stocks was then brought down and fastened, imprisoning her neck and wrists. Her legs were fastened as far apart as her leg chain permitted.

Diana was now bent over, her legs apart, her knees bent, her head and shoulders thrust forward, her buttocks nicely presented for the thick rubber paddle that one of the executioners was already swinging through the air, and which he suddenly brought down with a thwack across her buttocks.

Diana screamed with the pain.

Carlos, still sitting on her horse, smiled and felt his manhood react as the second stroke came down. He had ordered twelve strokes only, and from the rubber paddle rather than the long black whip usually used to discipline his women - he did not want Diana to be seriously hurt, or marked, lest her forthcoming training might be delayed. The rubber paddle stung and made a lot of noise, but did not seriously harm a woman being punished.

The third stroke came down and then there was a pause.

The public flogging of a white woman was a rare event for the others. Now stood at ease by their overseers, many of them were pointing to Diana's reddening bottom - and to her hairless sex lips that were so blatantly displayed as she was rigidly held, bent over for her punishment.

Diana herself scarcely knew which was worse, the pain that the heavy rubber paddle inflicted, or the humiliation of being exposed in this shameful way before so many women and their male overseers.

She vaguely understood that her hanging had been commuted to a flogging. However, she did not know how many strokes she was to receive. Nor did she know that a pause was always made after each batch of three strokes so as to draw out the agony, and to make the flogging a more impressive and awesome ceremony for those watching.

She could not of course see anything behind the board of the stocks that held her neck and wrists. The masked executioners, however, were now standing in front of her, and suddenly the one who had given her the first three strokes formally handed the paddle to one of his colleagues, who went out of sight behind her.

Diana shivered with fear and anticipation, clenching her buttocks desperately. She heard the overseers calling their companies to attention. She saw the women in front of her come smartly to attention, their eyes to the front. Another word of command and each woman turned her head to look at her.

There was a whistling noise behind her and the heavy paddle struck across her buttocks. Her little whimpering cry was heard all around the parade ground, and a few seconds later was followed by a scream of pain as the next stroke fell in the same place.

To the delight of the flogger, and of the watching Carlos, the pain made Diana give a little dance of pain, shaking her buttocks and lifting her separated legs quickly one after the other, to the extent that her chains permitted.

The flogger, his eye gleaming behind his mask, waited

for her to calm down, waited for her to keep still, and waited for her buttocks to stop juddering. He also waited for her to unclench her buttocks momentarily and then brought the paddle down low across the back of her thighs, which up to now had not felt the paddle. Again her scream echoed across the parade ground.

Then once again there came a long pause with the women being stood at ease again.

This time, Carlos got off his horse and, handing its bridle to a groom, walked to the platform. "So, my little slut", he said with a mock smile, "you aren't enjoying your flogging? Well, for the next three strokes I want to feel your tongue licking the soft palm of my hand. I want you to show your Master what a big brave girl you can be, and to take three strokes without crying out. I want you to show all these wretched women how brave a white girl can be! If you do cry out, then the stroke will not count. So it's up to you!"

The paddle was handed to the third executioner. The companies were called to attention. Carlos held out his hand to Diana's tongue. Obediently and docilely, Diana started to lick his palm, just as she had had to lick his manhood in his bed.

Suddenly the paddle came down. The pain was excruciating, but somehow Diana managed to keep licking her Master's palm. Down came the next stroke, and again she managed to stifle the scream in her throat.

Carlos patted her head. "Good girl! Now there's only one more stroke!"

The last of the three strokes came down, this time low down on the back of Dianas thighs. She couldn't help screaming. "No, please! No more, please!"

"Well you silly girl, that one doesn't count! so now you'll just have to have another stroke."

This time poor Diana succeeded in keeping quiet and in continuing to lick like a little dog.

125

"That's better," smiled Carlos as the overseers bawled out their orders to the women to stand easy. "Now I'm going to give you the last three strokes myself. And to really impress my strength and personality on my women, I want to hear you bawl your lungs out with each stroke. Do you understand? If I don't get enough noise out of you, I'll go on until I do!"

The executioner ceremoniously handed the paddle to Carlos. The companies were called to attention. Carlos went behind Diana as she clenched her buttocks. He raised the paddle high in the air, so that the all the women could see it and would realise that it was indeed their dreaded Master who was now flogging the white woman.

Carlos brought the paddle down hard onto Diana's left buttock. Diana screamed aloud, sobbing and begging for mercy.

Carlos raised the paddle again. Then he lowered it and made Diana bend her knees more so that she was displaying herself even more blatantly, before her raised the paddle again and brought it down hard across Diana's right buttock. Again the parade ground echoed to her cries.

Only one stroke more!

Carlos adjusted her stance and this time brought the paddle down across Dianas unsuspecting shoulders. There was no denying the reality of her scream of pain this time!

Carlos turned, handed the paddle back to the executioners, and walked down the steps of the platform, back to his horse. The women were marched off, company by company, by their overseers to their barracks, the pregnant women of each company forming a little advance guard, their bellies prominent but their arms swinging as smartly as those of the others.

Diana was left all alone tightly secured to the stocks, sobbing with the shock, pain, and humiliation. But perhaps the worst part was the realisation that, despite the pain, she had been aroused by being beaten by her Master. Even now the memory of how he had made her lick his hand whilst he had her beaten made her moist with excitement. What a slave she was! Her Master's slave! She would, she realised, do anything to please to him.

## 21 - IN TRAINING

Back in her cage in the stables, Diana was forced to submit to the same routine as before. Pedro gave her a day to recover from her flogging and used the opportunity to make her submit to the indignity of again being dewormed.

He then concentrated on getting her fit again. He made her spend long hours every day in the riding school, trotting round and round at the end of a lunging rein, her speed being varied and controlled by his long carriage whip. She spent further hours secured by the neck, together with other women and horses, to the long arms of an automatic exercising machine as they went endlessly round and round.

Every day her Master would come and discuss her progress in voluble but incomprehensible Spanish, calling her over to the front of her cage so that they feel her thigh or arm muscles, or her calves or shoulders.

Clearly Carlos was delighted with her body. She began to feel rather proud of the way that he patted her in a proprietary way. She was thrilled that he was evidently pleased with her.

She began to realise that she was under training, just like a race-horse. A race-horse! She was going to be raced! Raced by her Master. Trained to win races for him!

She did not know whether to to be shocked or thrilled. She longed to ask more about it, but did not dare do so. She realised that her Master saw no reason to tell her what she was being prepared for, any more than his horses in training understood about their training. Nor did she know whether to be shocked by the way that her body was constantly becoming intimately aroused by the idea of racing in public as one of her Master's pony girls.

Gradually she realised that she was going to tried out as a steeplechaser - carrying a boy jockey over a series of jumps. This sport appealed more to the Latin American temperament than using pony-girls for show jumping, in which they could only compete one at a time as opposed to the excitement and thrills of a competative jumping race.

As a first step Diana was made to run round the riding school with a weight strapped to her back and over her shoulders. At first the weight was only twenty pounds, but then, as her muscles grew stronger, it was gradually increased to forty.

Simultaneously she was also taught to to jump over brushwood fences that increased gradually from a height of only one foot to the full height of three feet. This was a height that was designed to tax a young womans agility and stamina to the maximum, bearing in mind that she would be carrying a young four stone Indian jockey at a fast gallop.

Carlos came frequently to the riding school to watch Diana being put through her paces over the jumps, and finally agreed with Pedro that she now showed sufficient promise to be saddled up for her first ride carrying a jockey.

Diana was both shocked and thrilled when she first saw the saddle being brought out, and as she felt the lightweight saddle being positioned in the small of her back by a broad leather girth strap. The weight of the rider was taken by two straps that ran from the front of the saddle over her shoulders and joined each other in a metal ring between her bare breasts. From the ring another strap ran down to fasten onto the front of her girth strap by her navel.

It was all rather exciting, she decided, especially when she saw that to keep the saddle properly down onto her waist, two straps ran down from the front of the girth on either side of her bare hairless beauty lips. They were held together by a horizontal strap that linked them just above her mound so that her beauty lips were nicely displayed between the narrow straps. These straps joined in a ring over her rear orifice, from which a rounded strap ran up her cleft, to be fastened to the back of the saddle.

Two very short stirrup leathers hung from the saddle so that the jockey's knees would grip her tightly around the waist, his spurs touching her hindquarters.

The saddle was, of course, specially made to be perpendicular to her back, its back sticking out horizontally to provide the jockey with a good support, though as with racing and jumping real horses, the jockey often partly stood up in his stirrups to reduce the impact on his mount's back when landing after a jump.

Although she did not know it, jockeys' weights were limited to four stone, and as with real horses the saddles were fitted to carry lead weights to make up for the weight of any under-weight jockeys, and for use in handicap races.

The pony-girls were only ridden by jockeys for steeplechase races. Flat races, for both horses and pony-girls, were always in the form of trotting races, in which the horses or the women both pulled lightweight two wheel racing sulkies.

This arrangement enabled pony-girls to be raced, over the flat, for distances of up to a mile, whereas, because the weight of the jockey on the girl's back, steeplechase races became too slow to provide good spectator sport over distances of more than a few hundred yards.

The races at each race meeting were alternately for horses and women, with steeplechases interposed with trotting races. There was always one joint trotting race, however, a special handicap, in which women, given a long start, raced against horses.

For all the races, the local Indian population betted heavily - as did the landowners who owned the horses and pony-girls being raced.

Some of the races for women were described as being for fillies, others for mares certified as having foaled, and others, to encourage breeding, were for two legged brood mares who were certified as being still under three or six months in foal.

The last race of the day was invariably a chariot race for pony-girls in which half a dozen young women from the same stables were each harnessed by a chain running from the back of a girth strap round their waists to the front of a lightweight racing chariot. The driver was often the young scion of a wealthy local landowning family, and they would use their long whips to drive the the women on and on at an excitingly high speed.

The skill in these races lay in steering the team of women round a short oblong course and in particular round the poles which marked either end - just as in Roman chariot races. With half a dozen chariots, each drawn by half a dozen frenzied young women, there were plenty of spills and excitements.

The pony-girls wore the usual girls double bridle with separate reins to their bits and to nipple rings. But all the reins fastened to the same part of each pony-girls anatomy were joined together into one rein before reaching back to the chariot. In this way the driver had only four reins to bother about, two leading down to the breasts and two to the bits. He held these reins tightly in one hand, and used them to control and steer all six galloping women, whilst with his other hand he whipped them into greater efforts as he jerked them tightly round the marker posts or overtook his rivals.

For the steeplechase races, however, bridles were changed

so as to meet the jockeys requirement for a different type of control. When being made to practise her jumping, Diana's reins, attached to her nipple rings, were led up through her bit rings, and then back over her shoulders to the jockey's hands.

Like the drivers in the chariot races, the jockeys would hold the reins in one hand, whilst using the other to whip their mounts into greater efforts.

The vital control in steeplechasing with pony-girls was to get them to jump at exactly the right distance from the fence, and for this the most effective control was a sharp jerk upwards on the nipple rings. Steering in these races was largely accomplished by the jockey swaying his weight from one side to the other, something which a pony-girl had to learn to respond to instantly.

The jockeys would also often seek to hold back an eager young mount so that she did not tire too soon, and then to using spur and whip to drive her on past her rivals to the winning post.

Diana was both frightened and affronted when, watched by her Master, a young eight year old called Pepe, racing whip in hand, swung himself up into her saddle for the first time and gathered the reins into his hands. Young though he may have been, he was nevertheless an experienced and successful jockey.

She had to bend forward against his weight. But this was now counter balanced by her head being pulled back by a special martingale strap that ran up from the front of her saddle to join another strap that ran round the top of her head. In this way, although the weight of the jockey made her lean forward, her head was held back, making her thrust her breasts forward - even more forward than when she was harnessed to a trap.

Pepe tapped her on the buttocks below the saddle with his

whip and made her trot forward. He held her bouncing breasts with the reins which now gently pulled them upwards towards her cheek rings. He ran her towards the first jump in the riding school circuit. Suddenly, a full yard and a half in front of the jump, he gave a sudden tug on the nipple reins, making Diana jump upwards with the pain and take off for the jump well ahead of it, so that she had to stretch her legs well out to clear it - the attitude that would be required in jumping at speed whilst carrying the boy's weight.

After a few circuits of the manege, she began to learn that she must leave it to her jockey to decide the moment she should start her jump, and that she must simply obey his signals. She was made to learn not to think for herself, but simply to obey his commands.

She learnt to feel his pressure on her nipple rings as he steadied her into each jump, then to feel the pressure from his knees on her waist as he forced her forward, and then finally to feel the jerk on her breasts lifting her up over the jump.

Hateful and shame-making though it was, as the days went by she felt a growing empathy between her body and the young boy who was forcing her over the jumps.

Several times, however, she tripped over the fences or on landing, sprawling on the soft peat of the riding school and throwing her furious young jockey. She soon learnt to fear the punishment for falling or throwing her jockey, a savage thrashing from the young boy's whip across her breasts and buttocks!

At the same time she was also being made to practice trotting races - racing against other pony-girls, all pulling sulkies, driven by young boys, on the much longer trotting race practice course. Here, wearing her normal double bridle again, she learnt to obey young Pepe's instructions, given through pressure on her cheek reins, to hold back and not to tire herself too quickly. Then, suddenly, she would have to obey his whip and a sideways pull on one of her nipple rings, passed on by the short linking chain to the other nipple, and increase speed and dash out to one side to break through a gap in the sulkies ahead of her.

Here again she quickly learnt after several thrashings that she must not think for herself but must simply obey young Pepe's pressures on her reins and the flick of his whip across her hindquarters.


Before Carlos could enter Diana in any of the forthcoming race meetings, she had to be passed by the Inspector of the all powerful Pony-girls Breeding and Racing Society. Although he was referred to as the Society's Vet by the Society's members, in fact he was a doctor with considerable experience of pony girls of different breeds.

As usual she had no idea what was going to be done to her until the strange man stepped into her cage with Pedro and Carlos. Once again her feelings were mixed as he started to feel her body all over, listening to her heart and checking that she was fit to race, and also checking her brand number, and entering it on her Registration Certificate and on his Record Card.

On the one hand she felt humiliated and embarrassed, but on the other she somehow felt rather proud that her handsome Master was taking all this trouble over her.

But she was mystified when the Vet made her bend over, whilst Pedro fastened her collar and her wrists to the bars of her cage, only a few feet above the ground. Then he carefully began to check that she genuinely was still a filly, not having yet carried a foal.

Finally satisfied, he straightened up, signed Diana's certificate, smiled at Carlos, and handed it to him.

The way was now clear for a new filly called by her registered name of Passion, registered number El Paraiso Y755, to compete in the races and other events that took place under the supervision of the Society.

Carlos patted Diana's cheek.

"You're going to win me a lot of money," he said. "You've made a lovely pony-girl."

Diana found her self blushing with pride.

## 22 - DIANA WINS!

After a couple of months of intensive training, it was time for Diana's first race meeting at a nearby village.

The horses that were going to be raced under Carlos' colours were carefully loaded up into the back of a large horsebox.

The women were put into a special compartment in the horse box, each carefully chained by her collar to a ring and each, of course, with her hands, as ever, chained tightly to rings on the side of her girth strap - for it would be disastrous if a woman exhausted her energy by playing with herself just before being raced! For the same reason the women were chained well apart from each other so that they could not dissipate their energies by rubbing themselves against each other.

The floorboards of the stall were covered with straw to absorb the wastes of the women and to encourage them to empty themselves before being raced.

At the race meeting, Diana could hear the cheers and yells of the crowd during each race. She could see the various horses and women being bridled and harnessed up for their races, then being led off to the paddock, and later, lathered in sweat, being brought back, their jockeys smiling or scowling depending on the results, whilst the horses or women were washed down in cold water.

Soon it was Diana's turn. To further hide her identity, special blinkers had been fitted over her head, leaving only small holes for her eyes, each with a leather eye-piece that prevented her seeing anything except right in front of her. The blinkers came down only to her nostril and mouth, leaving her nostril ring exposed and enabling the thick rubber bit to be forced into her mouth, whilst its supporting bridle was fastened over her now hidden head.

Only the whiteness of her skin, now gently tanned all over by the sun, gave a clue that she was really a white woman.

Diana's first race was to be a steeplechase. She was saddled up, and the special short breast-training chain was clipped onto her nipple rings - for Carlos wanted her new filly to look her best. Then the reins were also clipped onto her nipple rings and passed up through her cheek rings.

The saddle's under-straps were fastened between her legs, leaving her hairless beauty lips very visibly on show, as were those of her darker skinned competitors. Blushing furiously under her blinkers at being seen naked and harnessed by several thousand people, Diana was led into the paddock where a dozen other pony-girls were being led round under the appraising eyes of the crowd. Diana's long white legs drew considerable comment, for she was taller than the native pony girls against whom she was to be raced.

Her vision being severely restricted on purpose by her blinkers, Diana did not immediately see Pepe dressed in white breeches and the black silk racing colours of Carlos.

"Jockeys to mount" was ordered and Diana was led into the centre of the paddock where Pepe was standing next to Carlos, who was smartly dressed in a white tropical suit and Panama hat, with his racing glasses slung over his shoulders. He was so handsome, even if he was such a swine!

Then she felt a burst of jealousy, for she saw that he was surrounded by a group of attractive young white women, dressed in well cut dresses, and wearing expensive looking wide-brimmed hats and long gloves that matched their dresses. The women were laughing and evidently teasing Carlos, who seemed a popular figure.

Were they daughters of other local landowners, Diana wondered? Was Carlos, despite his affair with Inez and his harem of indentured servants, regarded as the local catch? Was he, a bachelor and the dashing owner of El Paraiso, locally regarded as highly eligible? No wonder he had re-acted so violently to her threatening his inheritance!

The contrast between these sophisticated and expensively dressed women and her own nakedness made Diana feel even more humiliated. And they were free and she was a mere pony-girl: to all intents and purposes a slave; reduced to the level of an animal; her Master's plaything. And yet these very thoughts were in some strange way rather exciting.

This same contrast aroused Carlos also as he looked at his admiring girl friends and then at Diana's bald mound and and beauty lips, at her naked breasts held unnaturally close together by the little chain between her nipple rings, at the big brass nose rings that hung down over lips of her mouth, between which was strapped the thick black rubber bit, and at way her martingale held her head back and and her breasts thrust forward.

He came over and patted her rump.

"Now little filly", he murmured softly in English, "let's see you win this race. I want you to put everything you've got into it, and if you don't I'll have you publicly flogged again back at the hacienda! I've betted very heavily on you, and as you are still unknown I've got very good odds. So, you're going to win a lot of money for your Master - or you'll feel that paddle again on your backside!"

With these terrifying words still ringing in her ears, Diana felt Pepe mount her, his weight making her take up the pret-tily curved S-shaped curved attitude of a woman carrying a jockey. He trotted her down to the start.

Through her blinkers she could see a line of brush fences

- they seemed terribly high! She could feel Pepe's knees firmly gripping her waist. She could feel his hands on the reins steadying her swaying breasts. She felt his spurs and his whip on her buttocks, as he drove her into a stall in the starting machine - the same starting machine that was used for both horses and women. She heard other women being forced into the stalls alongside her, but because of her blinkers she could only see the start of the course, and the wires that held her back.

Pepe pulled on her reins to lift her up onto her toes, inside her light running boots. Suddenly the wires in front of her flashed upwards, and Pepe drove his spurs into her buttocks, pushing her forward at a fast gallop.

They were off!

The course was a semi-circle some four hundred yards long. This gave the spectators a good view of the performance of the human animals on which they had all heavily betted and whom they were cheering on. There were a dozen jumps, including a deep waterjump that was intended to make the women really stretch out if they were to avoid falling into it. The jumps were high so to test their agility and, incidentally, to provide the falls, often painful for the heavily laden women, that so excited the crowd.

Diana, driven on by Pepe's whip, raced towards the first jump. Through her blinkers she could just see another woman slightly ahead of her on one side, and she could hear the grunting and panting of others all round her. Suddenly her breasts were tugged upwards by her reins and automatically and obediently she hurled herself into the air, one leg stretched forward and the other bent sideways. She had cleared the first jump. This gave her confidence and she hurdled the next few jumps in fine style.

Coming to the big water jump she was lying second. The woman in front of her failed to clear the deep stream that lay hidden beyond the jump. She fell, almost in front of Diana, who, given a double tug on her breasts by the jockey, realised that she must make an extra long jump this time. She just managed to avoid tripping on the sprawling woman.

Diana was now nearing exhaustion from carrying her jockey over the jumps. She was panting desperately. She was in the lead as they came into the final straight. Pepe's whip and the memory of Carlos's awful threat drove her on, and somehow she managed to race first across the finishing line!

Then she staggered into the winners unsaddling stall, where, sweating and panting, she was unsaddled whilst Pepe, saddle in hand, went off to the weighing room. His win was confirmed and Carlos, occasionally remembering to pat Diana's heaving shoulders, was the centre of a crown of people congratulating him and asking about his new white filly.

"Where did you get her?"

"Is she for sale yet?"

"Are you going to breed from her?"

"I've just the stallion to put to her!"

"I must say, she's got excellent conformation and bone!"

Carlos simply smiled at his friends and questioners, and made no reply. They would get an even greater surprise when they saw Diana in the fillies trotting race later that afternoon!

Diana had now got her breath back and was led back to the horse box. After being sponged down all over she was tied up in the stall with the other women, none of whom dared to speak. She felt rather proud. She had won! She had won for her Master!

Pedro massaged her legs and an hour later she led out to be harnessed to a racing sulky. In these trotting races the women were allowed to pull not only with their bellies and with their girth straps linked by short chains to the shafts, but also with their elbows round which a little strap was also fastened which led back to another chain attached to the shafts. The woman's wrists, of course, were fastened to a ring on the side of their girth strap, so that they were pulling in effect with their shoulders, as well as with their bellies.

Pepe, once again wearing Carlos's colours, drove Diana down to the paddock. Once again she had been blinkered. She was made to walk round the paddock pulling her light sulky, swaying her breasts and shoulders, as she had been taught, to show off her figure.

This was a race for big breasted fillies and Diana had to submit, like the other women, to her breasts being measured by the judges, so that their handicaps could be judged. All the races with good prize money were for big breasted fillies and mares, for racing such women was much more interesting spectacle for the spectators!

However the swaying of their heavy breasts would make them slower than a flat cheated woman - hence the importance of the handicaps and of measuring their bosoms at the start of a race - and for the pony-girl's trainer to ensure that her breasts met the minimum measurements without being unnecessarily large, heavy or pendulous.

If the trainer was in doubt as to whether a particular young woman's breasts were large enough, he would inject a special silicone mixture into them to increase their size. Diana had watched with horror in the stables as the other women had been tied by the neck and the waist to the bars of their cage, with their breasts thrust out through the bars to enable the veterinary surgeon to inject a little silicone through the nipple so as to distend the breasts sufficiently to give the right measurement.

Luckily, so far, her own breasts had remained big enough, even though her figure had been fined down by her strict training and diet. This was much to Carlos's joy as having to give a woman an injection of silicone into the breasts might reduce her value as a brood mare, since perfect natural conformation was so important for breeding.

Soon the half dozen racing sulkies were lined up for the start.

The starters flag fell and they were off on their half mile long trip round the big circular course. Pepe held Diana back at first, letting the other women exhaust themselves in making the running. Then, with a furlong to go, he drove her through a gap between two sulkies ahead of her and, whip flying, forced her to stride out with her long legs and overtake the other women, winning by half a length.

This time the champagne really flowed in Carlos's box in the grandstand, as more and more people asked about his new human filly, who meanwhile was only being allowed to drink from a bucket of water in the horse box.

Carlos had won a considerable sum of money from Diana's two wins, both in bets and prize money. He was particularly delighted that Diana had proved to be a success both in steeplechasing and in trotting, for it was rare for a woman to be a good performer at both.

He consulted closely with Pedro, her stud groom and trainer. He realised that he now had a potentially very valuable brood mare in his hands. It was vital, however, that before Diana was put to a stallion she should win a major trotting race - the short steeplechases were not considered so important in establishing a pony-woman's stamina. It was accordingly decided to enter Diana in the pony-girl Derby for fillies, a trotting race that would be run over a mile in a month's time.

Diana was brought to a new peak of fitness and obedience. Her diet and her wastes were meticulously supervised. To keep her breasts well balanced and big, they were massaged twice a day, which kept them well stimulated and firm, so that she would have no difficulty in meeting the minimum breast measurement requirement for the Derby.

The Derby meeting was the biggest of the year with, as

usual, separate races for horses and women, and for mares and fillies. The races were held some fifty miles away from El Paraiso, and Diana was allowed to squat down on the straw in the horse box as it jolted over the rough roads.

At last they arrived at the crowded race course with its flags, the flower decorated stands and boxes for the landowning class, and the enclosures for the many humble Indian peons who had come to watch and bet on the horses - and in particular on the women runners.

Although Diana was to be raced in blinkers, this time they were attached to her leather bridle, and not to the cloth head cover that had been used before. This meant that her shaven head, as well as her brilliantly polished nose and nipple rings, were all now visible. So too, of course, were her infibulation rings and the criss-cross lacing over her beauty lips. These all caused a great stir. Indeed she became a great favourite with the crowd as she was paraded in the paddock amid cries of 'Mira la calva!' - Look at the bald woman! - and 'Mira la zumbada!' - Look at the ringed one!

As he watched Diana being paraded, Carlos was congratulated on the appearance of his prize filly, on her glossy skin and evident fitness. He had decided that if she won this important race, then he would be time to earn a large sum from hiring Diana's body out to another breeder. He himself did not at present have a suitable stallion at El Paraiso. But he could make a lot of money by selling to another breeder the right of having Diana covered by a stallion of his choosing and subsequently of keeping the foal, or the first foal if there were twins.

Breeding from a successful winner was, of course, all part of the fascination of owning pony-girls. But in the case of Diana, quite apart from the money, it would, as he told Inez, be a delicious revenge if the woman who had tried to take El Paraiso away from him, ended up as one of his brood mares.

But really, it was more the feeling of power that really excited him - the power of deciding to breed from her, of virtually playing God and of having absolute power over the body of a beautiful Englishwoman.

Once again, Pepe kept Diana well back at the start of the race and, once again, made her spurt forward for the last few hundred yards, winning handsomely in a dramatic and exciting finish.

Again the champagne flowed in Carlos's box, whilst the sweating and panting Diana was unharnessed from the sulky and chained up again in the winner's stall, proud to have won again!

## 23 - DIANA BEGS TO BE MATED

It was now a few days after Diana's triumphal win at the Derby. She herself was elated, and despite being kept stabled and dumb like a real filly, she could not help being proud of her success, proud of having won for the Master she had come to - to - yes, the Master she had come to adore.

She was standing naked and helpless in her cage, with the heavy chain fastened to her collar and to the ring at the back of her cage. As usual her hands were chained to her side - fastened to the ring on the bottom of the extension piece that hung down her thighs from the girth strap round her belly. This extension piece was held in place by a strap which went round her lower thighs above the knee.

In the cage looking at her, as well as Pedro and Carlos, was an immaculately dressed and cruel looking man of about fifty. All three were carrying riding whips which they tapped against the palms of their hands or against the sides of their riding boots, terrifying poor Diana.

Their immaculate dress contrasted with Diana's nakedness which, as always, was alluringly set off by her subju-
gated helplessness.

The older man looked Diana up and down, like a horse
dealer making up his mind whether to put in a bid for an
apparently attractive buy. He felt Diana all over, carefully
and methodically, commenting in Spanish on her body as he
worked his way slowly down.

First he examined Diana's head and eyes, and then, lifting
up her nose ring, her teeth, before feeling her shoulder and
arm muscles and her breasts and nipples. He bent down and
ran his hand over the filly's belly and over her thigh muscles
and felt down her calves. Then he stood up and pointed down
at Diana's beauty lips.

Pedro bent down and unlocked the fibulating padlock.
Diana could feel her beauty lips splaying open, like a flower.
Then, with his dog whip, Pedro tapped the insides of her
thighs indicating to her to open her legs for a more intimate
inspection.

Senor Ortega, the well known and highly successful, leading trotting-horse and pony-girl breeder, for that is who he
was, parted Diana's beauty lips. He wanted to feel up inside
her to satisfy himself that she could carry a heavy mulatto
foal, or even twin foals. Diana, meanwhile, had gone scarlet
with embarrassment, wondering who on earth this awful
person was, and why he was examining her in such an intimate way. He certainly did not appear to be a doctor!

The man stood up and wiped his long fingers, wet with
Diana's natural juices, on a silk handkerchief. He turned to
Carlos.

"Well Senor, you drive a hard bargain."

"Please speak in English," interrupted Carlos. "I want this
filly to know just what we're planning to have done to her."

"I can certainly see that her win at the Derby was not
mere luck," said the man, now speaking in English. Diana

could not help preening herself. "I must admit that she is a magnificent specimen. With her long legs, her well developed muscles and her docile nature, she should win you many more races as a filly. But I want her blood in my own breed of pony-girls."

He casually weighed one of the blushing Diana's breasts in one hand and went on.

"I want her stamina, her conformation, her bone and her strong breasts in my own line of future Derby winners. I have just the stallion to mate her with - 'Black Beauty', a huge black Negro with a jet black velvet skin."

Diana gasped. Mated! With a black Negro! Only a warning tap on her bottom from her Master's whip stopped her from screaming out in protest.

"And he's got a fine record of throwing twin filly foals," went on the older man, to Diana's mounting horror. "Your filly would nick in very well with him, and their progeny would be unbeatable."

Diana listened, appalled, as she heard her Master reply with a confident smile.

"Well, Senor Ortega, you can use her for a half a million pesos. And if she has twins then I shall want to have the right to buy her second one for a hundred thousand. You can have first choice. Well?"

"As I said," replied the cruel looking Senor Ortega with a laugh, "you drive a hard bargain. I go to all the expense of experimenting with a stallion, and of proving that he is good at throwing twins, and you then want his second progeny!"

"It'll be the filly's second progeny," corrected Carlos with a laugh. "No, that's my final offer - that is, if you want your stallion to cover her."

"Oh come now, Senor. Be reasonable!

"No, take it or leave it! I've had other offers, and I've been thinking of breeding from her for myself. Whether she has one or two fillies, you'll still have made yourself a fortune. You'll be able to sell your foal immediately for a very large sum - and you know it!"

"Well," muttered Senor Ortega, stroking his chin reflectively and knowing when he was beaten.

"You will have first choice of the foals," smiled Carlos, "and it'll be yours to collect as soon as she has foaled. I'll let you know as soon as she starts so that you can come over here for the big event. Meanwhile I'll warn you when you when she next comes into season and then, ten days later, bring her over to be covered by your stallion. If you put her to the stallion on two successive days that should be enough."

"It's a deal!" exclaimed Senora Ortega, shaking Carlos's hand.

"Alright", laughed Carlos, "but I think I'd like to be there on both occasions - for personal reasons. Can you put me up?"

"Of course! And we'll have a special party for you, to celebrate the new breeding line."

"Yes! I'd like that," agreed Carlos.

"Good!"

Diana saw the two men shake hands. Shake hands on her mating! She watched them leave the stables together, deep in friendly conversation, obviously still discussing her.

Pedro tightened the laces over her beauty lips again, and adjusted them so that they were again held tightly pressed one against the other. Then he straightened up, and, whip in hand, stood guard over her until her Master returned and ordered her intimacies to be sealed again with the laces locked together.

Carlos stroked the now tightly compressed lips. It was, he reflected, like guarding a very valuable piece of jewellery - or, rather, perhaps more like guarding the entrance to a cave in which the jewellery was lying - waiting to be discovered by the invading seed of the stallion that had been chosen to cover her. Thanks to her wins, and his training, this girl's intimacies were now one of the plantation's most valuable assets - and they were in his care!

"Well, Passion, aren't you thrilled?"

It was a few minutes later and instead of ordering Diana's lips to be resealed, Carlos had instead ordered Pedro to loosen them again.

The tip of his whip had been going on and on, tantalisingly running up and down Diana's exposed beauty lips. She could not help writhing in a mixture of pleasure and shame, as Pedro held her tightly, helpless in front of her Master. Her legs were wide apart, and her knees bent. With one knee in the small of her back, Pedro made her thrust her belly forward - for the attention of her Master. Her head was held back, so that she was looking up at the iron bars that went across the top of her cage.

"And aren't you thrilled," she heard her Master continue, "that your Master has decided to breed from you! As you heard, you're going to earn so much money for your Master! So you're soon going to be such a proud little mother, carrying her precious progeny for her Master!"

Diana jumped as her Master's finger replaced the tip of his whip. Oh the ecstasy! Her Master's touch! And his hypnotic voice went on and on, as the roving fingers aroused her slowly to greater and greater heights.

Diana shivered, but was it she asked herself, a shiver of dread - or of excitement at the thought of being made to conceive, whether she liked it or not?

"Down! Get down and kneel at your Master's feet!" she heard her Master order. As if hypnotised, she let Pedro position her, humbly, on her knees. "Now lick my feet as a sign that you really want your Master to have you mated. Beg for it! Beg with your tongue!"

Oh yes! Oh yes, she thought, submissively licking his shiny leather riding boots. Oh yes!

Above her humbly, and yet happily, lowered head, Carlos smiled knowingly at his Stud Groom.

## 24 - PREPARATIONS

There was no easing of Diana's daily routine, for Pedro was of the firm opinion that a girl would conceive and carry more easily if she was kept really fit.

So it was that she was now exercised every day with several other pony-girls who were either already expecting, or who, like her, were awaiting their visit to a stallion.

Like them, Diana would have to run round and round the indoor riding school at the prancing trot with her hands clasped behind her neck and her knees raised high in the air. This would be interspersed by having to goose-step round and round at the walk, having to keep each leg quite straight as she brought them up to the horizontal.

The slightest sign of easing off would bring Pedro's long carriage whip cracking across her backside. They were both exhausting exercises but excellent for the all important belly muscles.

So it was that Pedro was delighted when Diana came into season on exactly the right date. He called Carlos down to the stables to show him the tell tale signs.

"Only another ten days!" Pedro exclaimed excitedly, for Senor Ortega had privately offered him the usual stud groom's large tip if Diana conceived.

So it was that, ten days later, early in the morning, Diana was taken in a horse trailer behind a Landrover to Senor Ortega's stud farm.

His entire plantation was given over to his breeding enterprise. Some thirty pedigree brood mares, four-legged and in-foal, were kept in well laid out paddocks surrounded by white painted fences. In the corners of the paddocks were simple field shelters for the horses to go into at night. In the opposite corners of the paddocks were the feeding and drinking troughs.

Ortega was a great believer in keeping his brood mares living out in paddocks rather than shut up in stables. Not only did he feel that it was healthier, but the mares kept themselves exercised and he was a great believer in the maxim that a well exercised mare rarely had trouble when foaling.

So each mare spent an hour a day on a rotary exerciser like that at El Paraiso, going round and round, attached with other brood mares to one of several long revolving arms.

Keeping his brood mares in paddocks also helped him to show them off to visitors and to potential buyers of their progeny.

He extended this routine to two-legged animals as well. Thus, it was not only his four-legged brood mares that were kept in paddocks. A similar number of half naked and valuable two-legged ones, nearly all in different stages of pregnancy, also lived out in similar paddocks - though in their case the paddocks were surrounded by high chain wire fencing.

There was, however, one noticeable difference between the four-legged mares and the two-legged ones. The two-legged ones all had been laced-up in the way that was used on Diana when she was first put into the stables. But now the purpose of the lacing was not merely to prevent a young woman from getting at herself to give herself pleasure, but primarily to make sure she did not interfere with the very valuable, but kicking, young progeny she was being made to carry.

For both types of brood mares, however, Ortega insisted on keeping their progeny in other paddocks out of sight of their dams.

"What the eye cannot see," he later explained to Carlos as he showed him round his immaculate premises, "the heart will not grieve for. My brood mares, both four and two-legged ones, are so valuable that they must be put to the stallion again soon after they foal, and they often don't conceive if they are feeding a young foal."

Ortega's famous stallions, one of which was the Negro 'Black Beauty' for whom the unsuspecting Diana was destined, were kept apart from the brood mares they had already covered, and equally out of sight of any young fillies to be covered.

Both the pampered human and equine stallions lived a life of luxury, hidden away in a special building in loose boxes or cages from which they would be led to the adjacent mating box. Here the waiting mare or filly would already have been secured, ready to be mounted.

In the case of human stallions their faces would be carefully masked, except for two eye holes - for while Senor Ortega wanted his stallion to be aroused by the sight of the trembling young woman he was to mount, he did not want her to form an attachment to the father of her future progeny.

Diana was put into one of the stalls used by visiting fillies and mares.

As a precaution in case she later lost control of herself in the mating box, when she realised that the moment of truth had arrived, they dosed her with a little castor oil and washed her down with a hose after she had emptied herself onto the straw.

Then, remembering that Senor Ortega had promised him a little reward for a successful outcome of the visit, Pedro unlocked Diana's infibulation padlock, momentarily loosened the laces, and carefully rubbed a little vaseline up inside her. This would make it easier for the stallion to penetrate her deeply and thus ensure conception.

Diana did not know where she was and still did not quite realise what was going to happen to her. She would therefore have been horrified had she heard the conversation between Carlos and Ortega as they breakfasted on the terrace of the latter's sumptuous hacienda after Carlos had driven over.

"I hope you don't mind me mentioning it," said Ortega, as he passed a cup of coffee to Carlos, "but I always like to cut down the food of a mare for a day before she's put to the stallion, especially if it's a filly being covered for the first time - and the same applies to a human filly."

"Oh, don't worry! I entirely agree," laughed Carlos. "I always have a woman mated on an empty stomach. Diana's had very little to eat since yesterday morning and Pedro will have ensured that she's emptied herself completely."

There was a pause as they both buttered their fresh croissants, and sipped their coffee.

"I know that she is going to be mated twice - today and again tomorrow," said Carlos, munching his deliciously flaky French bread, "would you mind, for the first time, if she's mounted from behind on all fours? I've been trying hard to make her think of herself as an animal, so I'd much rather she was mated like an animal for the first time - of course tomorrow you can have her serviced in any way you like!"

"Oh yes, I too like to see a girl being mounted from behind for the first time," said Ortega.

Carlos was thoroughly enjoying this conversation and the way they were discussing Diana as if she were a helpless beast. He was used to discussing such matters in these terms when it was about his native or crossbred women, but the fact that it was now about Diana added special poignancy.

"We'll have the mating fetters put on her," went on Ortega, pouring Carlos another cup of coffee. "I always like to use them so that a girl can't kick out at my valuable stallion."

Carlos's eyes glinted at the thought.

"But if she is going to be on all fours when the stallion penetrates her," Ortega continued, "then I do insist on two conditions. Firstly, to ensure the stallion's manhood penetrates deeply, I want my stallion handler to insert it himself."

"Of course!"

"Secondly, I want to make sure that the seed runs down inside her and not out of her! So I like to keep a girl's buttocks high and her shoulders down level with the ground - moreover she must be kept in that position for a good hour after the stallion has withdrawn. I have a special apparatus for this - perhaps you do too?"

"Yes indeed."

"Of course there's always the problem of whether she should be aroused before being covered. 'Black Beauty' tends to thrust in and out very violently, unless of course he is restrained by his handler."

"As violently as you like," interrupted Carlos his eyes gleaming.

"But then he tends to ejaculate quite quickly."

"Excellent, I don't want that slut enjoying herself!"

"My own experience," said the rather serious Ortega, "is that a little arousal does assist the fertilisation - but as you want the first mating to be as an animal-like as possible, I suggest that we strictly limit it. However, I'd like to have her warmed up a little both before and afterwards! It always seems to assist fertilisation, especially in the case of a nervous young girl."

"Feel free to warm her up as much you like!"

"And the next day," went on Ortega," I envisage the mating being done with the girl on her back with her legs and arms raised high in the air and most her weight being taken by her shoulders so that we get the deep penetration again, and downwards. This time I think she should be thoroughly aroused."

"Exactly!" murmured Carlos, smiling.

There was the noise of a car driving up to the hacienda.

"Ah! This must be the is the Breeding Society's vet. He's come to certify the mating." Ortega rose to welcome the visitor who was carrying his white operating gown and carrying his little black case. "I suggest we all adjourn to the mating box, where some refreshments are waiting for us!"

First, however, they went to the stall in which Diana stood chained to the wall by a heavy chain fastened to her collar.

As usual she was deprived of the use of her hands, as her wrists were strapped to the girth strap that went tightly round her waist.

Her mound and beauty lips had both been freshly shaved, powdered and polished until they gleamed. She made an erotic sight, and one that was now further set off by scarlet painted lips, made up eyes, and well polished black leather laces across her beauty lips.

This effect was further accentuated by her special head collar. This consisted of just a narrow strap that went over her head, and which divided into two on the bridge of her nose. The two side straps ran across her cheeks and were buckled together under her chin, making it difficult for her to open her mouth properly.

Where the straps passed the corners of her mouth they were joined by a rubber bit fastened to two metal rings in the cheek straps. To make quite sure that she could not get the bit out of her mouth, further straps went from the rings and were buckled together at the back of the wretched girl's neck where they met the other end of the narrow strap going over her head.

Carlos was not going to risk Diana disclosing her real identity whilst in Ortega's stables!

Carlos snapped her fingers and Pedro came forward with a long beautiful white lace bridal veil which he proceeded to put over Diana's head.

"And I think a further little bit of modesty would not come amiss."

He snapped her fingers again, and this time Pedro brought forward a white frilly skirt, no more than a few inches long in the front and slightly longer at the back. He wrapped it round Diana's waist. In front, it covered her brand mark but showed off her beauty lips, prettily covered by the criss-crossing leather laces, with the little locking padlock hanging down between her legs. Behind, it covered just the top of her buttocks.

"Charming," said Carlos. "That makes her much more decently dressed for her first meeting with her bridegroom."

Carlos and Senor Ortega now left to join their guests who had come to watch the mating of Carlos's now famous European filly, an event which had aroused widespread interest amongst their neighbours.

## 25 - COVERED!

It was a jolly and animated group of men and women who watched from the gallery that overlooked the mating box as Diana was led in by Pedro. They were sitting in comfortable chairs, laughing and gossiping amongst themselves, champagne glasses at the ready.

In one hand, Pedro held a rope lead that had been snapped onto one of the rings of Diana's bit, and in the other his dog whip with which he was tapping her naked buttocks below her tiny white frilly 'marriage skirt'. He was making her prance into the room, raising her knees high into the air but covering little ground as she was put through her paces.

There was an expectant buzz from the spectators at the sight of Diana's beautiful and well exercised and groomed body, and Pedro proceed to put her through a miniature dressage display, making her break into a goose step as he marched her round the room, her legs raised up high in front of her. This was followed by an extended walk and a collected trot. Then he halted her in the middle of the room.

The inspector from the Breeding Society came into the loose box. Gravely he lifted up Diana's little skirt and noted the numbers of the brand on her belly and had her turned round to check any other distinguishing marks, such as a small mole on her back and the bright blue of her eyes. Then he handed Pedro a bottle into which Diana was to pass water so that he could later certify that she was not in foal when she was covered by Black Beauty in his presence.

Pedro had specially not allowed Diana to stale for several hours and except for the embarrassment of having to straddle her legs and slightly bend her knees in public, she was almost glad to be able to relieve herself at Pedro's command. Soon the bottle was filled and Dina was made to stand at attention.

Then the door at the back of the mating box was opened and a huge naked negro was led in, his well oiled torso glistening, his well developed muscles bulging, and his face disguised and half hidden by a mask that gave him a grotesque and repulsive look.

His handler, a young Indian girl, led him up to Diana by a lead attached to a collar round his neck. His hands were free. Except for the collar he was stark naked. Diana shrank back as he was brought towards her, her eyes inevitably fastened on the huge manhood that dangled between his legs and which at the sight of her was already beginning to stiffen.

She turned to run, but Pedro held her tightly and she saw that the only doors out of the box were firmly shut. There was no escape.

The negro now stood right in front of her. She could smell his musky odour. She could see his piggy eyes, gleaming bright under his mask. She wanted to push him away but with her hands still strapped to her girth strap she was helpless.

"The bridegroom may now kiss the bride!" came Carlos's laughing voice.

Diana's white white bridal veil was removed. The black man's huge arms went round her in a powerful hug and his lips searched for hers. She tried to turn her head, but Pedro held her head rope firmly. The negro's tongue forced its way onto her mouth, past her bit. She felt his hand on her breast and his now erect manhood thrusting up under the absurd little skirt. Then, to her horror, she felt Pedro unfastening even this. She was now completely naked, naked in the arms of an equally naked huge black man! Naked in the arms of her black lover!

"Aren't they a pretty pair!" cried one of the spectators.

Goaded on by Diana's protesting wriggles, the black stallion was now getting very excited.

"Back, Black Beauty! Back up!" called out his handler as she jerked his collar leash backwards, anxious to prevent any risk of a premature climax. She nodded to Pedro who led the horrified and still trembling Diana into the centre of the room, towards a leather padded metal ring, like a circular bar. It was set on metal supports some two feet above the sandy floor. In the middle of the ring was small ringbolt cemented into the floor.

Diana was made to get down on her knees in front of the padded ring. Her arms were unfastened from her girth strap and instead fastened to the ring at the back of her collar. Her head was then pushed down towards the ringbolt with her belly resting high up on the leather padded bar. Her collar was fastened to the ring, so that she took some of her weight on her elbows, with the rest of it on the bar under her belly.

Pedro now produced the mating fetters. These were in the form of a three piece chain, joined together with a ring. Two ends were fastened around each of her ankles. The third end was led up up under her belly to her collar, so that she was kept tightly bent over - and unable to kick out at the stallion who would shortly mount her. Her ankles were now fastened well apart.

Pedro then bent down, unlocked Diana's little infibulating padlock, and eased the laces. Her beauty lips began to open.

The huge black needed no further encouragement. He knelt down between Diana's outspread legs, and like a dog with a bitch began to lick Diana through the loosened laces.

The shock of the negro's tongue made Diana jump, but the chains held her tight. All she could do was to try and wriggle away. But this only made her seem even more enticing - much to everyone's delight.

After a couple of minutes, Pedro put his hand down under Diana's twisting tummy and felt her. Despite all her writhings of protest, nature had had its way and she was beginning to be wet with her arousal.

"She's ready now," he announced with a knowledgable air, "not too much, just right!"

The Negro's belly was now right up against Diana's buttocks, his black manhood thrust forward and probing. The handler looked up enquiringly at Carlos and Ortega in the galley. They both nodded.

Pedro bent over Diana and with both hands separated the laces and held her lips apart. The young handler gripped the negro's manhood and inserted it through the laces. Then she gave Black Beauty a smack on the buttocks, making him thrust forward with a jerk. Through her bit, Diana gave a shriek, a shriek of pain, protest and horror, as she was suddenly and deeply penetrated.

Black Beauty began to thrust in and out. His body half collapsed over Diana's back. His hands groped for her breasts and then pulled her thighs close to his. They were coupling like two animals, much to the amusement of the spectators sipping their champagne and nibbling delicious biscuits.

The watchers had a good view of the strong black manhood as it thrust in and out of the white girl's body, with the stallion now gripping her round the waist and breasts. They could see the look of horror and repugnance on the face of Diana, but they could also see that despite herself she was beginning to respond to the thrusting.

Indeed she soon she found herself thrusting her buttocks back to meet the next downward thrust.

It was at that moment that Carlos got up and quickly ran down the steps that led down from the little gallery into the mating box. Quickly he came behind the stallion and watched as the girl handler reached down to feel the heavy black scrotum. He wanted to watch the moment of discharge deep down into Diana. He wanted to witness the moment of the conception that was being carried out at his orders.

The touch of the girl handler's cold hands acted as a catalyst, and almost immediately Carlos was thrilled to see the seed being pumped out and down the manhood.

A suppressed scream came from Diana as she felt the seed jetting into her. A moment later the stallion collapsed over her, and then withdrew. His handler pulled him back and he stood up, his eyes gleaming under his mask. He bowed to his Master and to Carlos, and was then led from the box.

Carlos knelt down alongside Diana. He put his hand down and stroked her belly. Then he stood up and went back up the steps to the gallery, where the guests were now refilling their glasses, standing up and chatting, oblivious of the helpless figure of Diana sobbing behind her bit.

Meanwhile Pedro had drawn the laces tight again and this time the inspector had carefully locked them together with his own padlock. It was a special high security one and only the inspector had the key. As if that was not enough, however, he then sealed the keyhole of the padlock.

It was indeed all a very neat way of ensuring that no other

manhood found its way between her beauty lips except that of the stallion whose name, Black Beauty, would be shown on the Certificate of Mating.

Ten minutes later the spectators had all left, but it was another hour before Diana was released and taken back to her stall - an hour in which she could feel the black man's seed still slipping down inside her. Back in her stall she was still kept lying down on the straw for the rest of the day and the following night, her hands once again fastened to her girth strap.

She was horrified, and yet as Nature took over, she also began to feel excited by what had happened, by what her all-powerful Master had done to her.

The following morning Diana was again led back into the mating box. It was still empty - no black stallion yet, no spectators, and no leather covered ring. This time she was fastened on her back, lying on the straw, and as Ortega had described to Carlos, her ankles were raised high in the air and fastened wide apart to two chains hanging down from the ceiling, and her wrists to two other chains. Once again she was bitted to prevent her from speaking.

After a few minutes, Carlos and Ortega and a new party of invited guests strolled into the gallery. Once again they were served cool refreshments as they looked down with interest at the helpless girl. Her eyes watched them helplessly, silently pleading.

She made a really pretty picture as she lay helpless on her back, and in order to make certain that the stallion's manhood would really be driving downwards when it penetrated her, Pedro now pulled her ankle chains slightly up so that her buttocks were raised off the ground. She was now positioned as if offering herself, with her weight on her shoulders.

The Breeding Society inspector who had witnessed and

certified her first mating checked the seal on the padlock that had kept the laces tightly fastened over her beauty lips. Then he removed it and unlocked the padlock, and Pedro came forward and again loosened the laces.

The inspector began to fill in the Certificates of Mating that would be handed over the owners of Diana and Black Beauty once it had been clearly established that the described filly had been fertilised by the registered stallion. A further copy of the Certificate would be kept in the Society's records.

He turned to Pedro and nodded, and Pedro began to roll Diana's nipples between his fingers. Then, pleased with the reaction, he began to stroke her sex with a feather. Slowly her breathing became more laboured. The spectators could see that her face and breasts were becoming flushed and that unable to avoid the tickling of the feather her belly was beginning to wriggle wildly.

She tried to call out, to beg him to stop, but of course her bit kept her mute and the devilish tickling went on. She was quite unable to prevent herself from becoming more and more aroused. The feather was now tracing a delicate path over her now stiff little nipples and then down again between her legs. Not until he saw that the filly's beauty lips were really glistening did Pedro cease.

Black Beauty had meanwhile been led in and was held by his pretty young handler in front of Diana's writhing young body. His manhood was again coming into a hard erection.

Black Beauty was now ordered to kneel down between Diana's legs. He knew, of course, what he was going to have to do. He had been used so many times to fertilise a pretty young filly! His black manhood touched her sex lips. The feather was withdrawn. His pretty handler reached down and gently rubbed the erect manhood up and down against the proffered beauty lips.

Diana found herself becoming almost mad with desire for this huge muscular giant.

The teasing went on and on. Diana was driven almost out of her mind. Then suddenly the young girl, still holding the erect manhood in one hand, gave the Negro a word of command and, with her other hand, hit him sharply across the buttocks with her whip.

Instantly the Negro drove his manhood downwards into Diana, once again between the loosened laces, penetrating deeply. The audience heard her give a choked scream from behind her bitted lips.

The stallion began to sway in and out. Soon the aroused filly found herself thrusting her belly up to meet his thrusts. At another word of command, the stallion went down on all fours, his hands reaching for her shoulders, her breasts, her hair.

Once again Carlos was amused to see the animal-like way in which the two of them were being forced to copulate. Pedro put his hand down to feel Diana's beauty bud, as the black manhood drove in and out, like a well oiled piston. It was erect and ready.

Soon Pedro was satisfied that Diana was ready to climax as soon as she felt the seed shooting into her. He looked up at Carlos and nodded. As before he quickly slipped down the winding staircase to the floor below. As he had done for the first mating, he came to the side of the copulating couple and watched the girl handler gently cup the stallion's bulging sack.

Then Pedro, his finger still on the the Diana's beauty bud, nodded to the stallion's handler. She raised her whip, and brought it down across the black buttocks in front of her.

"Go!" she cried.

The stallion gave a tremendous jerk, and moments later suddenly climaxed, pumping his seed down into Diana, who in turn gave another choked scream and a violent wriggle as she too came to a violent climax.

The stallion, grinning under his mask with the knowledge that he would be rewarded for a job well done, was led out.

Pedro carefully drew the laces tight again. None of the precious seed must be wasted! The inspector had a careful look at the now exhausted and sobbing Diana. Then, as before, he locked the two ends of the laces together with his special padlock and sealed the keyhole. This time he would only remove it against the written certification of a vet approved of by the Society that the filly was well and truly infoal.

More champagne was offered to the guests. Poor Diana was left lying on her back with her chained legs high in the air to help the seed to slip down well inside her.

For another hour she was kept like that, and it was not until the following day that she was sent back to El Paraiso, still not certain whether to be thrilled or horrified at having been put, like an animal, to the negro buck.

## 26 - THE BROOD MARE

As with the dressage for real horses, there was a complicated routine for the pony-women entered for the driven dressage competitions in the local horse shows.

Controlled only by their reins and by the whip, they had to follow their driver's orders exactly and unthinkingly as they criss-crossing the little arena from one mark to another, and whilst avoiding the obstacles, they had to vary their speed and type of step according to the complex laid down routine.

It was a test of complete obedience and control - just as it was with real horses.

One pace late in breaking from the slow walk into the extended trot on passing a particular marker, or the failure to stop dead after ten paces at the fast trot on turning a particular corner, and the woman would lose her driver several marks. All movements had to be done smoothly and beautifully; the slightest sign of stumble or hesitation would lose more marks. Hence the need for hours of daily practice whilst being driven by Carlos himself, for it was he who was going to put Diana through her paces at the horse show, pulling Carlos's pretty surrey with its fringed sun canopy.

Dressage competitions, and straight forward pony-girl showing events, were both considered very suitable for pregnant pony-girls. Carlos reckoned that the sight of Diana's very white body with its gradually swelling and shiny belly, erotically matching her white shiny bald head, together with her laces and nose ring, would greatly impress the judges. Accordingly Diana was kept out of the sun as much as possible, being continued in the early morning and evening.

The competitions for pony girls at the shows consisted not only of dressage but also of brood mare showing classes, which involved a careful examination of the woman's body, her bone structure and her breast size, and muscle development, with marks being awarded for good conformation, pleasing appearance, and docile but eager appearance.

To encourage breeding, large prizes were reserved for the best mares in foal, with marks being lost if the mare appeared to be overweight, or if her breasts were not also showing signs of adequate future milk production, or if it was felt that her hips were too narrow to allow a quick and easy foaling.

The judges paid considerable attention to the hang of the breasts, often eliminating women whose breasts pointed slightly outwards. Breasts that pointed forward were easier to control with the steering reins when the girl was harnessed to a trap, and of course looked prettier.

The hang of Diana's breasts had been partly corrected during her previous period in the stables, and now the short chain, with its tightening bottle screw, was again fastened between her nipples to complete the correction.

Forcing a woman to submit to dressage training was, of course, very erotic for their Masters, or Mistresses - for the patience required for exerting the strict discipline of dressage training tended to attract women as well as men.

It was, therefore, noticeable that the pony women entered in the competitions were nearly all very attractive light coloured young creatures. Their Masters and Mistresses much enjoyed making a beautiful woman submit to their complete control - a control that later was often continued in more intimate surroundings!

As a confirmed voluptuary with a penchant for young obedient girls, Carlos similarly took great pleasure in dominating Diana and in forcing her to abandon her own will and to submit to his.

She herself was so busy learning her new role as a potential dressage prize winner, that she had almost forgotten about the terrifying scenes with Black Beauty at Senor Ortega's stud farm.

But in reality, of course, as well as preparing Diana for the horse shows and dressage competitions, great care was being devoted to ensuring that she successfully carried her valuable twin foals - for almost from the start the size of her gently swelling belly made the experienced Pedro correctly suspect that she was carrying twins.

Unknown to her, a series of simple pregnancy tests had confirmed that she had conceived by the huge negro stallion. These had been accepted by the Breeding Society and their inspector had removed his special padlock that kept her laces taut and her intimacies locked-up. But immediately Pedro had replaced it with his own infibulation padlock, the one that she had formerly been made to carry.

Now, every week, the locking padlock was removed, the laces eased, and she was examined by the estate vet, who treated her just as he would one of Carlos's real in-foal mares, whilst mysteriously commenting in incomprehensible Spanish to the watching Carlos and Pedro.

On these occasions, Diana would be tied with her back to the bars of her cage, and her girth belt would be removed to enable the vet to have a better feel of her soft and gently swelling belly. Then using a scanner, with the monitoring screen carefully positioned so that Diana could not see it, he would point out the progress of what were clearly two tiny little female embryos.

Carlos had been delighted with the news and invited Senor Ortega to come over and see the pictures on the scan for himself.

As Diana's belly gradually swelled so her girth strap had to be slowly let out, though it still acted as a corset supporting her belly, and of course still played a key role when she was harnessed by it to her Master's surrey.

Under the vet's supervision, her feeds were increased with the addition of the special high protien nuts that were routinely fed to mares in foal to bring on their milk and to ensure the proper growth of the foals.


The day of the horse show arrived. Diana was entered in the top class of mares in-foal. Harnessed to her Master's surrey she put on an almost perfect display of dressage, changing her step and her pace with perfect grace under the control of her Master's whip.

It was of course an embarrassing experience to have to perform naked, harnessed and now noticeably pregnant - and in front of a small crowd of smartly dressed landowners and their friends, many of whom themselves were showing horses or pony girls or both.

It was only the sheer fear of Carlos's long carriage whip that drove her on and made her concentrate on obeying the orders being given to her by the slight touches on her nipple and cheek reins, and on the check rein now fastened to her nose ring.

With her belly now more pronounced than when she had started her dressage training, Diana found it more difficult to carry out many of the required paces. One that was particularly difficult was the slow prancing trot in which she had to raise her knees so high that her thighs were perfectly horizontal. Another was marking time on the spot at the same prancing speed, knowing that the slightest change in speed, or failure to achieve the horizontal, would result immediately in a flick of Carlos's whip across her hindquarters.

Diana had learnt the hard way that Carlos could tell at a glance whether she was performing the required movement to the best of her ability. She also had learnt that Carlos made no allowance for her condition. She was just there to perform to his orders - and to perform perfectly.

After completing the course, Carlos lined his surrey up with those of the other entrants in the mares in-foal class. They made a pretty sight - two dozen beautifully groomed and turned out light-skinned young women: all naked; all showing a distinctly swelling belly; all rigidly harnessed to a variety of beautifully painted traps; all bitted, bridled, and dumb; but all showing, by their jealously flashing eyes, that they still had human feelings.

Half of the pony-women were driven by men, cruel men like Carlos who enjoyed showing off a pretty young girl and making her perform like a circus animal through fear of their whips. The remaining girls, however, were driven by women who enjoyed the complete domination of another woman that dressage training provided.

Two of the drivers were themselves the pretty young spoilt daughters of wealthy landowners who, having originally been fascinated by training horses to do dressage, had later found an even greater fascination in training and breeding from grown women older than themselves.

Because of the sexual background to the ownership and driving of pony-girls, many a favourite pony-girl might be brought from the stables to spend a night in their master's bed in the 'macho' households of the big landowners. Indeed it often suited the convenience of a wealthy master for his mistresses to be kept in his stables, living the life of a pony and kept well groomed, cleaned and healthy by the stable lads. Nor did all the women object to such treatment. Many found it exciting and a relief from the cares and worries of the real world.

Such women were available at any time to be brought to the bed of their Master or Mistress. They would often be brought still bitted and bridled to keep them silent, and with their hands fastened to their girths to ensure their helpless acquiescence to the lusts of their owner.

Indeed many a shrill young woman, kept by a rich admirer in a flat in the capital city, had paid the penalty for nagging too much, for having too many tantrums or for being unfaithful with a younger man, and had found herself installed as a pony-girl in the stables of her admirer's country hacienda.

Similarly many an over-proud but poor young woman had paid the same penalty for resisting the advances of a wealthy landowner - abduction and incarceration in his stables!

Carlos and Diana were lying in second place after the dressage part of the competition. This was very good bearing in mind that it was the first time that Diana had had to perform naked before a crowd.

Now came the critical part of the competition - the judging of the pony-women's bodily conformation and physique. Diana with her dead white skin had clearly caught the attention of the judges and of the spectators.

The ideal conformation for a pony-woman had been laid down by the Breeding Society and it was against these requirements that the displayed women were judged, still harnessed in their traps.

To encourage the breeding of pony women who were stronger and taller than the ordinary Indian women of the country, various ratios had been devised for the ideal pony-woman: the ratio of the wrists and ankles to the size of the hips, the ratio of the size of her neck to her bust measurement, the length of her legs as compared to the distance between her beauty bud and her nipples and so on.

High cheekbones were desirable, as were long necks. Nipples had to be large and breasts hang closely together. Beauty lips had to give a little girl effect with no sign of the inner lips protruding, even with the legs apart. Knees had to be quite straight and so on. The way the body moved at the walk and at the trot was also important.

Diana was both humiliated and nervous when the judges came down the line to examine her. They measured her in every possible way. They stood back and looked at her from every possible angle. They felt her arm and leg muscles. They made her open her legs to judge her beauty lips more closely, and even asked for the laces to be removed entirely for a moment. They lifted up her breasts and measured the droop. They asked Carlos to drive the surrey round in a tight circle, first at a walk and then at a trot.

Whilst the judges considered their verdict, a more light hearted competition took place: a 'Concours d'Elegance' for the drivers and carriages. The vehicles paraded round in front of the stand, their drivers showing off their smart clothes and beautifully painted and varnished traps. Carlos was looking remarkably fetching in his smart European dressage outfit: black silk top hat, double breasted black swallow tail coat, white cravat and gloves, tight white breeches and gleaming black boots, as he drove the surrey with its bright fringes round the little circle, flicking his whip occasionally across Diana's hindquarters. He was the clear winner.

Diana felt proud of her handsome Master as she realised that he had won. He might be a cruel and capricious Master, but at least he was a good looking, and took a pride in his appearance!

Then the judges announced the results of the main competition. Diana was first! As Carlos had anticipated, her physical conformation fitted very well into the ideal laid down for pony-women and she was awarded the championship cup.

This, coming after her win at the Derby trotting race, would make Diana even more sought after for breeding purposes, and would make her an even more valuable brood mare, with half the breeders in the country anxious to try out their best stallions on her. Further wins at other shows would make her even better known and increase her value yet more.

Carlos drove Diana at a fast extended trot round the little arena in a lap of honour to celebrate her win before joining his friends in the bar to drink champagne from the newly won cup.

Meanwhile a small crowd of well dressed men and women were taking a close look at the new champion as she stood naked and harnessed to the surrey, her bridle held by the Pedro, now proudly showing off his charge.

"So clever of Carlos to have her head shaved. She looks so sweet without a mane," said one woman.

"I wonder if Carlos would sell her after she's foaled?" said a wealthy looking man. "Wouldn't mind having her in my stables, or my bed!"

"She's a good looking mare. Carries her foal well too."

"I hear they are expecting twins from her."

"I like a pony girl when she's got an interesting little curve to her belly! I often have my own mares brought to my bedroom when they're in foal," laughed another man coarsely.

"Darling," whispered one smartly dressed woman to another, "wouldn't it would be delicious to feel that little bald head between one's legs! Perhaps I'll try it out on you!"

Finally it was time to unharness Diana, to put her into the horse box and take her back to the stables at El Paraiso, where as a reward a pile of horse and pony nuts and special mares nuts lay waiting for her in her feeding trough.

## 27 - THE HAPPY EVENT AND THEN ...?

A few months later, after several more wins at different local Horse Shows, Diana foaled, in the traditional way, standing in the the foaling box in the stables.

She was watched by Carlos and Ortega and a party of their friends who had driven over to El Paraiso for the exciting event - the foaling of Carlos's very valuable prize mare. The inspector from the Breeding Society had also arrived to witness the birth of her valuable progeny.

Her hands had been fastened to a beam above her head to keep her standing up, though she was able to bend her knees. To prevent her cries from disturbing the stables or from upsetting the watchers, she had once again been bridled and bitted with the thick black bit forced into her open mouth, keeping her dumb like an animal.

To hide any unpleasantness from her guests, Carlos had ordered that a little waist high screen be erected in front of the girl. It hid her intimacies, whilst showing the straw filled basket into which her progeny were to be dropped.

This was to be a happy event, and to hide Diana's contorted face, the grinning rubber mask of a smiling girl had been fastened over her face, through which she could see nothing.

Pedro was pleased with the way he had delayed matters until the guests had arrived and were comfortably seated, the usual glass of champagne in their hands, and, perhaps more important, until the Breeding Society inspector had arrived.

Pedro went behind the screen to reactivate matters. Satisfied, he called the Inspector to join him and to authorise him to loosen the laces.

The vet stood by in case he was required, but Carlos liked his mares to be left to foal as naturally as possible. Indeed, thanks to Pedro's experienced ministrations, and to the exercising that he had put Diana through during the previous couple of months, she dropped her mulatto foals quickly and, thanks to her muzzle and her mask, with little apparent fuss.

But also thanks to her mask she never saw them, nor with her hands fastened above her head was she able to hold them. Pedro did not intend her to bond with them them in any way.

As expected, and to the great delight of Ortega and Carlos, the foals were twin fillies. The inspector marked them and then handed the Society's Certificates of Birth and Breeding to Carlos and Ortega.

The two valuable little fillies were now removed from the foaling box. One was handed over to Senor Ortega's stud groom to be raised on his hacienda. The other was quickly taken away by Pedro and handed over to Carlos's head breeder who would be responsible for its rearing.

Diana scarcely saw them. She wanted to protest, to beg that they should not be taken away from her, but she could not say anything. Under her pretty mask, two large tears ran down her cheeks.

Pedro then refastened the laces. Diana was far too valuable for uncontrolled access to be allowed to be body. Any more breeding from Diana was going to be carefully planned and controlled!

The vet now reached up to give her an injection to stop her milk from coming on. But Carlos put out a restraining hand. He pointed to one of the girl's nipples which was showing a little drop of white.

"No!" he explained, Diana had been specially 'steamed

up', to use the parlance of Carlos's dairyman, during the last few weeks and her breasts had come on well - thanks to the special high protein nuts she had been fed. "Anyway not yet. I have other plans for her!"

Indeed, Carlos' thirst for revenge was still not slaked, and he was planning further humiliations for Diana.

But first, to get her milk really well established, Carlos had decided to take certain special steps!

## 28 - THE REARING PENS

Later that day, blindfolded, Diana was taken out of the stables and led to another building. She was still wearing her bridle and bit to keep her muzzled.

She was made to kneel down. She felt her neck and wrists being clamped into a strong wooden stocks. She heard the creek of something be lowered over her and felt a metal bar pressing against her raised buttocks.

Then she felt hands reaching down, and her blindfold was removed. She looked around and saw that she seemed to be in a kind of pen, rather like a pig pen, with bare whitewashed walls.

She looked around anxiously, but behind her head were the hinged planks of the stocks, preventing her from seeing what was happening to her body, and in particular to her breasts, nor, of course, was she able to use her hands.

The height of the stocks had been been adjusted so that her swollen breasts hung down, on the other side of the screen, some six inches above the straw on the cement floor. Metal bars covered the top of the whole pen. They were sufficiently spaced for someone to be able to reach down into the pen, but close enough to prevent her from standing up, even if she were not locked into the stocks. She gasped as she saw that looking down at her, was the grinning face of Juan, the plantation's head livestock breeder, his stock whip in his raised hand.

Diana heard the noise of voices approaching. Then, looking up again, she saw Carlos and some friends, including Inez, pointing down at her through the bars and laughing.

She saw Carlos say something in Spanish to Juan who then disappeared out of sight behind the stocks. She heard the creak of a wooden door being opened.

Suddenly, she heard a little cry from behind her, a babylike cry. Suddenly she felt little feet, running over the back of her calves.

Then, suddenly, she felt a soft wet nose and little hands touching her belly, her breasts and finally her nipples. Her nipples became erect. Something small was sucking at them, sucking hard, thirstily and persistently - and at both of them.

The sucking and squealing continued. She shook her breasts to try and throw off whatever it was that were suckling her, but they hung onto her nipples. Gradually she felt her milk begin to flow. For the first time in her life she was beginning to give suck...

Carlos's smartly dressed woman friends laughed and pointed down at Diana, chattering in Spanish, as they watched the young Englishwoman unknowingly suckling a pair little crawling black babies that were being reared as future indentured servants for the El Paraiso plantation.

"Let's have a closer look at them," she heard Carlos say to Juan.

The head livestock breeder bent down behind the stocks. Diana felt the bar over her buttocks being raised.

The women gave little cries of delight and one of them bent down behind the stocks and lifted something up.

"Oh, isn't it sweet," Diana heard her say in English.

Diana looked up at her with horror. She was holding a

little black baby! Clearly it was too old to be her own.

The pulling on one of her nipples continued. She was being suckled by two such little creatures, used as a wet nurse in the plantation's rearing pens!

"Oh no!" came a scream from behind her bit.

Carlos reached down and smacked Diana's face.

"Don't you dare argue with me! I'm your Master! And anyway just you remember that animals can't talk."

Diana fell silent. She saw the woman who had picked up the little creature, bend down and put it back. It seemed to push the other one aside. Then both of them were once again suckling.

For half an hour Diana was kept in the special stocks, her neck and hands held rigid, whilst the little black creatures got used to suckling her. Meanwhile the head livestock breeder was checking that her steadily increasing flow of milk was going to be sufficient for her new role.

Soon Diana learnt that if she tried to shake off the hungry little creatures by shaking her breasts, or by jerking away from their eager little mouths, then Juan would lean over, lift up the grill, and give her a smart crack across her naked buttocks with his short stockwhip.

Carlos was delighted as his elegantly dressed women friends found it exciting to watch the naked Diana being forced by the whip to keep still and to let the little black creatures get at her milk.

"You'll make a fine little wet-nurse for my plantation, Diana," said Carlos as he prepared to lead his friends back to the big house for an evening swim in his swimming pool - to be followed by a night of fun and games with the young girls that Carlos kept locked up in the 'harem' wing of the house.

Diana heard the little creatures being taken away. Then

Juan lifted up the bars, and stepped into the pen. Before releasing her from the stocks, he snapped a chain lead onto her collar and put her hands as into what seemed to be a kind of boxing gloves.

Although Diana did not yet realise it, these gloves would not only prevent her from using her fingers to harm any of the hungry little creatures that she was now going to have to help rear, but also prevent her from easing her increasingly milk laden breasts by trying to squeeze out any of her milk. Only by giving suck to little black creatures were her swollen breasts to get any relief.

There was also another cunning purpose behind the big unwieldy boxing gloves - Diana would later learn that these bulbous gloves would also prevent her from trying to part her laced up beauty lips to reach her beauty bud with even a little finger. The head livestock breeder was a firm believer in all a girl's energies going into her milk production!

But that was not all for just as, when Diana had been treated as a bitch, she had had to wear a dog mask, so now she was fitted with a very realistic black rubber human mask so as not to frighten off the black infants.

Under her mask, a muzzle prevented her from opening her mouth properly to bite or to talk. However it still allowed her to suck up the sloppy high protein mixture that was fed to wet-nurses in the human rearing pens of the El Paraiso hacienda to increase their milk production.

It was a firm rule that the wet nurses had to remain on all fours so that their increasingly heavy breasts hung down below them. Raising his whip menacingly as he lifted the top half of the wooden stocks, Juan pointed down to the floor of the pen.

"A gatas!" he ordered. Diana might still not understand much Spanish, but the livestock breeder's order to remain crawling was quite clear.

Juan opened a low wooden door, and giving her lead a tug, he led her out into what seemed to be corridor running between numerous other pens, each with a low wooden door with numbers painted on them. Crawling along behind Juan she could hear little baby gurgling noises coming from behind the walls. He opened a door, unsnapped Diana's lead from her collar and pushed her inside.

There in front of her, kneeling on all fours, was a pretty, naked and remarkably buxom young negress. Her surprisingly large breasts were hanging down below her.

Her hands, like Diana's, had been fastened into the same type of gloves as Diana now wore - for the same reasons. A ring hung from her nose, and, as with Diana, a little bell had been fastened to this ring.

The pen was divided into two parts separated by a vertical metal grill fitted with rollers on each side, enabling the grill to be raised or lowered from outside the pen.

Diana gasped as she saw behind the barred metal grill, half a dozen little black piccaninnies crawling on the straw covered cement floor of the pen. They were crying and vainly trying to get through the bars to the black girl. Each one had a different coloured ribbon tied round its neck.

The grille would hold back the piccaninnies in the other half of the pen, whilst the breasts of the black girl, and now those of Diana too, were being rested and recharged. Then, every few hours, at feeding time, the head livestock breeder or his assistants would raise the grill to allow the little creatures to get at the milk of their wet-nurses.

This pen, like the testing pen, was covered by metal bars that kept them crawling on all fours.

The black girl looked jealously at Diana and at her hanging breasts. Then she smiled welcomingly, as she realised that that Diana was also in milk. This white girl's breasts could help spread the load of feeding the demanding piccaninnies.

Appalled as she increasingly realised what was now to be her fate, Diana crawled into a corner of the small pen. The head stockbreeder looked down approvingly at the two girls through the bars. They would be made to become a perfect team.

He looked at his wristwatch. The next feeding time in the pens would be in three hours time. This would give Diana's breasts time to recover from their successful trial run in the testing pen.

He turned on his heel and left to enjoy a good lunch and a little siesta.

Three hours later, there was a sudden ringing of a bell. Recognising the bell, the little piccaninnies came to life on the other side of the grill.

The black girl went to the centre of the pen and knelt on all fours, her breasts hanging down beneath her, her head up and her eyes fixed ahead. She started to shake her head, making her bell ring clearly and distinctively, which yet further excited the little creatures beyond the grille.

Suddenly there was a crack as the angry head livestock breeder brought his stockwhip down across the still dozing Diana's back. She hastily copied the other girl, shaking her head and making her bell ring too.

Juan nodded to his assistant at the far end of the pens. He pressed a button and immediately all the grills in the pens were raised. Diana heard several squealing and hungry little creatures crawled into their half of the pen. Mesmerised by the sight of Juan's stockwhip Diana did not dare to look round or down.

The little creatures started to fight for the four nipples now on offer. Once again Diana found her natural repulsion being overtaken by a strange maternal feeling as her nipples were sucked by one baby after another.

When Carlos and his guests, out for a morning ride after their night of love making, came over to see how Diana had settled down, they laughed to see her and her companion slurping up her special feed.

Minutes later the feeding time bell rang, and again they laughed to see her line up next to her companion, shaking her bell and awaiting the onslaught on her hanging breasts.

Diana felt hideously humiliated having to do this in front of them all, but Juan's raised stockwhip kept her just kneeling in the centre of the pen whilst the six little creatures struggled for a teat.

Soon, however, her maternal instincts were fully aroused and the spectators laughed as they heard her happily grunting behind her black mask.

Diana's whole world now revolved around giving suck to her demanding little black charges. She began to distinguish between them recognise them, between the greedy ones who pulled painfully at her nipples, and who pushed the other ones out of the way to get at her milk, and the more gentle ones that the livestock breeders had to make sure were getting their share of her increasing prolific amount of milk.

More and more she began to associate herself as a plantation wet-nurse and with her lovely little charges, sharing with them, and her companion, her now simple life of eating, sleeping and giving suck.

This association was of course heightened by the realistic black woman's mask that was strapped over Diana's head, by the way that her bell rang with her every movement, and by the way the bars over the pen kept her, too, down on all fours on the cemented floor, and by the fact that her world was limited to the walls of her pen.

Only the daily visits of Carlos, immaculately dressed in breeches and boots, and often accompanied by the smartly dressed Inez, brought back the realisation that, under her mask, she too was a pretty and attractive woman.

## 29 - THE MILKMAID

To Diana's utter dismay, after two weeks of feeding her charges, they were suddenly taken away, and Pedro came and started treating her like a pony-girl again.

The humiliating black mask was removed, and then in the passageway outside her pen she was hosed down and then scrubbed down, a worming paste was injected into her mouth, and her head, mound and beauty lips were shaved and powdered again. Then her wrists were again fastened to a leather girth strapped around her belly, and her own bridle and bit were put back onto her. Once again she was a muzzled pony girl!

She was then put back into her cage in the stables, wondering what new horror her cruel Master now had in store for her.

She was soon to learn!

She heard a trundling noise coming along the passageway. She saw that a young Indian boy, accompanied by Pedro, was pushing a trolley towards her cage.

Suddenly she recognised it. It was the portable milking machine that she had seen, her first day in the stables, being used on a wretched young woman. She remembered, now with horror, how she had been fascinated at the way the pulsating machine had thrust little jets of the girl's milk into a glass jar. And now this same awful machine was being brought to her cage!

Impeded, as usual, by the heavy chain fastened to her collar, she backed away to the far side of her cage. Was she now, she wondered, going to be introduced to the delights of Carlos's milking machine. Oh, no! No!

Terrified, she heard the crack of a whip. She looked up. Pedro, whip in one had, was silently and slowly beckoning her forward, with his other hand, towards the front bars of his cage.

As if hypnotised she found herself slowly going over to him. He pulled back a little panel of bars in her cage. They were level with her breasts. Again he beckoned her forward. Again she found herself obeying. He stood back, still beckoning her forward until she was pressing up against the bars, with her breasts sticking out through the small gap in the bars.

The young Indian boy deftly fastened a strap around her neck, from the bars above the gap. Then he fastened another from below the gap round her waist. She was now held pressing up against the bars, her breasts exposed.

Pedro snapped his fingers and the Indian boy switched on the machine on the trolley. She heard a pulsating noise, and watched in horror as the Indian boy lifted up two rubber cups. He placed them over her breasts. She heard a sucking noise. She felt her breasts being drawn out. The boy took his hands away, the cups remained as if glued onto her breasts.

Then the boy made another switch, on the side of the machine. Instantly she felt one of the cups contract onto her breasts and then release it. A second later it was the turn of her other breast, and then the first one again. Her breasts were being massaged! Massaged against her will! She caught her breath as she felt her nipples becoming erect.

They boy switched on a loudspeaker. She heard quiet, soft, reassuring and gentle music. She could not help relaxing. And all the time the pulsating cups were still massaging her breasts. She could not help feeling excited. If only it was being done by a man, especially her Master, and not by this awful machine. And it was so humiliating the machine being controlled by a mere boy.

The boy put his had down between the bars to where her

belly was held by the strap. He unlocked the padlock and loosened the laces. She felt utterly ashamed, but she simply could not stop herself from parting her legs. The boy felt her beauty lips and gently parted them. They were now nicely moist!

He looked up at Pedro and nodded. Then with his free hand he turned another switch.

Instantly there was change in the note of the machine. Diana realised that it was now not only massaging her breasts, but with every pulsation there was also a strong sucking feeling. She saw little jets of milk being squirted into a glass jar.

She was being milked! Milked for her Master's table!

## 30 - A NEW BRAND

Diana had been branded on her belly with the diamond-shaped mark of El Paraiso and with her number Y 534 taken from the hacienda livestock register.

The Y stood for 'Yegua' or mare. When she had been successfully covered by Black Beauty the letter V should of course have been added, standing for 'Vientre' or belly, since 'Yegua de Vientre' is the Spanish for Brood Mare. The purpose of adding the V was to make it clear to anyone intercepting an escaped brood mare that she was a particularly valuable animal, for whom her owners would pay a large reward if returned, particularly if the mare was in foal when she escaped.

However, Senor Ortega had specially asked that her additional branding be deferred until after she had foaled lest the shock might make her slip her valuable progeny.

Diana's identity tag that hung from her collar had been altered to show that she was now a brood mare, and Carlos now wanted her belly to show it as well. An escaped mare might with difficulty succeed in ridding herself of her collar but her belly brand would be there for life.

So it was that one morning Diana was led out of her cage and taken to the blacksmith's forge. Carlos and Inez, fresh from another night of love in each others arms whilst being aroused by Carlos's well trained troop of young girls from his harem, were again sitting comfortably around the branding post to which Diana was to be tied. Once again Diana was to provide erotic entertainment!

To save them from the annoyance of Diana's inevitable pleadings when she realised what was to happen, she had been bitted and bridled. So all they heard were urgent little whimperings, as Diana was strapped with her back to the branding post, with her arms fastened high above her head to pull her belly up nice and taut for the branding iron.

Her subdued whines and sobs in no way reflected the desperate state of her mind. She was going to be branded again! Why? Where? She had seen at the horse show pretty young pony women with their breasts branded. Oh no! Surely they were not now going to brand her breasts, swollen and tender as they were from being in milk?

She remembered the awful pain from last time. She wanted to beg Carlos not to brand her again, not to mark her body again! She wanted to grovel at his feet! Anything, but not the branding iron again!

But she was gagged by her bit and tied tightly to the branding post, and could only whimper and whine! Tears began to roll down her cheeks as she saw the powerful blacksmith thrust a branding iron into his furnace, and then pull it out red hot and gleaming.

The negro blacksmith thrust the branding iron back into the furnace and then came over to the cringing Diana. To mislead her as to where she was going to be branded, he started to fondle her big breasts, heavy with milk and ready for the milking machine. He lifted up her right breast as if looking for a good site for the brand on the curve below the nipple, and Diana trembled with fear.

The eyes of Carlos and Inez were gleaming as they watched the spectacle, and as they saw Diana's breathing become quick as she panted with fright. They stretched out for each other's hands, pulling them furtively down onto each other's laps, as their own erotic excitement grew.

The blacksmith turned his attention to Diana's other breast as if looking for a suitable place above the nipple. Carlos and Inez could see that Diana's swollen breasts were trembling deliciously.

The blacksmith moved his hands up to Diana's shoulders, but then, before Diana could sigh with relief that it was not her breasts that were to receive the brand, he brought his hands back to her two gently curving under breasts as if deciding that they would be suitable. Diana held her breath in trepidation.

The blacksmith carefully noted her new stretch marks and saw the place carefully left last time on her belly for the addition of the V mark. There would be no difficulty in placing the brand neatly after the existing numbers on her belly, he decided, provided the woman was made to take in a deep breath to tauten the skin of her belly just as the iron was applied.

He started to feel her shaven sex lips as if seeking a suitable place there. Diana shook with terror as he opened up the lips, seeking her beauty bud.

Leaving Diana mystified and fearful, the blacksmith went back to his furnace, where his assistant was now holding a heated brand. It would be the assistant, a young Negro, who would now play a key role. It would be he who would give Diana a hard sharp stroke with a dog whip across her breasts, just before the brand was applied, so as to make her body jump up with the pain and thus tauten her belly muscles.

The blacksmith took the branding iron from his assistant

and turned back towards Diana. His assistant picked up his dog whip and also went towards her.

Pedro, the stud groom, quickly slipped the thick rubber bit out of Diana's mouth, so that Carlos and his mistress could hear her screams. But for the moment Diana stood open-mouthed in horror, her eyes riveted on the small bright red hot branding iron that was pointing at her.

Suddenly the blacksmith's assistant brought his dog whip hard down across Dianas breasts. The surprise was complete. She jerked upwards in her bonds, tautening her belly and crying out.

Instantly the blacksmith pressed the branding iron against her belly. There was a smell of burning flesh. Dianas cry became a scream, a desperate scream, an appalling scream.

Carlos's eyes glazed with satisfaction...


## 31 - A DINNER PARTY AND A CHANGE OF PLAN

Two days later Carlos drove his surrey around the hacienda, and was delighted to find that Diana was pulling well. The new V brand on her belly was still sore and red, but under stimulus of her Master's whip she was made to thrust her belly forwards and take the surrey along at a spanking trot.

At last he halted the surrey in the shade of a large tree. With a shudder, Diana recognised the place as where Carlos so often used to lie on the grass and arouse her with the tip of his whip. But this time Carlos was more interested in quenching his thirst!

The tight bearing strap kept Diana's head well back, and she could not look down at her swollen breasts. She had been surprised when she was not put to the milking machine that morning. Now she was now going to learn the reason, for having carefully caressed one of her breasts, Carlos put his mouth to the nipple and started to suck. After a few seconds he felt Diana's sweet warm milk jetting into his mouth. It was delicious and refreshing and the girl's nipple rings did not hinder his sucking.

Tethered tightly between the shafts of the surrey, with her breasts thrust forward by the double effect of her head and elbows both being pulled back, Diana was forced to offer her milk to her Master. It was to be the first of many such offerings both when harnessed between the shafts and at other times as well.

Carlos was so pleased with the delicious taste of the milk, and the way it had been brought on by the dual effect of the piccaninnies and the milking machine, that he had Diana produced at the end of a big dinner party he gave a few days later.

Diana had been washed, scrubbed, dosed, douched, whisped and even scented. Bitted and bridled as for pulling the surrey, with her head pulled back and her wrists fastened to the top rings on the side of her girth strap, she was led into her Master's dining room just as coffee was being served. The same scarlet lipstick adorned her hairless sex lips as adorned the lips of her mouth. Her eyes glistened with glittering make-up, and gave her an erotic look.

"My dear friends," Carlos called out along the length of the table, "please help yourselves to the milk of my Derby winning mare! I promise you it is exceptionally delicious!"

Diana was led up to a good looking young man seated opposite Carlos. The young Indian boy who was leading her tapped her shoulder with his stockwhip to show that she should lean forward so that her breasts hung over the young man's cup. He reached up and squeezed one of the breasts, and after a moment a little jet of milk hissed into his cup!

Diana felt shamed and humiliated at being in treated in

this way, but, bitted and harnessed as she was, she had no alternative but to obey the dairyman's whip. She was led to the next guest, a cruel looking older woman, who eagerly and painfully squeezed her other breast, and so on right round the table.

No one paid any attention to her and the laughing and chattering in Spanish continued, as if the presence of a naked young woman being forced to offer milk was a normal dinner party practice.

Then she was made to stand at attention, with her back against the wall, whilst the guests sipped their coffee. Although her head was pulled back, she could see the expensive and brilliantly coloured dresses of the women, their beautifully arranged hair and the sparkling of their jewels. She could see the suave, dapperly dressed men, their faces lit up by the light of the candles on the dining table. The brilliance of the scene only added to her own feelings of submission and humiliation. She was being ignored. She was a mere naked indentured servant, little more than an animal.

Carlos took in the scene with satisfaction. He relished the way he had further succeeded in debasing Diana. Mentally he began to make plans for her future. She would be entered in the milking competitions at the forthcoming dairy show, where cows and heifers and female indentured servants in-milk were entered in several different classes to have their milk judged for both quality and quantity. She would be entered in the special trotting races for human mares in-milk where each woman was given a handicap depending on her breast size. She would be entered again in the dressage competitions, but this time competing in the class for mares in-milk.

Perhaps it was also time Diana spent a little time as his pet dog again, perhaps for a longer period this time so that she could be put to Inez's dwarfs again and again during her safe periods. Perhaps, he thought with a laugh, he might even let her conceive. Who knows what the result might be! A cross between a blond Englishgirl and a black dwarf! A new breed of pony-girls? It was a fascinating thought.

Perhaps Diana might even be allowed to grow her lovely hair back again and be locked up for a few months with the other young women in his secret harem, to be put through a proper training course!

No, Carlos decided, she was too valuable as a brood mare for any such ideas. Indeed, more practically, it was time to think about her next mating.

What stallion should she be put to this time?

Should he hire her out as a brood mare as he had done with Ortega, who was only too keen to put the girl to Black Beauty again! And he had had numerous other offers.

What was he do with Diana's little foal which was now in his rearing pens? It could be sold now for a large sum - and for considerably more in, say, ten years time. Or should he keep it to start his own breeding strain from Diana?

With Diana producing one or two valuable foals every year or two, he could soon build up a fine stock of very valuable fillies. He might even send for the seed of a famous white athlete that she had heard was now being discreetly marketed - although the Breeding Society did not approve of artificial insemination yet!

Certainly, Carlos thought as he looked at the trembling, white skinned girl, with her long legs, her strong thighs and her big delicate breasts, he was going to enjoy for many years having Diana as one of his indentured servants in Costa Negra.

But there was something nagging him. None of these plans for Diana really excited him now. Instead, he had to admit that his feelings towards the girl had changed. He no longer resented her. He no longer sought his revenge. He was past all that now. He simply wanted her! She was an attractive, well educated, and, above all, now submissive young Englishwoman. Clearly she was half in love with him. It was such a pity that fear of her escaping prevented him from treating her more as the companion he so much needed.

"Why don't you marry her?" said Inez. "She obviously adores you."

It was later that evening. Diana had been sent back to the stables and the guests had gone, leaving Carlos alone with Inez. She had noticed the pensive way that Carlos had been looking at the girl. She was genuinely fond of her lover and concerned abut his future happiness.

"What!" exclaimed Carlos. "Marry an indentured servant!"

"Why should anyone know her background. She would just be your step cousin from England."

"With her shaven head and her branded belly!"

"Send her to me to keep her locked up and hidden for a few months whilst her hair grows. No one would recognise her then, and no one knows her voice. Meanwhile I'd use her as my ladies maid and keep her locked up in a cage off my bedroom at night - if she wasn't in my bed. You could come over and enjoy her too - and train her in her future marital role! We'd soon teach her a trick or two! And as for her her brand marks, well there's no need for them to be paraded in front of everyone. Of course, you'd have to take off her nose ring and collar - but you could still keep her laced-up with Gamba keeping the key of the padlock and could still keep her nipple rings on - both as a salutary reminder that you are still her Master!"

There was a long pause.

"She'd make you an ideal wife," said Inez. "She enjoys being submissive - and she's already had first hand experience of plantation life!"

"But what about us? I'm not giving up seeing you."

"Well, much as I love having an affair with you, I'm certainly not going to give up my independence and marry a selfish swine like you!" laughed Inez. "But I don't see why life shouldn't continue much like now. After all she'd be far too grateful to me for having rescued her from the life of a pony-girl to bother about making a fuss about you seeing me from time to time. And any way I shall insist on using her just as I have in the past! So you'll have both us in your bed!"

Carlos laughed. "Well it certainly sounds exciting!"

"And I think I'll even come on the honeymoon," went on Inez. "We might as well start as we intend to go on. We'll travel as the husband and wife, with Diana as my pretty young ladies maid. She'll be well trained by then - and loving it."

"But will she agree?"

"Obedient wives dont argue with their husbands! And you'll just have to make it all a condition for releasing her and marrying her. I think she'll jump at it. After all, you'd still be her Master - and that's what deep down she wants!"

"But what's to stop her from trying once again to get El Paraiso into her hands?"

"Don't forget that here in Costa Negra, a wife can't sue her husband - and anyway she's in love with you. She'll be getting her precious El Paraiso, though not quite in the way she anticipated! Just think what you'd be getting: a loving, beautiful and well disciplined wife with an inside knowledge of how you run El Paraiso."

"Well, why don't you take her with you tomorrow? I can't wait to come over and see her dressed as your maid!"

"No, you must give me a month to get her settled down - a month in which she'll be missing you badly. Then she'll be thrilled to see you again and to learn about the marriage!"

It was a brilliant scene as Carlos and his beautiful English bride came out of the Church, followed, firstly, by Inez, as matron of honour and by several pretty coffee coloured bridesmaids from Carlos's harem of indentured servants, and secondly by a crowd of landowning neighbours.

Diana looked up admiringly at her husband. He was so handsome, so dashing. Moreover, as the tightly drawn laces, carefully locked together, constantly reminded her from under her gorgeous wedding dress, he was also so excitingly dominating.

Inez smiled as she looked at the lovely bride, her newly grown blond hair gleaming under her thrown back veil. They would all be spending a rather unusual wedding night together!

## BONUS PAGES - START HERE!

We continue to develop our Bonus pages - which you get for free
in addition to the usual full length novel.

The author of Hacienda, Allan Aldiss, is also the author of the
Barbary series (Barbary Slavemaster, Barbary Slavegirl, Barbary
Pasha, Barbary Enslavement and Barbary Revenge), and we give
an extract below from Barbary Revenge, which is the subject of a
special offer to introduce the Barbary series. This offer is open to
everyone on our mailing list (or who joins it now!) - merely send
£4 requesting 'Special Offer BE' quoting your number.

PART 1: MERCHANDISE

The nubile young woman awoke naked and terrified, gagged
and blindfolded.

All around her a ship creaked and groaned and the engines
vibrated beneath her.

She quickly discovered that her hands were tied together and
confined in thick mittens which denied her the use of her fingers.

There was dread in her heart as she lay trembling there and
wondered what had happened to her and where she was being taken.

She had no way of knowing that they were steaming into a
modern version of the days when the Barbary corsairs carried so
many women away to slavery in Arabia -

His Excellency Prince Rashid bin Murad al Salia sat back on
a long sofa in the private office of his large palace, sipping his
sherbet, triumph lighting his thoughts. Outside, in the grounds of
his palace, the sun shone down upon fountains and date palms and
beyond that heat shimmered on the endless sand dunes.

He smiled as he studied the photographs of Amanda Aston,
together with her passport which had been furnished as proof of
identity, and contemplated Hassan Atala, the dealer, who stood
diffidently before him on the priceless rugs.

"Yes! That is the one that brought shame upon me! You have

# Bonus Pages

done well!"

Hassan bowed respectfully, rubbing his hands in anticipation of profitable business.

He coughed, a wary eye on the Prince. "Your Highness will, I trust, bear in mind that the abduction of this particular woman was extremely difficult and expensive. I had to wait until she was on holiday in the Mediterranean by herself - and then move fast and bribe many people to turn a blind eye, so that she just disappeared and cannot be traced."

He paused and coughed again, even more significantly.

"Your Highness will be aware that several other leading Arab personalities have also been insulted on her television show and have expressed a desire to get their hands on her."

"Very well, Hassan," the Prince replied at last. "You are a trader and your price will be high. Name it!"

"But Your Highness!" protested Hassan. "It is a little early yet for that! I just thought that Your Highness would be interested to know that she will shortly be on the market - but not yet! Indeed, she is still on her way. Then I shall make a video -"

"We need not wait for that. I wish to buy her now."

"Oh, Your Highness!" exclaimed Hassan with a gesture of despair. "There is nothing I would like to do more than to oblige you, but that would cause grave offence to some of my oldest and most influential clients. I have had to promise them that she will be sold by auction to the highest bidder."

Prince Rashid's lips tightened and he frowned ominously and Hassan rushed into nervous speech.

"Sheik Turki, for example, has expressed interest -"

"That - that upstart!"

The Prince jumped to his feet and strode up and down, mastering the inner rage which it would be demeaning to show before this mercenary rogue who dared argue with him.

"I am sorry, Your Highness. Truly, I had no choice."

"Very well, Hassan. I am not pleased, but I shall be there. What do you think she will fetch?"

"Your Highness, I will do all that I can to help you acquire her, but I must warn you that bidding is likely to start perhaps as high as a quarter of a million dollars."

Prince Rashid nodded nonchalantly. "I shall be there, Hassan.

The higher the price the sweeter the revenge!"

Hassan bowed deeply, hiding his inner delight.

"There will be several other white women, Highness, including a most attractive and unusual couple - an aristocratic English mother and daughter, and couple of beautiful blonde Norwegian nurses."

There was no reply. The Prince was no longer interested. He had turned away. The interview was over.

At the door Hassan salaamed again.

The matter was going well, but there remained much to see to.


Hassan inserted the video cassette that had been made for his approval and switched on the player.

The screen showed two very pretty tall young women on a little stage. There was a background of Arab music. The women were dressed in long nurse's uniforms that buttoned down the front. Their hair was hidden by their nurses' caps.

Hassan smiled approvingly. He liked his clients to be first shown white women as if being auctioned but dressed as they would normally have been if they had still been free. Not only did this serve to show the client the background of the woman being displayed, but also accentuated the fact that a once free Western woman could now be bought as a mere concubine.

The women were smiling nervously at the video camera.

"My name is Ingrid," said one of the young women in a charming Scandinavian accent.

"And my name is Brigit," said the other in a similar accent.

Their lips had been painted scarlet, and their eyes had been carefully made-up and outlined with kohl in the Eastern fashion. Their eyes seemed unnaturally large - thanks to drops of belladonna.

Again Hassan smiled approvingly. The sight of respectable European women erotically made up like Arab dancing girls never failed to arouse interest.

But even more erotic was the sight of each tall woman now being led round the stage by a small black boy holding a dog lead fastened to a collar round her neck. The black boys were dressed in red baggy trousers, embroidered waistcoats and big silken turbans. The Eastern opulence of their dress acted as a further erotic contrast to the simple Western uniforms of the women - and so did their small size and the little dog whips with which they were tapping the buttocks of their tall charges.

The women were in fact a couple of Norwegian nurses who had been working for an aid organisation in Eritrea. They had been captured by guerillas when the isolated village in which they had been working was overrun. The guerillas very short of money had sold them to Hassan's local agents.

Now being sold as a matched pair, Hassan was confident that they would reach a good price at his next auction - provided the video showed them off well. Copies of the video would be discreetly sent to the chief black eunuchs in charge of the harems of certain wealthy Arab clients whom Hassan thought might well be interested in this pair. At the auction telephone bids would be taken as well as bids from those present in the auction room.

The video continued to show the two young women being walked up and down by their small black keepers, their high heel shoes showing off their carriage. The video now zoomed in to show each of the young women's breasts wobbling entrancingly under the thin nurse's uniforms and on their excitingly swaying buttocks.

Then a larger and stronger-looking black boy entered. He was carrying a pair of shiny metal handcuffs. He gripped the wrists of one of the young women and pulled them behind her back, making her grimace.

"No! No!" she shouted. She started to struggle but there was a clicking noise and her hands were now helplessly fastened behind her.

Hassan nodded approvingly. It was important that the video showed the woman off as if she was being auctioned.

The larger boy, still standing behind her, now gently removed her nurse's cap, letting her long blonde hair tumble down. Then he expertly arranged it so that it hung entrancingly over one shoulder.

The sight of this silken cascade of honey coloured hair made even the jaded Hassan catch his breath. Blonde hair always had an electrifying effect in the Arab world and this would really make the rich viewers sit up!

Then her small black keeper, still holding her lead in one hand, slowly began to unbutton the front of her uniform. The larger boy, still standing behind her, suddenly jerked the top of the uniform down over her shoulders, baring her breasts. The young woman wriggled with delightful embarrassment as she vainly tried to cover them with her hands.

"Be still!" the boy shouted giving her a hard tap across her buttocks with his dog whip. "Head up! Shoulders back!"

The terrified woman's firm breasts were now thrust forward. They were surprisingly large. Her nipples were also surprisingly prominent - and painted the same shade of scarlet as her lips.

Again Hassan smiled. Arab men liked large breasts and nipples. Clearly, the breast enlargement and nipple stretching treatment that he had ordered for these women had been a great success. The latest laser American equipment had been expensive, and so he had been sending one his black assistants to learn how to use it. But it had been well worthwhile, and a little breast enlargement and forming was now standard for most of the white women who passed through his hands.

It was a more difficult decision to decide whether or not a particular woman should have another certain little operation - one that greatly increased the value of a woman in the eyes of some men. It would much reduce the pleasure felt by a woman, but without reducing her ability to give pleasure. Indeed it made the girl concentrate more on the pleasure she was giving to her Master. It also largely removed the temptation to deceive her Master with another woman, or even with another a man or by herself. Above all, it greatly increased the feeling of power felt by the Master, and although it was cruel and sadistic, it had been considered perfectly normal in much of Africa and Arabia for centuries - and still was.

In its simplest form, it was such a simple operation - just a little snip and a woman's main source of pleasure was removed. Many African women had the operation done when they were children, but the idea of it being done to a grown white woman was one that greatly appealed to some of Hassan's clients - but not to all. Many men preferred the feeling of making his woman respond, even against her wishes.

Hassan often liked to offer in each sale at least one white woman who had been cut and to offer to cut another free of charge if bought by the same customer, either before delivery or if she was subsequently brought back for it to be done.

Hassan rubbed his nose. Should he have had these Norwegian

## Bonus Pages

girls cut? Probably not. He turned back to the screen.

The small black boy was continuing to undo the buttons. Soon a narrow waist and flat belly were displayed. Hassan had ordered both of the young women to be put on a strict diet and kept well exercised. He was delighted with the result, for the contrast between the prominent but firm breasts, the slender waist, and the hint of the swelling but still hidden hips was very arousing.

The larger boy now went over to the other young woman.

Despite her protests, she too was handcuffed, and her equally lovely blonde hair carefully arranged. Then the top of her uniform was undone and jerked back over her shoulders to display her big firm breasts, stretched nipples and slender waist.

They really were a matched pair, thought Hassan, and as such would sell very well indeed.

The two black boys delicately finished unbuttoning the uniforms and then dramatically pulled them back to disclose long white legs and hairless mounds, under which their equally hairless but scarlet painted beauty glistened provocatively.

Then, not giving the viewers more than a glimpse of these delights, the camera came behind the two young women, displaying their long backs, slender waists and voluptuous buttocks.

Hassan lent forward and switched off the video. It would do very nicely and copies should be sent out immediately to the black eunuchs in charge of the harems of a dozen or more potential buyers. By working through these influential personages he was able to ensure a steady flow of continuing business with his clients, since the eunuch was able to take the credit for finding these new acquisitions for his Master and would be keen to arrange for a repeat order!

AND NOW HERE IS AN EXTRACT from our next title, ANGEL OF LUST. It is by Lia Anderssen, author of Bikers Girl, Bikers Girl on the Run, The Hunted Aristocrat and Bush Slave. We are back to Bikers!!:-

Charlie's heart was beating fast as she rummaged through the mess that was Garth's locker. It bore no resemblance to Zep's, the clothes simply flung in with the rest of his things. Judging by the smell, many of the garments were long overdue a wash. Delving through the piles of dirty clothes, pornographic magazines and weapons of all sorts she finally found the whip tucked at the back. It was made of fine leather, long and thin and extremely flexible. She ran her fingers down its length, shivering slightly as she did so. She thought of the beating she had received in the clubhouse, the marks from which were still visible on her backside. Would Garth also wish to beat her bare behind? Surely not. Not in the open air and in front of all the other bikers?

She searched further and found a bag full of lengths of rope. It was a coarse hempen rope in strands of between three and six feet. In addition there was a mallet and some metal staves that resembled tent pegs. Charlie pulled the bag from the locker and closed the door. Then, her stomach full of butterflies, she began to make her way to the meeting area.

Once again a large crowd met her eyes as she walked down the slope to where the campfire still smouldered. There was a real buzz in the air, and all eyes turned towards her as she came into view. She searched around for Zep, but he was nowhere to be seen. Garth was there, though, standing by a sturdy tree in the centre of the area, his arms folded as he watched her approach.

Charlie felt very nervous indeed as she made her way towards him, clutching her load. But as well as the apprehension, there was another feeling as well, one which she couldn't explain. It was a feeling of intense excitement. Not for the first time since being forced to join this strange and lawless gang, Charlie was realising that there was something about the way these people treated her that appealed to her basest desires. She knew she should be at home now, unpacking her supermarket shopping or hanging out her washing. Instead here she was in a strange country amongst a group of anarchic misfits, about to submit herself to a public and humiliating punishment. And, despite herself, the thought was beginning to arouse her more than she would have thought possible.

She stopped in front of Garth and held out the whip and the bag of rope, which he took from her without speaking. He quickly checked the contents of the bag and nodded.

"At least you can get something right," he said. "Now, stand over there by the tree. And stand like a good apprentice should,

197

hands behind your head and legs apart."

Charlie moved across to the spot he had indicated, and took up the stance. All around more bikers were arriving, squatting down on the grass to watch what was to happen. Charlie knew she was the centre of attention, as she had been on the stage the day before. On that occasion, though, the bikers had been intent on pleasure. This time she knew that Garth had punishment on his mind.

She stood for about ten minutes , feeling very lonely and isolated from the crowd that surrounded her. It was almost as if the anticipation was worse than the punishment itself, and she guessed that that was precisely why Garth was making her wait. She determined not to show herself to be intimidated by his tactics, though, holding her head high and staring out into the middle distance. Meanwhile still more bikers were arriving until she was sure that nearly all the occupants of the camp were gathered round waiting to see what was to follow. The one person she couldn't see, though, was Zep.

At last Garth moved across to where Charlie was standing. He stood close to her, looking her up and down.

"Thought you could get away with slapping me, eh?" he said quietly. "Well, you're about to learn who's boss. Understand?"

"Yes Sir."

"Hold out your arms."

Slowly Charlie stretched out her arms in front of her, and Garth began wrapping the rope about her wrists. He tied it tight, knotting it so that the rough cord bit into her tender flesh. He secured a length to both wrists, then threw the ends up over a branch that ran out parallel from the trunk of the tree above her head. The branch was at such a height that Charlie could barely reach it, even standing on tiptoe. He tied her arms about three feet apart, leaving her hardly able to move.

He hadn't finished yet, though. From the bag he produced the mallet and stakes and drove two of the stakes into the ground on either side of where she stood, at a similar distance apart to the bonds on her arms. Then he took hold of her ankles and, hauling them apart, began to secure them to the stakes.

By the time he had finished, Charlie was totally helpless, her feet barely touching the ground, her body spreadeagled and held in the most excruciating tension, her wrists and ankles burning with the pressure of the ropes. It was the most extraordinary experience for the girl, to be thus totally at Garth's mercy, yet at the same time there was something strangely erotic about her situation. The notion of her subservience to the bikers had been something that had been a turn-on to her since she had joined the gang. This bondage took her one step further towards servitude, and once again she wondered as she felt her masochistic tendencies come to the fore.

What happened next took her totally by surprise. All at once Garth stepped forward and, taking hold of the neck of her blouse in both hands, ripped it open. Buttons flew in all directions as he rent the garment apart, tearing the material from her shoulders until he held no more than two useless rags in his hands and Charlie was naked to the waist. The blood ran to her face as she stood facing the crowd, quite unable to cover herself, her plump, delicious breasts on display to all.

Garth reached out and cupped her breast, squeezing it from underneath and pressing the nipple upward. To Charlie's embarrassment she felt the brown flesh harden at once into a solid knob and she avoided his eyes as he grinned at her.

"Still feeling tough?" he asked, flicking at her rubbery teats, clearly enjoying her discomfort.

Charlie said nothing.

His hand dropped to her shorts, and he ran his fingers down between her legs, pressing the thin material against her sex. Charlie gritted her teeth, trying hard not to display any emotions as he rubbed her in her most sensitive spot, his fingers pressing insistently up into her crotch, making her body writhe slightly as he felt her up.

He reached for her fly, and, as he began undoing the button, Charlie realised that her worst fears were about to be realised. She opened her mouth to protest, but thought better of it. No objection by her would stop Garth, and to do so would simply give him satisfaction.

He pulled down the zip, so that she knew the dark curls of her pubic bush would be showing. Then he grasped hold and, as with the blouse, ripped her shorts apart in a single movement.

A murmur went up from the crowd as Charlie's last vestige of modesty was removed. She watched them as they craned forward, anxious for a look at the gorgeous young apprentice strung up naked before them. A lot of them had already seen her nude the day before, but most had not, and there was no doubt that she was the centre of attention. She glanced down at herself. Her nipples were harder than ever, pointing upwards and outwards from the firm globes of her breasts. Her belly was flattened by the tension in which her body was being held, the paleness of her skin contrasting with the darkness of her pubic triangle, beneath which she knew they could see the open lips of her sex. Once again a flush of shame coloured her face, yet at the same time the thrill of arousal coursed through her. There was something totally sexual about her situation which she was quite unable to deny. Something which, despite herself, brought a warmth and a wetness to her crotch that she feared might soon become visible to the onlookers.

Garth was in front of her again now, and this time he was holding the whip in his hand. Charlie watched fearfully as he flexed it, his eyes burning into hers.

"Now, my little beauty," he said. "How does it feel to be in the power of a real man?"

Once again Charlie remained silent, unwilling to betray how excited she was by her situation. The proximity of this powerful, muscular man with his male smell was having a totally unexpected effect on the young captive, and, despite her dislike for the rough, uncouth biker, she felt her body respond to his closeness in a totally physical way that shocked her with its intensity.

Garth seemed to sense her arousal, as he gave another grin.

"All in good time," he murmured. "First of all, there's a little score to settle. Ten strokes I think."

The sound of the words sent a shiver down Charlie's spine. Ten strokes of the whip! And on her bare backside in front of all these people! She could scarcely credit what was happening to her.

He ran his fingers over the soft swell of her behind, squeezing the flesh.

"Yes," he mused. "A few stripes across your lovely rear will look very pretty indeed."

He moved round behind her and tapped her with the end of the whip. Then he drew it back...

ERICA by Rex Saviour - revised, extended and serialised. The complete book is out of print but (like all our titles) is available on floppy disk or for download over the internet - see end of this book.

Episode 7 - Can be started anywhere, though previous episodes are included in our last six books. Desensitization means exposing the patient in gradually increasing doses to what she fears most in order to cure her of that fear. In the case of Erica it has not worked too well in previous episodes:-

"Being locked up is very bad for her," I said to the lawyer. "She has extremely strong claustrophobia. Prison for her would be catastrophic."

She was whimpering at the very thought of it, quite a pathetic sight.

"I see." He coughed and put his fingers together - I could see how this was turning him on. "It is essential, then, that this desensitization treatment is continued and succeeds. You are gravely at fault so far, Mr Saviour. I am going to insist, on behalf of your step-daughter, that desensitization is pressed to its limit. To its limit, I say. May I write that into the new agreement we are about to sign?"

"Certainly," I said. "To the best of my ability, yes, I will try very hard to effect a total cure, no matter how harrowing I find it. Yes, that seems entirely fair."

"Shyness, being touched, being locked up - or tied up, I presume, or shut in a dark place -"

Erica was shivering, a delightful sight. "Yes indeed," I said, "that too."

He took off his glasses and polished then, and eased his crotch. "Or beaten?" he asked.

"She does react rather strongly when I beat her."

"You must do it a lot then. For her sake, you must not hold back... Now, is there anything else? You, young lady, what have you to say? What other phobias to you suffer from? Come now, must I repeat that this is a legal matter and requires an answer."

"Nothing -"

# Bonus Pages

"Oh. but there is," I said.

She looked at me, and saw that she must admit to it. "S-s-"

"Yes? You are under oath. You must speak up!"

"S-s-snakes."

"That's enough!" I interrupted. Erica was on the verge of hysteria. "It's very painful for her to be reminded of childhood traumas. They are far too severe for this sort of treatment. Surely there is no need to drag up all that filth?"

"Well - do you agree, my dear? I will put snakes on the list in a general way without any more information. It seems to be a critical area, and no doubt he will do his best. Do you agree not to be any more precise about that?"

"Oh God yes, I agree, I agree!"

"Very well." He turned to me. "Now, to clarify one matter, does sex-slave imply she be at the disposal of your friends if you so command?"

"What would the law presume?"

He licked his lips and eased the bulge at his crotch yet again. "I think the presumption would be in the affirmative, the way I have drafted the clause." He turned back to Erica. "Is that in order, my dear?" As she hesitated he added: "Or would prison be preferable?"

"No, no, not locking up, anything else, anything!"

"Very well, so be it. You accept three years as a sex-slave as defined in this document, and your step-father accepts the responsibility of curing the specified phobias listed by means of desensitization, which means exposing you to what you fear most in increasing measure until you cease to fear it." He paused and looked at us both, receiving nods. "And then, of course, my dear, we shall meet again on your twenty-second birthday, when we shall wash the blood and finger prints from the hammer and I shall destroy the photographs and testimonies regarding the murder of your father and your step-father will sign a release from your bondage to him. Is it all agreed? Yes? Very well."

For a while he scribbled away at the agreement. "Ready for signature as amended," he said at last, sticking a red seal onto it with a satisfied flourish. "I shall witness both signatures myself." Again he eased himself. "Personally!" he added. He was, after all, a genuine lawyer.

I signed the document and handed it to Erica.

"Read it," I said. "Sign only if it is correct and remember that nobody is forcing you."

She bit her lip and frowned over it, but a few minutes later the heavy document was signed, sealed and witnessed. It was all very solemn, and I could see that it impressed Erica greatly. I am sure it was no more legally binding than the original one, but the fact remained that she was at my disposal with or without an agreement - after what had happened in her father's cellar she would do anything to avoid being locked up.

She handed the agreement to John and looked at me.

"Good," I said. "You can tell them to serve lunch now." When she came back, I added: "You won't need those clothes any more, now you are my slave. I will get new ones for you that are more suitable."

She hesitated, looked at the document for a moment, then took off her clothes, ever so slowly. Then she folded them neatly, laid them on her chair and stood very erect behind it. The deportment training I had been giving her was working well. I beckoned her into the open, where we could see her properly. She looked from one to the other, fidgeted a little, glancing uneasily at the door although it would be a few minutes before the meal arrived, then put her hands behind her neck, as custom was when she was naked or doing nothing.

"Sherry before lunch?" I suggested.

Erica went to the side-board for the decanter and returned, graceful as ever, to pour for John and I. As we sipped, she moved respectfully aside, trying unavailingly to shield herself with the little tray.

"Erica dear," I said, "how about going out tonight? A little birthday treat?"

"That would be nice, Uncle Rex - b-but I haven't any clothes at all now?"

"In actual fact," said John, "you don't have anything now. Nothing."

She looked at him, a little startled.

"You don't even own your body - in future you do with it as you are told - come here."

She glanced at me appealingly, but I nodded, and John smiled in appreciation as she inched even closer to him.

"Now Miss - good, good - you don't own this fine body you live in - no, not even that part - shy, are we?"

She started to cry.

"Yes, well, don't worry, you shall be cured of. As arbitrator to this agreement, I am obliged to ensure that you receive the treatment to which you are entitled. In full. I believe that I and your owner, as we may now term him, are treating you for shyness at this very moment. Am I not right, Mr Saviour?"

"Absolutely! And don't worry about clothes, Erica dear. I have some for you already and I shall dress you myself for our little outing. You'll look great, I assure you. Everyone will look your way, never fear. We must remember to be back early, though, for the punishment session."

"Oh God! B-but what am I to be punished for?"

"Blasphemy," I said. I took from my pocket the little black book I had bought specially for the occasion. "That's another black mark."

She bit her lip and said nothing.

"And," I added, "not finishing your exercises this morning."

"Oh G- I mean, mayn't I do that now?"

"Very well," I said. "I shall continue to be reasonable, I hope."

"Yes, Uncle, but - well -" She was looking at John and thinking also, no doubt, of the servants. "Upstairs? May I go upstairs?"

"No, no, it's cold up there." There was a knock on the door. "Behind that curtain, then, do them there." She was greatly relieved as she quickly disappeared. The exercises do exhibit her superb young body rather blatantly, specially where I have shaved her.

There was a brief interruption whilst the table was laid, then I refilled our glasses. "Now John," I said. "Watch this."

I activated the motor that parted the curtains and Erica was revealed, dimly lit. I pushed the dimmers up. Spot lights shone out, highlighting all those delicious curves. She was on a small round glass stage in a corner that had mirrors for walls, ceiling and floor. I had worked hard on this, for I anticipated that she would spend a good deal of time on display in one way or another: whilst I watched television, for example, it would be nice to have her posing there, just to glance at from time to time, or maybe feel her up a bit.

Opening the curtains had caught her in one of her those poses, like a statue reflected from all angles. A living statue, for at that moment she made the transition to the next and even more revealing position.

A touch on another switch. The little stage began its slow revolving, and John started to clap. He had done his bit well and deserved a reward. "Come back this evening, if you like," I said. "I shall hold a punishment session at eleven to deal with the black in this book, and any more she may receive this evening."

"Shall I be able to help?"

"Certainly. You can bring a belt?"

"Well, I have a luggage strap. I should think that would be quite effective." There was a definite relish in his voice and although the room was quite warm, I saw Erica shiver with anticipation in the middle of an exercise.

There was a knock on the door, and I saw how near she was to jumping down before she realised there was nowhere to hide. The butler entered with the first course, and lunch passed pleasantly. The male staff were in and out more than usual, perhaps, but at last everything was cleared away.

Erica had finished her last exercise and stood to attention, very upright and motionless, naked under the spotlights on the revolving stage.

I raised my glass.

"And now," I suggested, "a toast: to Erica!"

"Yes indeed." John patted the signed document. "To Erica, property of Rex."

2-2

"Time to dress for dinner," I said.

Erica came reluctantly down from her stage and stood erect before me, a beautiful naked doll that would look more erotic than ever when I had dressed and decorated it.

I ran my hands over her beautiful smooth olive-brown skin for a while, just to savour the shrinking away of her nakedness. Some

## Bonus Pages

of my feelings, like the pleasure I had just taken in her dread of my touch, were disturbing. It troubled me a little until I remembered that only if I acted in this way could the the desensitization succeed, and how essential to her whole future it was that I cure her of her excessive shyness: and now I was legally obliged to do so.

Thoughtfully, still full of self-doubt for the moment, I brushed her shining hair and created two short plaits, one on either side. Was plait the right word? I looked it up in the dictionary: 'interlacing of three or more strands of hair, ribbon, straw, etc.' Yes, that was it. Then I tied the two plaits together in a reef knot at the back of her head. That made a nice convenient handle and looked quite acceptable when I tarted it up with a bow of green ribbon that complemented the reddish sheen of the hair.

"Go and fetch your nipple rings and chain."

She hesitated, but only for a moment, before fetching them from the bedroom. I love to see her go up and down the stairs. I have trained her to do so with her hands on the top of her head and she gets a spanking if she does not wiggle her bottom sufficiently for my approval.

The rings had not been used for some time, but they still fitted the nipple piercings easily enough. The trouble was with the chain. I clicked it onto the left nipple ring and passed it round her neck beneath her hair and down over the right shoulder, but when I attached it to the other nipple I had to pull rather hard. Her breasts must have developed a little since we last used it, and wearing it distorted them, just a little but in a way that did not appeal to me at all.

"Go to the kitchen," I said. "Ask chef to make those rings oval. Nut crackers should do it. If not, try the chauffeur - he should be in the garage."

She made to take them off, but I stopped her.

"It will be easier with them in place, I think. Let whoever it is see the problem. If he wants them off, he can do it himself."

Ten minutes later she was back. There was still the trace of a blush on her cheeks, but the formerly round nipple rings were now oval, and the pull from the chain round her neck no longer distorted her breasts, just lifted them a trifle and made the nipples more prominent.

She paraded again. Much better but not perfect. When she came back to me, I separated out a small strand of her long hair and twisted it around the neck chain in a clove hitch at the back of her neck.

This time the walk up and down was much better. Her head was held up as well as her breasts. She would not be able to look down, but that was of no consequence since it improved her whole posture.

Next I put a garter belt and black stockings on her, smoothing the stockings with great care, and gave her a smart pair of high heel shoes, also black.

Then I unpacked something I had prepared and had been looking forward to seeing on her: upper-arm bands and wrist bracelets.

"A birthday present," I said. "Do you like them?"

They were made of silver, in the form of snakes, and she could not conceal the shudder that went right through her when she saw them.

"They are to help cure you of your fear of snakes."

"Yes Uncle, I - I know. Th-thank you."

"Come here, then, don't shrink away when I want to put them on."

I fitted the upper-arm bands first. These were hinged, and clipped into place above the elbow. The heads of the snakes pointed upwards, as if they were crawling. Tongue and tail were bent into little rings. The bracelets for the wrists had snaps designed to self-engage with the tail rings.

"If you hold your arms behind your back," I said, "you can snap your wrists to the arm-bands of the other arm. Try it. There, you see, it isn't too hard is it?"

"No, but -"

"But what?"

"How do I undo them?"

"You don't, you wait for someone else to undo them. Show me how you walk like that."

She was looking really good, but still not perfect.

"Get one of the staff to cut the heels off these shoes," I said. She looked really exotic from behind as she swayed from the room on those high heels, well worth opening the door for, and even better when she came tip-toeing back, even more erect with no heels at all. And yet I doubted if people would notice their absence, for the only way she could walk in those shoes was on tiptoe as if the heels were still there.

I released her arms with some reluctance and buttoned on the off-the shoulder top I had ready, then paraded her again. After minor adjustments with a couple of pins it looked as if the nipple chain round her neck was holding up the garment, so nobody could complain. She was erotic but decent: or, rather, she would be decent when I chose a suitable skirt and put it on her.

"Let's have a break," I said. "Be a dear and ring for a brandy."

There was plenty of time, so, whilst Erica walked up and down displaying what I had done so far, I brooded on the best skirt to set off the outfit. I hardly noticed when the brandy came, or when someone came to clear it away, or when the fire was made up.

After Erica had modelled all the skirts, I chose the shortest because none of the others showed off her legs so well. It verged on indecency, I have to admit, but can't have everything. It must be prevented from riding up. I intended, after all, to take her to a very respectable restaurant for her birthday treat.

"Ask the gardener for some twine," I said. Scissors I already had.

When she came back I had her stand in front of me with her legs wide apart. I had always found it hard to resist sliding my hands up the insides of her legs in such a situation, and now I need not even think of resisting temptation. Indeed, a duty to succumb to any such temptations had been laid upon me! After a certain amount of wriggling on her part, I pierced the skirt near the top at the front, then, feeding a doubled up length of twine from inside, took it round the top edge and pulled the ends through the loop thus formed.

"Turn round."

I passed the dangling twine between her legs and pulled the two strands up, adjusting them until they were equal.

"Oh, oh, oh!"

The garden twine was, perhaps, a little rougher than I had anticipated, but she would soon get used to it. I made holes for the two pieces of twine at the top of the skirt at the back and, allowing for some slackening during the evening, pulled both ends really hard before tying them together.

"Oh! Oh God!"

I made another note in the little black book.

Now, when she paraded for me, there was definitely an added wiggle to her walk because of the cord between her legs, specially seen from behind, and the skirt would not ride up - not the top of it, anyway.

"Excellent!" I said. "Now these ear-rings and you'll do!"

The ear-rings I had bought for her were large ones, like silver snakes biting the lobe of the ear, and rather pretty silver bells dangled from them.

"Those are to help you stop fidgeting. If the bells ring I shall be angry. Very angry. Very angry indeed. Do you understand?"

She stood very still. "Yes, Uncle!"

At that moment there was a knock on the door: "May the staff come in, Sir? We have a present for Miss Erica."

"Well, that is thoughtful! Come in, come in. Walk up and down, dear, without the bells tinkling, let them all see how well you behave and how fine you look."

"How Miss Erica behaves is up to her, Sir," said the butler. "It is not for us to express disapproval..."

I cut him short. "If she misbehaves in my absence," I said, "you may punish her."

"Any of us, Sir?"

"Certainly. Take the belt she wears to her. It is nice and wide and very supple - the most pain for the least damage, and that is why she wears it. I would appreciate your help in making sure, for example, that her posture reaches a very high standard at all times."

"Very well, Sir. Her posture does you credit when you are here, Sir, if I may say so, and we shall certainly watch her on your behalf in future... but we are a little concerned about the way she dresses, Sir. We thought these might be useful."

He held out his little tray. A bra and a pair of knickers!

"Why of course," I said, "of course she must put them on, the brazen little hussy. At once, Erica dear, at once!"

She was blushing as she began to strip. She never seems to get used to being seen naked, even by the staff.

It is nice having staff, by the way. Only day staff, of course - they all go home at night. That is when I like to be free to express myself.

# Bonus Pages

Heads certainly turned when Erica and I entered that crowded restaurant and started slowly down the five splendidly carpeted steps - it was the contrast between her so obvious shyness and the flagrant way I had dressed her. It was mainly the skirt, the shortness of it, and the rather nice wiggle to her walk imposed by the tightness of the twine in her crotch.

That walk must have seemed erotic but natural to other diners. Probably nobody noticed that she was tip-toeing.

"Head up!" I whispered on the second step.

"Yes, Uncle."

It already was up, of course, because of the strand of hair attached to the chain round her neck: the rest of her hair was an auburn cascade down her straight back, pouring through the loop of the two plaits.

"Straighter!" I said on the third step.

"Yes, Uncle." She tried, but it was hardly possible.

"Ah, waiter - for two, the alcove I think. My niece likes to be admired, don't you Erica dear?"

"Yes, Uncle." It was the last thing she wanted, of course, we both knew that, but she had given the right reply. The waiter certainly admired the way she mounted the three rather steep steps to the alcove.

I had added a brooch to the ensemble at the last moment, a large silver snake, specially made, every scale a masterpiece. I had chosen it as further help to overcome her fear of snakes. The outfit was black but the silver theme was continued in the bracelets and arm bands. She also now wore the usual leather belt for my convenience, and the silver buckle with 'REX' on it matched perfectly.

When we were seated and I had ordered our meal, I had time to look her over properly. Delightful. She was, as I now demanded, holding the tip of her tongue between her fine white teeth, so that her luscious red lips were invitingly parted. I was only thinking how gorgeous she was, sitting so upright like that, but she began to tremble under my scrutiny, and before long she squirmed in her seat until there was a faint but unmistakable tinkling from the little bells on her ear-rings.

"Erica, my dear," I said, "do be still."

She flushed and braced herself even tighter.

"I have warned you about fidgeting!"

"Oh God, I'll try harder, truly I will!"

"Yes, you really should behave better by now."

"Yes, yes, I know."

"This is your birthday, after all. You're nineteen now, not a child any more. You will have to be punished, of course."

"Yes, Uncle."

"In addition to the punishment for blasphemy you already have coming."

"Yes, yes, I know - please don't talk so loud. Please?"

I glanced round. Other tables were rather near, but the diners were chatting to each other again. I saw no reason to whisper. I pushed back my chair to make room for her over my lap.

"Oh please Uncle, not here, beat me as hard as you like, but not here - oh not in front of all these people - oh God, Uncle, do it at home, beat me at home, oh please, take me home to beat me -"

"Very well, if you prefer it." I drew my chair in again. "I suppose it will keep till we get home, since this is your birthday." I saw the relief in her eyes - I had spanked her in public once or twice when she was younger and she hated it. I buttered a roll as we waited for the chicken to come. "How about the cellar?" I asked casually. "Then Mr Smith and I can play chess in peace. Would being sent there be a good punishment?"

She went quite white. "Oh Uncle! Please not!"

"Shouldn't we try it, now you are older? You have to be cured of this fear of being locked up."

"Not yet, not yet, mayn't I be beaten instead?"

"Speak up!"

"Please may I be beaten?"

"Louder," I said.

"PLEASE MAY I BE BEATEN!"

Heads were turning, people, interested by her posture and the shortness of her skirt from the moment we entered, were getting more and more interested.

"How many?"

# Bonus Pages

She hesitated. "Is it a number game?"

"Yes, the one where if you say less than I have already decided it shall be three times what you say."

She licked her red lips: I had applied a little make up, not too much. Then, glancing round uneasily, she took off the broad leather belt and kissed it four times. She hesitated, then kissed it once more before putting it back on.

"Five?" I asked mockingly, taking a sip of wine. It was dry and properly chilled. "Only five? Are you sure?"

She hesitated again, biting her lip this time. She frightens very easily, my girl Erica. She glanced round as if she could run away, then, as I expected, she took the belt off again and kissed it twice more.

"Are you quite sure?"

Again she hesitated, biting that delightful lower lip. "Yes, thank you - Uncle -"

"Well?"

"Did I guess right?"

"You'll find out later, my girl."

"Yes Uncle. Please Uncle -"

"Well, what is it this time?"

"Please don't talk so loud. Please? I think the next table heard, and the waiter."

"I am not ashamed of beating you. Why do I do it?"

"F-for my own good."

"Again." This is something I need to drill her in.

"You beat me for my own good."

The waiter had been hovering and listening.

"You're upsetting the waiter now," I said. "You'd better explain yourself."

"Oh - yes, well - potatoes, yes thank you - Uncle does beat me sometimes, he's going to do it when we get home tonight, but - but it's for my own good, so it's alright -"

He served us, speechless and somewhat pop-eyed, and for a while we concentrated on the meal. The conversation was pretty boring. At last I said: "About this beating you asked for. You had better prepare yourself, my dear."

"Oh! You don't mean - I thought we could go home for it?"

"So we shall, my dear, so we shall. But you may as well get

212

ready."

"Oh no, not in front of all these people!"

"No sense in putting it off."

"Oh God!"

"Blasphemy!" I said. She watched me making yet another note in the little black book, then got up ever so reluctantly.

"Now, Uncle?"

"Oh yes." My theory is that as much preparation as is reasonably possible in advance concentrates the mind on a punishment. She knows the correct punishment dress excludes underwear. That had always been the case, though it was seldom relevant as she never had any in her wardrobe.

"Just the bra," I said.

Her breasts are high and neat, firm rather than large, but without the bra the staff had so thoughtfully given her the nipple rings might show because of the chain. However, she smiled, grateful that the knickers had been excused, and set off for the ladies. Reaction from those around was restrained, in keeping with the high-class nature of the establishment, but was gratifyingly noticeable nevertheless.

When she came back she stood beside my chair, waiting for permission to sit.

The coffee had come by now and I was ready for my cigar. "Do sit down, dear," I said. "It's irritating to have you hovering like that."

"Sorry, Uncle. Here is the bra."

"You'll have to carry it." She doesn't have a handbag. I have never allowed her any money because she had once stolen some, before I had her, so a hand bag would have been superfluous.

When she was seated, I said: "Now for the knickers."

"Oh God no!"

"I beg your pardon?"

"I mean, yes Uncle, yes yes I'm going!"

There was a definite hush as she set out on her second walk, descending from the alcove with flushed cheeks, carrying the bra and pushing through the close-set tables. I almost expected them to start clapping when she squeezed back carrying her knickers as well, but it was definitely not that sort of place: she came through in dead hush, blushing like mad.

## Bonus Pages

When at last she took her seat again her bare bottom must have well prepared her mind for blushes of another sort. Her lower lip was quivering and she was blinking away tears, though she still remembered to keep the tip of her tongue between her teeth. She did not have a handkerchief - no handbag, no handkerchief, I suppose.

I wondered about sending her to remove her suspender belt and stockings, but one doesn't like to be over the top.

"You can go now," I said. "Wait in the car."

She tried to say something about keys, but I waved her away. I wanted a little peace, not to be troubled with trifles.

I poured cream into my second cup of coffee.

She'd be safe enough, after all. The street was well lit and would be quite busy. There had been a home match that night. And there was not much wind, not really.

Here are more items from VICTORIAN SCRAPBOOK by Stephen Rawlings, the author of the very popular JANE AND HER MASTER:

MARIETTA AND THE ROD

Naturally, as any other respectable young woman of her eighteen years, Marietta would not have dreamed of appearing in public unless tightly restrained by the comforting confinement of her stays, but the delicate and fashionable garment she favoured did not apparently satisfy her newly appointed guardian, Sir Frederick Lingham, into whose care she had been committed by the unfortunate death of both her parents in a coaching accident in the Italian Alps a few months previously.

In Sir Frederick's opinion, she had been allowed too much licence by her indulgent parents, and required strict discipline to restore her to that state of mind and body that would render her a suitable candidate for matrimony, and the disposal of her considerable inheritance to a deserving husband. To this end, he had decided that, amongst other things, she should be more strictly corseted and advised her that they would be shortly visiting a certain Madam Berthenon.

"She is a corsetiere," he informed his ward, "whose care of your figure will help you to achieve that straightness of deportment that should reflect a firmness of character and good moral fibre, while she has other means at her disposal to help you with the latter. I shall be taking you to meet her tomorrow after noon. Please ensure that you are suitably cleansed and clad to enable her to examine you and fit you for a proper corset, rather than those frivolous and flimsy stays you at present wear. I shall have the carriage called for two o'clock."

Now the carriage had deposited them at the door of a discreet establishment off Wimpole Street, in the newly fashionable part of London. They were evidently expected and a neatly dressed maid ushered them into a well furnished drawing room, where they were soon joined by a rather severe looking woman of about fifty, with iron grey hair drawn back in a bun, but with the upright carriage and slim figure of a much younger woman, though the stiffness of her pose suggested that this owed much to the excellence of her own products.

After the minimum of polite exchanges, she went straight to the purpose. While her guardian watched, Marietta was made to remove her outer clothing and submit to being measured carefully, over her shift, from neck to knee, including, not only the usual assessment of her waist and bust, but also various dimensions through her crotch, from navel to the top of her buttocks' divide, the width of her shoulders and much else besides, until Madame was satisfied she had a complete record of her shape in every particular. She left them for a few minutes, then returned with a stiff unyielding contraption of steel, whalebone and kid leather, with satin cups for Marietta's breasts, and strong laces to bind it tight around her.

Naturally, as a well brought up young lady, she would not think of going abroad without the security and decency of stays, but her own garments were feminine and of soft satin, boned but not harshly so. The new garment was of unyielding kid leather with pockets formed in its strong cambric liner that were separated only by a single row of tight stitching, the thick whalebone slices almost touching to form a rigid carapace, the stomach kept flat, and the back straight, by a broad strip of spring steel, which ran from a point between her breasts, flattening the slight roundness of her soft belly, and fitting closely against the pouting mound at the top of her thighs.

"This will serve to hold you in order for the time being," Madame informed her. "Your personal tight lacing will be ready in twenty-four hours."

The next day saw again guardian and ward in Madame's drawing room, and, as promised, the new corset was ready for her. It was much as the temporary device she had adopted the previous day, though tighter now, constricting her waist even more firmly, and requiring the help of a maid to ensure the laces were pulled tight enough for the two halves to meet on her back, forcing her buttocks to swell beneath it, and her breasts to even greater prominence above. She feared, indeed, that the pressure they were under might result in them being squeezed out of their lacy cups, to expose the nipples to her disgrace and shame, but Madame had anticipated this risk.

"Do you wish her to have modesty rings?" she asked Sir Frederick. "It would be safer so, and no risk of Mam'zelle's nipple making an unannounced appearance."

Her guardian considered the option offered.

"Best be sure," he said. "Besides, it embellishes a woman most uncommonly, and a suitor will appreciate it."

"Out with your teats then, Mam'zelle," Madame instructed and then, when the girl hesitated, "tsk, tsk! Such modesty!"

She plunged her own fingers into the cups of the corset, lifting out the cherry nipples, that were about to burst their own way to freedom in any case, and left them resting on the rim.

"Ah, nice and fat. They'll take the needle well, and you can have full thick rings, with tension on them."

Now Marietta understood, and shuddered. The corset she had 'borrowed' overnight had had a small hook sewn into each half cup, and her new one was equipped with the same feature. She had heard of such devices, but had not thought of it being applied to herself, but now she was to have her teats pierced and rings inserted, so that they could be placed under the hooks and prevent any possibility of unwanted exposure of those most intimate parts of her bosom, while enabling its snowy abundance to be prominently displayed.

It was not a quick operation. Madame declared that it was better to suffer a little pain now, rather than be burdened with piercings that were not truly symmetrical and which she would regret the rest of her life. The needle was placed with utmost care against the side of one delicate dug, then pushed through with agonising slowness, while Madame maintained it absolutely horizontal as it traversed the flesh, chiding the girl for flinching and endangering her aim. The insertion of the thick gold ring was even more painful and, when Marietta had ceased whining at the anguish in her left teat, it was all to do again with her right but, eventually, she was the proud possessor of a pair of handsome and practical rings set in rather inflamed, and still sore, nipples.

Madame addressed Sir Frederick again.

"She is well formed, but I always think a really prominent nipple is a great asset in a girl. The gentlemen seem to think them so at any rate. Would you wish me to stretch her a little?"

"A good idea. A man likes a dug he can pull on. See to it, will you."

Now she whines again, for the rings are withdrawn, and small rods inserted in their place, with several shaped washers under each, dragging the nipple out of its areola to stand out prominently.

"Now, Mam'zelle, I have put two spacers under each. You must wear them so, every night, though you will need to use rings in the day, to maintain decorum. After a week you should add another spacer to each side and, in a month, yet another. We will see how much progress you make at that time, before deciding if further stretching would be advantageous."

"That's her bodily requirements seen to," Sir Frederick remarked, as Marietta stood with tight pressed lips, the rods pulling painfully on her stretched nipples, "but there are other uses for your admirable whalebone; a discipline for her soul as well as her body. I am determined," he declared, "that she should learn to be a compliant and obedient young woman, and to that end should feel the rod. I shall send her to you for regular exercise of that instrument, and supplementary visits when there are specific shortcomings to be rectified."

Up to this point Marietta had submitted without fuss to all the demands made on her, including the not inconsiderable pain she had suffered during the piercing of her nipples and their subsequent stretching, but now she pleaded strenuously that he should

# Bonus Pages

not subject her to a whipping, as being too undignified for a girl of her age, and she could not bear to be treated so.

"I did not take you for a coward, Marietta," her guardian admonished her. "Why even a school girl learns to take the birch without whimpering and you, by your own estimation, are a woman."

He turned to Madame.

"You see how justified I am in my decision that she should feel the rod. I think it would be appropriate to let her learn what is involved as soon as possible. At this moment in fact."

"But Sir..."

"Silence girl. No more argument," he thundered, and Marietta bit her lip and looked down.

"Now, kindly remove your drawers and lift your chemise."

Marietta coloured deep crimson.

"Ah, Sir," she pleaded, "not in front of a man. It would not be decent."

Sir Frederick and Madame exchanged looks before her guardian nodded to himself.

"Very well," he conceded, "you may take her into the fitting room. I will wait here, but tight mind you, and two extra for her ungentle protest."

"Ah no," Madame explained, "I do not carry out the corrections myself. I employ Mam'zelle Hortense for the purpose. She disciplines the girls in the sewing room, and many of my clients send their girls here to be corrected as well. I also arrange for her to pay home visits," she added. "It is a matter for speculation whether it is more salutary for the young lady to wait in her own home for the appearance of the disciplinarian, which may not be announced to her, or to be brought or sent to her here. Each approach has its merits."

"I will bear that in mind," said Sir Frederick, "but in the mean time, I would be grateful if you would send for Mam'zelle Hortense and have her take this rebellious young lady into the next room and deliver six with a stiff rod to her naked posteriors, plus her extra tally of two for her unwarranted protests."

And so it was done. Marietta walked with stiff back, and chin held in the air, through the communicating door, though one could detect a slight trembling of her lower lip. She was accompanied by

218

the tall austere figure of Mam'zelle Hortense, and an awesome length of thick whippy whalebone that that lady had brought with her, nearly three feet long, tapering from the thickness of a woman's thumb at the gripping end, to that of her second finger at the other, though with a very slight thickening at the very tip, which formed a distinct 'bulb'.

Sir Frederick and Madame, seated at their ease in the drawing room, could hear little at first, just some low murmurings, and, once, the scrape of a chair on boards.

"Will it be long?" he asked his companion.

"It will happen now," she assured him. "It is the girl's first time, and she has to be shown how she must bare herself, and the position she must adopt. It is kinder not to make a girl bend unsupported for a flogging. Here we have her bend over the back of a chair and grip the seat in her hands. Of course her punishment would be severe if she failed to maintain this pose until she is dismissed."

Now, at last, came the sounds he had been waiting for, a crisp snapping noise, as of a brittle twig stepped on in the forest, a gasp, not a true cry, but loud enough to be heard through the intervening door, a pause, and then the cycle repeated. Four times the rod cracked on naked flesh, and the girl gasped out her breath at the shock and pain of it, hissing in again afterwards as fire raged in her hinds. After the fifth stroke there was a break in the inexorable rhythm of the agony.

There was a growl from Hortense, a whimpered response from the girl, then, separated by a short interval, two pairs of sharper snapping sounds, each accompanied by a squeal, quickly suppressed, from Marietta. Again Sir Frederick turned to his companion for an explanation.

"I fear the girl has been foolish enough to seize her buttocks in her hands, to try and ease the pain," that lady explained. "It often happens with inexperienced girls, but they soon learn their lesson. What you heard was her taking two cuts on each hand, to remind her to keep them off her bottom, and on the chair. Hortense will ignore the stroke, naturally, and we will hear her proceed now."

And so it proved to be. Four more times the snap of rod on bare flesh penetrated the door, and each time Marietta's gasp grew stronger, until it was almost a cry, and her whimpers afterwards, as she tried to absorb the welling pain in the burning stripes on her bottom, were more and more clearly audible. It was over at last and, after a pause to enable the girl to resume the clothing she had discarded or lifted to expose her buttocks for correction, she was ushered through the door into the room where her guardian waited.

Her face was flushed a deep red, her under-lip was swollen and bruised, where she had bitten on it to suppress her cries, and she held her hands tightly clenched at her sides, though whether to conceal their equally bruised condition, or to try and ease the throbbing pain that infested them, was not clear. In a trembling voice she thanked her guardian for taking such good care of her, a lesson obviously instilled by the redoubtable Hortense, and one she was in no mood to forget.

Sir Frederick accepted her thanks graciously, and gave his own to Hortense, with the added remark that he would be making use of her services regularly in future, in view of the excellent results obtained on this first visit. As Marietta walked stiff legged to the waiting carriage, for the bulbous tip of the rod had wounded her sorely on her flank, and placed her cringing bum on the leather of the seat, she was only too aware that she would be returning here for similar, or harsher, treatment, many times in the future.

AN IMPORTANT ADVANCE IN MEDICINE, AND THE MANAGEMENT OF WOMEN'S DISORDERS - From the Morning Courier.

[Readers who normally allow their female dependants to read all or part of the this newspaper may, at this point, wish to shield them from the details on the grounds of delicacy but, so important is it to their health, both mental and physical, we earnestly urge them to at least impart the gist of the contents to those who would most benefit from them.]

At a meeting of the London Gynaecological Society last night one of its founders, and most experienced practitioners, Dr. Isaac

Baker-Brown, delivered a lecture of the first importance.

Woman is so ruled by her body, Dr. Brown tells us, that her brain, being smaller and weaker than man's, will often collapse under the strain, resulting in the manifold ailments of the mind that so afflict the fair sex. Moreover, he has discovered, nearly all such cases can be traced back to unnatural vice.

[We will spell out here, once and once only, the exact nature of the evil. The learned Doctor refers to female masturbation. Once again we caution our readers against allowing this article to fall into the hands of their womenfolk, without, at least, preparing them for the contents. So that there can be no ambiguity, we will go further, and define it as the stimulation, manual or by means of an instrument, of the pubic nerve, or clitoris, until passion over-spills in spasm or paroxysm]

Masturbation, Dr. Brown makes clear, leads to lassitude, hysteria, inflammation of the spine, mania and, eventually but inevitably, death. There is only one certain cure for this condition, once the habit has been formed, and that is the surgical removal of the organ responsible, the enlarged ending of the pubic nerve, sometimes known as the clitoris. He recommends a radical incision with the scalpel, on either side of the clitoral ridge, followed by cauterisation with a hot iron, to stem any flow, since the area is well supplied with blood vessels. Since the procedure is comparatively quick, it is best not to risk the newly introduced methods of anaesthesia. In any case, this operation has been made necessary by the woman's own unacceptable behaviour, and any suffering she endures may be thought of as part of her penance.

Total success may be anticipated, the lecturer not being aware of any woman who did not become submissive and tractable after such treatment. The cases of several women, whose instability of mind was demonstrated by their wish to take advantage of the recent relaxation of the laws governing divorce, were advanced as proof of this assertion. After the surgery they all returned to their husbands and no longer spoke of such nonsense.

In a further reference to the connection between a female's mind and her bodily functions, it was stated that, at the menopause, many women are stricken by unnatural cravings for sexual attention. All husbands of such women were earnestly recommended to deny them such stimulation, which can otherwise be expected to result in the same grave consequences as unnatural vice in the younger female. In really severe cases, he recommended, the same surgical solution should be employed.

Other eminent medical men have also commented on this domination of the female mind by her bodily functions, including the deleterious effects of menstruation. Mothers are earnestly advised to take precautions to delay the onset of this dangerous phenomenum, with its mood changes often bordering on madness, by keeping their daughters in the nursery, restricting diet and exercise and, especially, forbidding the reading of 'novels' which so inflame the female brain.

How about some reader's letters for the bonus pages? We won't publish name and address unless you ask us to.

# Out of print Titles

Available on floppy disc
£5 or $8.50 postage inclusive
(PC format unless Mac requested)

All Silver Moon titles are also available on floppy or for
download onto a browser as txt (ASCI) files to be copied and
saved for reading in your favourite word processor.

<u>Mail order or Internet only</u>
http://www.thebookshops.com/silver

All our titles can be ordered from any bookshop in the UK and an
increasing number in the USA and Australia by quoting the title and ISBN,
or directly from us for £5.95 each (UK) or $10.50 (USA) postage included.
Credit Cards read EBS (Electronic Book Services - £ converted to $ and
back!)

# TITLES IN PRINT

## Silver Moon

## Silver Mink